THE WINNOWING

GHERBOD FLEMING

First edition March 1998.
Printed in Canada.

White Wolf Publishing
735 Park North Blvd.
Suite 128
Clarkston, GA 30021
www.white-wolf.com

CONTENTS

CHAPTER ONE

Rage drove Nicholas on through the night. His thirst for vengeance would be sated only by blood, and it was the thought of that blood that fueled his fury. Blood that once, maybe a thousand years before, had run through the undead veins of his ancestor across the seas. Blood that had been stolen from Blaidd, the murdered Gangrel. Blood that Nicholas would reclaim for his lineage, for his clan.

But it would be another night that would see Nicholas's vengeance satisfied, for the moon had already run its course across the blue-black sky. Mighty Orion, the hunter, had also completed his trek, and the faintest traces of pink and orange were becoming increasingly evident on the eastern horizon.

Unrelenting, Nicholas pressed the limits of his wolven form. Mile after mile fell away behind him. Already the wide plains of the Midwest, empty except for acres of winter wheat and the wind that danced through the stalks, were only a memory. It was on those plains, less than a day ago, that the truth had been revealed to him. Visited by another of the waking dreams that had plagued him over the past weeks, Nicholas had seen through the eyes of his great-great-grandsire as the most heinous of crimes among the Kindred had been committed against Blaidd. And though the deed was nearly a millennium past, Nicholas had laid eyes upon the perpetrator less than a fortnight ago, and each step, each mile that receded in the distance, left Nicholas closer to the criminal. Closer to justice.

Countless rolling hills of bluegrass passed almost without notice. Horse country. Nicholas had stopped only briefly to feed from an old roan, a creature that in ages past might have been a proud beast roaming the plains, but instead was the broken-down beast of burden of a struggling farmer. With an animal so large, it was easy for Nicholas to drink his fill without too adversely affecting his prey. As Nicholas fed, he grieved for the beast, fenced in amongst such squalor. Had Nicholas been in less of a hurry, or had there been signs of abuse on the horse, he would have stormed into the farmer's shack and fed instead from him and his family. But what would have been the use? The roan, utterly domesticated, would have squandered the gift of freedom. Even without fence or tether, it would merely wander until other mortals placed a rope around its neck. It pained Nicholas to see the spirit of a fine beast so completely broken by the mortals.

Feeding was painful for Nicholas in other ways as well. For weeks now, as long as the dreams had been assailing him, each feeding had brought not relief from his hunger, but increased pain. It burned from within, as if his very blood boiled. Tonight, only the fury of his running had kept Nicholas from falling to the ground or going mad from the agony.

The blood curse. Nicholas had seen it in the city, had heard stories from Edward Blackfeather. Nicholas had hoped that returning to the nurturing wilds would cure him, but although the wide open spaces had helped him control the hunger and the madness somewhat, the curse clung to him like the stink of the city that could not be washed away.

Ahead, the Smoky Mountains loomed, less obstacle than milepost to Nicholas. It was a shame, he thought, that the dawn was breaking so chill and clear. The mountains, when bathed in the fog and mist for which they were named, were truly an awesome spectacle, and on the darkest and most overcast of mornings, Nicholas might have stolen another hour from the sunrise. But his time was nearly at an end for now. Soon he would have no choice but to sink into the ground, into the welcoming earth that protected him from the day.

Tomorrow night. He would enter again the accursed city, and vengeance would be his. Nicholas would exact justice. He would tear it from the flesh of the Gangrel-killer. Owain Evans. The Ventrue elder played the part of civilized gentry. He was gracious and polite, offered refreshments to his guests. But in his past, secrets were buried that, without question, damned him. The modern businessman had, at one point in time, dirtied his own hands. Nicholas had seen through curse-born dream the cruel pleasure Evans had taken in destroying the Gangrel's great-great-grandsire. How many other Kindred had Evans murdered likewise in the intervening years? How many, Gangrel or otherwise, had fallen to this respectable elder? The other clans, Nicholas knew, derided the Gangrel, mocked their "beastly" ways. But who was the real beast— he who dealt forthrightly with his peers and was tied to no single place, or he who clung frightened to his city and fed upon his own, while pretending to adhere to some higher, sophisticated code?

Nicholas grunted. Too much thinking. He had been among the city Kindred too much of late. A burning was beginning to grow within him. He was so exhausted from his two nights of running that he couldn't tell whether the pain was the protestation of muscles pushed beyond their limits, or the tiny pin-pricks of the sun's first rays sizzling his skin like the bacon his mother had fried over an open flame back in Kiev so long ago. Or perhaps the pain was the hunger demanding attention, the yearning that only grew worse after any attempt to appease it, a reminder of the curse that had latched onto Nicholas his last time in the city. How would he bear it this time, going back among all the kine and their buildings and roads and automobiles?

But that was not the most important problem, Nicholas reminded himself as he began to sink down into the rich earth. There were age-old wrongs to be redressed, offenses ten times Nicholas's age to be set right.

Owain Evans would pay for his crimes. That Nicholas swore. On the blood of his ancestry, the blood that Nicholas would savor as he drained it from Evans's tattered body, Nicholas swore. As he became one with the soil beneath the emerging rays of the sun, his pain, for a brief while, drained away. His fury did not.

Owain had retreated into the study to seek the comfort of solitude. He wanted nothing to do with his uninvited houseguest, or with the swirling tempest of Atlanta's Kindred politics, which Owain would doubtless be dragged into more fully. There were also the day-to-day responsibilities that he had been ignoring for the past few weeks as other matters had loomed, and without his servant ghoul Randal to attend to such details, more of the burden fell back onto Owain.

Damnation! he thought. *How, of all things, can I run off to Spain right now?*

With Prince Benison's decrees of the night before clamping down on the liberties of the anarchs, trouble was sure to follow. Owain, as elder and all-but-in-name primogen, might be called upon to help maintain order. Or there was always the possibility that he might be able to gain some advantage through the likely turmoil. Benison's wife Eleanor, Ventrue like Owain, would be in a difficult spot, her loyalty tested between her husband and Baylor, her justicar sire who would undoubtedly frown upon Benison's decrees. Antagonizing the anarchs was most likely not at the head of the Camarilla agenda these days. Anything that distracted from the organization's endeavor to survive the curse would be a liability. For Eleanor's position to be compromised, either she would have to become estranged from Benison, or more likely Benison himself would be disciplined by the Camarilla for his rash actions. The prince could be censured or even removed from power. But who would step in to pick up the mantle of authority in Atlanta? Certainly neither brainless Marlene nor

Thelonious the Brujah. Aunt Bedelia was too far removed from reality, though less than she let on, Owain suspected. Aurelius would never leave the sewer long enough to be of any use, and though Hannah would be an able administrator, she was far from inspiring, and at any rate, it was doubtful the Camarilla would let a Tremere move to the fore. There was too much distrust from the other clans.

Owain's eyebrows rose at the thought that no suitable successor to Benison dwelled within the city. None except perhaps…Owain himself?

He smacked himself lightly on the cheek several times. *What vampire in his right mind would even want to be prince?* Owain wondered. *In his right mind. That explains how Benison got the job.* Owain couldn't believe that he'd even entertained the ludicrous idea at all. He was not enough of a recognized factor within the Camarilla to assume a position of such prominence. He was too much the outsider, too much an unknown quantity. And that was how he liked it. Owain had had his day in the sun, so to speak. He had been the controlling force behind the small Welsh kingdom of Rhufoniog for two hundred years. There was more to be gained, he had finally realized, from remaining even further behind the scenes, and he had stuck to that strategy for the past seven centuries or so.

No point tampering with what works, he decided.

But was it working? He had survived longer than most of his kind, but after the past few weeks, nothing in his undead existence was certain. The predictable routine that Owain's nights and months and years had fallen into was utterly shattered. The siren had seen to that. Owain stretched back in his chair. He pressed with his hands against the large ornate desk at which he sat. The solidity and weight of the piece of furniture was reassuring, as was the smooth grain of the black walnut. A very hard wood, it had not been easy for the carpenter to work with, and Owain had paid a handsome price for the desk, even back in the century of its origin. Later modifications, such as the installation of an intercom into the structure, were regrettable concessions to modernity that displeased him more and more as time passed. He wished he had not sullied its pristine beauty so, but had refrained from having the situation corrected for fear of further marring the integrity of the piece. What was done was done. The desk served as something of a grim reminder of so many unfortunate decisions.

The commonplace book that lay on the desk before Owain was a reminder in different ways. The cover of the book was several shades lighter than the walnut beneath. There were no markings or inscriptions on the smooth leather. It had been disturbing enough when the original embroidered cover had deteriorated well beyond the possibility of repair. Owain could still envision the design that had graced the cover—Welsh grouse trussed, from the crest of House Rhufoniog—when the original owner had given him the book. *Angharad*. She had been done such a great disservice by House Rhufoniog, but still she had retained her loyalty. So had Owain, until years later.

He had hated to replace that cover, but still the book held special meaning. Even without markings, Owain knew he could never mistake it for another, or another for it. Place it amidst a library of thousands identical to it, and he would pick it out with hardly a glance. Unlike many elder Kindred, there were few heirlooms that Owain valued, but those that he did—this book, his sword—were irreplaceable for reasons beyond the reach of his vast wealth. The contents of the book were largely inconsequential: handwritten bits of scripture, common sayings, countless scribblings in two distinct hands and a handful of languages. But still Owain could not bring himself to relegate it to a glass case where its life might be lengthened.

What kind of life would that be? he wondered. A book like this was meant to be handled, to be touched. That was what Owain needed it for, at any rate—reminding him of and connecting him to his humanity of centuries past. There was little other actual use for the book. Finding the reference to absinthe several months ago was probably the first time he had needed information from the tome in several years. And when was the last time he had written in it? Curious, he took it from the desk and gingerly turned the stiff parchment pages, so as not to crack them or strain the aged binding, until he found the last entry. The legible but less than technically perfect handwriting was unmistakably his own, though the words were rendered in Spanish. After all, he remembered upon seeing the text, he had been living in Toledo for over a hundred years when it was written.

Earlier tonight I sat atop the walls near Bad Yehudin, Jews' Gate. Behind me, fires burned in the Jewish quarter. In the days to come, the Jews will be blamed for the fires—"criminals hiding evidence of their crimes," people will say, or "laying deathtraps for devout Christians." But it was those "devout" Christians who could not even wait to loot until the Jews were driven from their homes. I have no religious sensibilities left to lead me to persecute them.

Before me as I sat atop the wall, an endless procession of Jews streamed into the night, beyond the Basilica de Santa Leocadia, beyond the limit of even my sight. Ferdinand and Isabella have their wish. The Jews will be gone from Spain, and both a proud people and this kingdom will suffer.

The Jews will suffer the most, however. They will go...to Portugal? France? Will they find any better there than what they leave? I doubt it will be so. Their possessions on carts, on horses, on their own backs, the descendants of Don Samuel are laid as low as any. And for what? For much the same reason I was chased from my lost Wales. At least I had the luxury of contributing to my own misfortune.

The last sentence surprised Owain. Seeing the words, he remembered crouching on the wall that night as the Jews were leaving the city, expelled as they were from all of Spain. But how could he have thought that he had contributed to his own expulsion from Wales? Obviously, not quite two hundred years after his exodus, he hadn't had the proper perspective, the broader historical overview, to realize that the fault lay entirely with the Normans and the Ventrue conquerors who accompanied them driving the native Ventrue of Britain before them.

At any rate, Owain reminded himself, his past misconceptions were of little concern. He had written that last entry just over five hundred years ago. Though he had not placed the commonplace book in a museum or in a hermetically sealed container, for more than five centuries he had added nothing new to it. *So why have I bothered to keep it?* he wondered. *Nostalgia? Self-pity?*

Owain's introspective mood began to turn dark. *For that matter, what have I done since my last awakening?* It had been roughly three hundred years since he had last emerged from torpor, and though in that time he had traveled across the great Atlantic and constructed a relatively vast financial empire, in many ways those endeavors had been merely going through the motions. Owain had taken little pleasure or satisfaction in his accomplishments. This book, the desk it rested upon, the objects that were of any value to him, these were only visions of the past. They held no meaning, no value, in and of themselves in this modern day. Owain felt suddenly, looking at the book, that *he* might as well have spent the centuries in a hermetically sealed pine box, himself a relic of bygone days, surrounded by the present but not really a part of it.

That was the predictable routine of his lingering nights that the siren had shattered. While the objects guarded Owain's memories of the past, the siren had reawakened the *feelings* of the past, emotions he had not experienced so acutely for centuries. He truly had been the living dead.

No more!

The commonplace book open before him, Owain reached for his gold-accented fountain pen. For the briefest of moments, he hesitated, nib fractions of an inch above parchment. Then he lowered the pen and wrote:

What would Angharad think?

The words, the last spoken by Albert before Benison had slammed a stake through the condemned Malkavian's heart, had been echoing in Owain's mind since last night. How ironic, Owain thought, that they should be given form in this book that Angharad had given him so long ago. Perhaps expelled onto parchment, they would not haunt him for countless nights to come. Perhaps.

Owain capped his pen. He reached for his blotter but then paused and just watched as the ink soaked into the parchment. The new words were so much darker than those that had been on the page for hundreds of years. The dichotomy was unnerving, this mingling of the ancient and the modern, but Owain would have to accustom himself to it. The past had been forcefully thrust upon the present in recent weeks. There were too many coincidences, Owain realized, seeing the patterns in hindsight. Reminders of Angharad—in the siren's song, in Albert's last words. And all had coincided with the spread of the curse.

Owain had witnessed the carnage of the Black Death during his years in France. Many had pronounced it a judgment of God, the coming of the apocalypse. This curse had made similarly deadly inroads among the Kindred as the Black Death had among mortals. Cainites were growing wary of one another, those who had not already succumbed to the curse. Some were calling it the onset of the Endtime, of Gehenna. Even Prince Benison believed the curse to be a divine reprisal against wayward subjects of the night. His decrees, basically repressing the anarchs, were supposed to rectify that situation somehow and restore supernatural favor. More likely, Owain suspected, the decrees would only serve to further damage the thin social fabric of the Kindred world, that which was already dangerously frayed by the curse.

The strange visions, too, that were plaguing Owain had begun shortly after the spread of the curse. Was there actually a connection running through it all, or like the inept historian, was Owain erroneously attributing cause and effect where there were none?

I am not your brother, Owain instinctively wanted to say, but he restrained himself. No good could come from unnecessarily antagonizing this irritating but dangerous vampire.

"The hour grows late," Miguel continued, unperturbed by Owain's silence. "We must leave soon. Are you packed?"

Demonstrating forced calm, Owain, the gracious host, smiled. "I'm afraid I can't get away this evening."

Miguel, remaining in the doorway, cocked his

head to the side and, with an exaggerated motion, cupped a hand by his ear. "*Que?*"

Owain maintained his rigid smile. "I must put certain affairs in order before I could go anywhere. But don't let me stop you. I can catch up."

Miguel laughed. It was a loud, grating sound. "But, *mi hermano*, I have made arrangements for *both* of us to travel."

The ticking of the clock on the shelf seemed to grow louder to fill the silence in the room. Owain took measure of his guest. Obviously Miguel had his orders and would not be swayed, and in the end, Owain would have little choice but to respect the summons from El Greco. Most likely it was pride that drove Owain, but he could not bring himself to give in to the perverse little Spaniard. Not yet.

"Well, *mi hermano*," Owain asserted through clenched teeth, "I suppose you will just have to make other arrangements."

Miguel, his patience cracking around the edges, stalked over to the desk and glared down at Owain. "You deny El Greco's request?"

Slowly Owain stood to his full height behind the desk, allowing him, in turn, to glower down at Miguel. "You misunderstand, my little *amigo*," said Owain. "Our mutual friend asked me in his message, which you seem to be familiar with, to 'come to Toledo *with all possible haste*.' For me to leave tonight—it is not possible."

The two faced one another across the desk. Owain knew he had made his point, but it was a victory of style rather than substance. He would be traveling with this detestable man soon.

Miguel took a step back from the desk. "Very well, then," he conceded. "When will it be *possible* for you to accompany me back to our lovely city of Toledo?" His tone was still demanding.

Enjoying the upper hand for the moment, Owain made a great show of mulling over this question for several moments. "Normally, I would say a matter of weeks at the very least." Owain almost laughed as Miguel tensed and his eyes grew wide. "But for El Greco," Owain continued before Miguel could protest, "I will leave…tomorrow."

For an instant, Miguel did not trust what he had heard. He expected trickery, or a challenge of some sort, but as Owain's response sunk in, a genuine smile blossomed across Miguel's face. He quickly tried to hide his relief, as if it was a matter of course that they would leave tomorrow. "Very well, then," said Miguel, businesslike. "Tomorrow. I will make the arrangements."

"You do that, Miguel," said Owain. He remained standing until Miguel had scurried out of the room and the door was again closed.

It was no use, Owain decided. He could not hide his dislike for Miguel. *The little weasel invades my study as if he were in his own home. What good is knocking if he doesn't bother to wait for a reply?* Of course, if Miguel had waited for an invitation, Owain probably would have left him standing in the hall the entire night. Miguel always had been a prickly type, and with Owain in a bad mood most centuries, the two had never gotten along particularly well. Owain took some small satisfaction in having delayed their departure; it had always been a question of *when* they would leave for Toledo, not *if*, despite whatever Owain might say.

As his thoughts turned to Toledo and El Greco, Owain's gaze drifted toward the chess board in the alcove before the window seat. He and El Greco had measured their gamesmanship, one against the other, for centuries now, and excepting this recent game, Owain had generally enjoyed the upper hand. Absent-mindedly, Owain stood and went to the board. Now that his energies had been drawn to weightier matters, he was able to examine the game a bit more dispassionately. He was still amazed at how El Greco had managed, in one move, to transform the game from a near rout for Owain to an assured victory for himself. Owain scratched the stubble on his young-looking face. Such subtlety, executed to perfection, was not the norm for El Greco. He aspired to subtlety, but rarely possessed the patience necessary to succeed. *An anarch who has survived beyond his time*, Owain thought of El Greco as, but the old anarch had certainly blindsided Owain in this game.

Though the anger was more controllable now, just looking at the board still raised Owain's ire and did little to ease the mood of the night that, already, Miguel had quite ably soured.

Owain returned to his desk. There *were* actually arrangements that needed to be taken care of. He had not put off Miguel purely out of spitefulness, though that was largely the reason. Owain had still not responded to Lorenzo Giovanni's request for information regarding several Atlanta Kindred. It was a simple enough favor and would go far in cementing favorable relations with the Giovanni clan's local representative. Also, Owain had not decided whether he should have his driver and most dependable ghoul, Kendall Jackson, accompany him to Spain, or if she should stay behind to manage the estate. She did not yet, Owain supposed, know enough about his financial affairs to be much help in Atlanta, so he might as well take her with him. Besides, she had proven herself useful in tight situations, and Owain didn't fancy traveling anywhere near his Sabbat "allies" without a pair of day-time eyes.

There were other details to attend to, though for a moment Owain entertained the perverse idea of having a bit of sport with Miguel and delaying their departure for another night or two.

Blackfeather curled inward—one leg folded beneath him, the other hugged to his chest. He beat time with one foot, marking the passage of clouds across the moon.

Wa-Kan-Kan Ya-Wa-On-We.

In a holy manner I live.

For the third time tonight, his quarry had narrowly eluded him, seeming to vanish entirely from the face of this world. Still, the beast could not be far and Blackfeather was a peerless hunter.

A lesser hunter would have given up the chase as darkness fell, masking the nearly imperceptible signs along the path—the bent stalk of grass, the crushed leaf, the displaced pebble, the nettle-snared tuft of fur. A mortal hunter scoured a trail in the wake of his prey. His gaze focused ever downwards, scrutinizing the earth, wringing it for answers.

Blackfeather had not even risen until well after sunset. He was not in the least inconvenienced by the shadows and silences that lay thick upon the land. Quite the contrary. It was the intensity of the light and bustle of the day that was most likely to distract him, to make him uneasy, to throw him off the trail.

His preternatural senses were finely tuned to the half-light of the stars and waning moon. He could travel more swiftly than a horse over treacherous ground without ever missing the small telltale signs of his quarry as he raced along.

But now the trail had grown cold and Blackfeather had come to rest. He sat in the middle of the trail, carefully folded in upon himself, slowly tapping one foot. He did not fear obscuring the subtle signs of the beast's passage. He knew full well that there were no such signs to obscure. This prey left no mark of its passing upon the earth.

Blackfeather ignored the ground entirely. His head was thrown back, his attention was turned upward. His gaze remained unfocused. His sight blurred at the edges as if scanning for something in the realm of the peripheral.

Nothing.

No sign of the beast, his counterpart, his nemesis. No sense of its presence.

The tapping of his foot slowed. Time seemed to stretch away before him, matching its pace to the rhythm of his foot.

The change was imperceptible at first. His first clue was that the cloud that was passing across the moon seemed to pause midcourse. It hung suspended, inverted, as if waiting for the next footstep to fall.

Then the moon itself seemed to stretch, to lengthen. It grew oblong, a lustrous egg perched high above him in a nest of translucent cloud. A shadow fell across Blackfeather's face and he thought of the Thunderbird, Lord of the Heavens, whose talons struck sparks of lightning from the mountaintops at the four corners of the world.

Blackfeather whispered a silent prayer that the beast might not take the form of the Thunderbird this night. He watched the egg as carefully as ever a mother eagle had sat sentry over her nest.

His fears soon proved groundless. The moon continued its transformation, and Blackfeather allowed himself a slight sigh of relief. By the time he had again drawn ritual breath, the moon had stretched itself into an arc, forming a wide road of light across the night sky. Blackfeather noted that the stars were likewise lengthening, expanding into the middle distance. They kept pace with the wayward moon, following its passage from east to west.

It seemed to Blackfeather that he was taking in their entire night's journey at a single glance. Time had spread its bounty before him. He picked out a single arcing star at random from the feast of lights, studied it intently. Rigel, he decided after a moment, the radiant heel of Orion, the Hunter. A fine omen.

He soon picked out Betelgeuse and, having caught the Hunter's eye, had little difficulty making out the three jewels of his belt. The constellation curled in upon itself as it stretched across the night sky in pursuit of its elusive quarry. Each of its component stars spanned the entire vault of the sky from horizon to horizon, both racing and motionless in the same instant.

Below, Blackfeather sat at the still point, gazing

up intently at the play of lights. His senses stretched away into the dim recesses of the night sky. He felt as if his very essence were being stretched thin. The shadows fell heavy upon him until he seemed more a shade himself than a physical being—a restless shade, summoned from the earth's arms to witness this strange motionless dance of starlight.

Yes, a shade, he thought. Something of the grave clung to him. A touch of shadow that was not cast from above, but drawn out of him and made increasingly obvious by the growing illumination of the night sky.

The streaks of light splashed a more sinister aspect across Blackfeather's features. They picked out the intricate network of lines carved into his leathery face. His visage was so deeply scored, it called to mind a weathered fishing net—crisscrossed, frayed, cracked by the sun. A person could lose his way among the lines of that face, fall victim to the subtle pattern of the labyrinth. Blackfeather gazed upon the world past a parched, cracked landscape of desolation. A maze of gulches, ravines, arroyos spread out across the badlands of his weathered features.

Above his head, stranger patterns still were forming—feverish matrices of fire and night. Like shooting stars run in reverse, the arcs of light appeared to burn out into the dim distance, to lose themselves amidst the smudge of the Milky Way.

Blackfeather raised one insubstantial hand in mute salute and let it fall again. He repeated the motion, watching his other hand drift leisurely earthward. He suddenly caught a vision of himself as if he were standing over his own shoulder. The curious shadowy figure seated before him on the trail appeared as a solitary phantom juggler.

Arms as insubstantial as shadow, translucent as cloud, waved slowly skyward then earthward, skyward, earthward. The limbs were beyond his volition, moved by a gentle breeze or a barely perceptible tug at invisible strings.

Above his head a thousand brilliant silver balls cut an arc across the sky. At its crux, triumphant moon bounded high and plummeted fast.

Blackfeather jerked, lunging to catch the moon as it streaked earthward. But his hand had no substance to it, no hope to arrest the fiery orb in its flight. It struck the earth with a sound that raced the length of Blackfeather's spine, cracking it like a whip. The concussion that followed a moment later pitched him into the air and sent him scrambling on all fours trying to regain some semblance of balance.

A great cloud of dust arose from the south, marking the point of impact. One by one, the stars dimmed and then fell from the sky with the sound of tinkling glass. The sky found itself once more in darkness. Cleansed of light. Primeval, pristine, pure.

Blackfeather was on his feet and racing southward. He hardly took note of his path in his headlong flight. His feet seemed sure of themselves, finding their footing of their own accord. His footfalls, however, sounded different now—the unmistakable slap of leather on wooden planks. The path had twisted unexpectedly, taken a turn not of direction, but of substance. Blackfeather found himself racing along disused railroad tracks towards some unguessed destination in the far south.

Even as the thought crossed his mind, he knew it to be untrue. His destination was not unguessed. Some part of him recognized instinctively the point towards which the tracks were inexorably leading him.

All roads, it is said, lead to Rome. When railroad men speak of the End of the Line, however, they have quite a different destination in mind—a place they once called Terminus.

Ahead of him, from beyond the expanding cloud of ash, Blackfeather could now pick out the first flickering hints of conflagration, little more than ruddy glowing coals on the horizon. Somewhere ahead, fields were burning. And surely buildings by the look of it, he thought. Many buildings. And there were mounted men with torches among the buildings.

Blackfeather shook his head to clear it. Surely

even his keen eyesight could not pick out such details at this distance. A riderless horse streaked past him, nearly knocking him to the ground. It stamped, reared in panic and raced on.

He could hear the sound of confused shouts and feel a searing heat stretching his face taut. A man in a blue uniform carrying a rifle swore at him loudly, giving him a rough shove. When Blackfeather failed to react, the man shouted again.

"...damned wind's kicked up and turned the flames back around! If you're not out of this field double time, you will be mustering out of General Sherman's army the hard way, soldier!"

Then the man was gone, vanished back into the maelstrom of heat and sound. Blackfeather heard a great roar drawing close and turned back toward the source of the blaze. There, rising from the cloud of ash that blanketed the city, a thousand tongues of flame rose, joined, blossomed heavenward.

Each tongue voiced a great cry. The shrieking cacophony rose ever higher, not a wail of despair, but the birth-wail of the beast, the phoenix, the city rising from its own ashes. Atlanta.

The great beast, the firebird, soared forth, revealed in all its glory.

Blackfeather saw his quarry resplendent in all its majesty, rising in the heavens like a newborn star. He let the terrible beauty of the beast, his beast, wash over him. He felt the sense of purpose quicken within him. The age-old chase was once again afoot.

There was no question of his running his prey to ground this night. Blackfeather rocked back on his heels and smiled, content to be bested. His thoughts were already leaping ahead, anticipating the coming hours of dogging his own personal star across the heavens.

Soon enough dawn would press him gently back into the earth. No doubt the first hints of sunrise would take him on the outskirts of Atlanta. He was not likely to lose the trail again now. But the night stretched away before him like a lover's promise. Tonight, there was the chase, the hunt, the quest.

The beast opened its maw with the sound of one hundred baying hounds and Blackfeather, peerless hunter, dutifully followed after.

It had been two nights since the gathering of practically all of Atlanta's Kindred, and still Eleanor had heard nothing from Benjamin. Of course they had to stay reasonably clear of each other when Cainites gathered—no point in inviting gossip, especially when it might be true—but what could be the harm in a private walk? An evening meal?

Eleanor paced about the parlor. This was her province, her contemplative retreat. Just as she left the library to Benison, aside from when she needed particular books, he left the parlor to her. Just because they were joined to one another for eternity, an unusual enough arrangement for vampires, did not mean that they didn't both need their privacy. Though each thrived on the other's company, they did both, in fact, spend much of their time in solitude. *Merely intensifies the time we spend together*, Eleanor reasoned.

At the moment, however, it was Benjamin, not Benison, who occupied Eleanor's thoughts, and solitude was not her craving. Theirs was a relationship of the mind, unsullied by the physical passion of mortals, though certainly not devoid of passion. Eleanor longed for Benjamin's companionship, his insight, his sharp wit—so cerebral, while Benison was…less so. What did Benjamin think of Benison's pronouncements? Would the anarchs respect the decrees and take up their places in respectable clans, or would unrest ensue? Did Benjamin think the Camarilla would intervene?

Actually, Eleanor was more knowledgeable on that front, with her connections through her sire and her own former position of archon. Even so, she could no more than guess. The Inner Council might step in, or they might have more urgent business elsewhere, responding to the ravages of the curse. Chicago, Miami, Washington D.C., London, Berlin—all maintained more precarious balances of power than here in Atlanta. Benison had a history of stability—for his city, not necessarily his temperament—on his side. He would have a certain window of time during which he must maintain control. Only no one had any way of knowing how large that window was.

But these were the thoughts she wanted to share with Benjamin! Eleanor realized that she was crumpling in her fist the lace doily on her writing table. She carefully smoothed the lace, then sat. This table, in other venues, had seen written some of the most influential epistles of the Kindred world. Eleanor did not feel she was flattering herself to think so. But she had left behind the larger world of Cainite politics to be with Benison. Sometimes she wondered if he remembered that. Tonight he was gallivanting around the city keeping an eye out for trouble—an important job, but if the prince saw to all that himself, why did they have hired help? It could be interpreted as weakness, the prince on patrol, and she had told him as much. But what good had it done? Meanwhile, she was here alone. No Benison. No Benjamin.

Why hadn't she heard from her childe? That was one secret that her husband need never learn—that she had Embraced Benjamin after her intellectual desire for him had left her little choice, other than to destroy him, and *that* clearly had not been a viable alternative.

Eleanor frowned at the blank stationary before her. Why hadn't he responded to her previous message? Her waifish serving ghoul, Sally, said she had delivered the letter. Again, Eleanor put pen to paper. Benjamin had often assured her that, though it tore a small piece of his heart away each time, he destroyed each of her letters to him, for the sake of prudence. Still, Eleanor generally tried to couch her phrases ambiguously enough that an errant missive would not be her undoing. This letter would be less ambiguous than most, she felt, as her aggravation with Benjamin flamed higher.

How long had it been since she had heard a tender word from him? How long had it been since she'd heard *any* word from him, other than the most perfunctory of greetings at a social gathering? Not since before that disastrous exhibit of Marlene-the-idiot-whore's so-called artwork at the High Museum, and that had been months ago!

Her pen bit into the stationary. She had been willing to play coy for some time, but enough was enough. In no uncertain terms, she let Benjamin know just how she felt about being ignored. *The ungrateful childe*, she fumed. Eleanor believed that affairs of the heart, unlike marriage, which was as much a political as an emotional arrangement, required brutal honesty at times, and she spared no brutality with Benjamin. She could understand, after Owain Evans's threats, Benjamin's wanting to thicken the veil of discretion beneath which their relationship necessarily existed, but she would not tolerate him using that as an excuse to slink away and leave her unstimulated intellectually. Because that's what was important really—the encounters with her in, and then out of, her negligée were mainly just a change of pace, to keep things fresh.

It all came back to Owain Evans, Eleanor noticed. If he hadn't tried to unduly influence Benjamin, then she would not have to be dealing with this personal turmoil. How much did Evans know? she wondered. There was no one other than Benjamin and herself who knew that he was her progeny, so there was no way Evans could have discovered that little tidbit. But then again, he had found out about her and Benjamin's…involvement, despite their precautions. An infuriating thought crossed Eleanor's mind. Had Evans merely suspected and taken a blind gamble, and Benjamin had panicked and confirmed Evans's suspicions? If Benjamin had been so clumsy, could he have discussed his Cainite lineage with someone as well? Perhaps; though her secret childe was superior to most intellectually, he was lacking in guile.

Eleanor completed her letter to Benjamin. Hopefully the expression of her displeasure would bring him to his senses. Certainly, she was sure, he could hope to do no better than her, neither intellectually nor socially, while her status was quite safe without him. Safer, in fact. And, she reminded herself, J. Benison was quite the adept debater. What his arguments lacked in subtlety, they made up for in conviction. Certainly she could be content without her wayward childe, if it came to that. *Yes, dear Benjamin had better just watch his step, or he might find himself walking all alone in the dark city*, she decided.

As she folded the note and applied sealing wax, Eleanor's thoughts turned again to Owain Evans. She needed to find out how much he did know; but more importantly, she needed to make him pay for dragging her name into his little schemes—regardless of the accuracy of his allegations. She would keep her eyes open, and she would find a way. Of that, Eleanor was certain.

Kli Kodesh walked dripping from the sea. The waters rolled back from his shoulders and fell away unnoticed in his wake. A tangle of long white hair, plaited with streamers of seaweed, stretched out behind him like a fishing net cast out upon the surface of the waters. His simple white linen robe clung tightly about him as he emerged. It had gone distinctly gray from exposure to sea and salt, and drew attention to the unmistakable bluish tinge to his features.

The lines of his face were striking—sharp, classical, almost sculpted. Sand and bits of shell coated his skin, glittered in the moonlight. The effect made him seem more a work of marble and artifice than a creature of flesh and blood. Even his bearing was regal, statuesque. He rose from the water smoothly, seamlessly, like the prow of a ship cresting the beach.

Kli Kodesh felt the water stream away from his chiseled features. He blinked experimentally. Once, twice. He had the unsettling impression of struggling to awaken from a dream. And it had been such a lovely dream.

He had dreamt of crossing a vast desert. The sands beneath his feet were cool and soothing, even at midday when the shadows themselves fled the desert wastes. The sky was a blue of infinite depth, ever-shifting. It filled the vault of heaven from horizon to horizon. Kli Kodesh had wandered that desert for forty years, moving with the languid grace of the sleeper.

But the sea had cast him up again. In all his years of wandering, he found that the oceans had, by far, the greatest patience. An ocean might spend the better part of a century worrying away the tip of a jetty, or a single brass fitting on a sunken ship. Even the long-suffering oceans, however, would not long abide his presence.

Kli Kodesh felt the night wind on his face, sharp and cool. He smiled, scoring deep lines into the layer of brine and sand that caked his face. Half of his expression cracked, broke away and fell to the beach. It was good to be back in the world.

But where, in the world, was he? Slowly, but without misstep, he picked his way to the top of the nearest dune. His garment hung heavily upon him. Even the weight of his skin seemed an unaccustomed burden. As he crested the ridge, a blare of lights broke over him, streaking upwards into the night, filling the vault of heaven.

Whites, reds, yellows—a city of lights flared outward. It etched its image into the underside of the heavy layer of yellowed cloud that hung in perpetuity above the city of men below. The greasy ring of cloud shone like a halo.

Kli Kodesh closed his eyes and swirled the murky clouds like tea leaves, turning them over and over again in his mind. Searching for some dimly remembered snatch of story or song or prophecy.

He had spent centuries watching cities gather and disperse, dissolve and resolve. He was an adept at sifting the jagged shards of civilization from the uncertain sands of time. He was a master of possibilities and permutations.

As he watched the play of lights, he could see cities long forgotten standing side-by-side with those that were as yet unguessed. He traced their growth and decline absently with one finger, as if following a treacherous route on a map. His mind raced down branchings of past and future that spread themselves before his scrutiny, butterflied, laid bare.

Ah. Just...there.

A Beacon on the Shores of the Western Nyght.

A City of Angels.

It has begun.

With great anticipation, Kli Kodesh descended upon the city. All about him were heard lamentations and the gnashing of teeth.

CHAPTER TWO

John Rotty knew there was going to be trouble as soon as he saw Thu come through the door. She was cracking her knuckles, and that chain hanging out of her jacket wasn't just for show.

Atlanta was dead these days, or more precisely, anybody who was anybody in anarch circles was dead. Tobias, Aaron, Eddie Cocke, Liza, Jolanda, Matt—the list went on and on. All dead. Bloated and belly-up. The few Rotty had seen had been pretty messy—bleeding out of eyes, ears, nose, among other places. Like there was too much blood for their bodies. *But everybody says,* Rotty remembered, *if the curse gets you, you starve to death. It doesn't make any sense.*

Rotty figured: it hadn't caught up with him yet, maybe he wasn't the right type for curses, maybe he was just lucky. Either way, he wasn't going to sit around and twiddle his thumbs in his room all night. He had been a vampire for about ten years now, and one thing he had decided long ago was that he had to keep moving. He didn't like the idea of spending the rest of eternity sitting on his butt, bored to undeath. So he'd checked out Underground. Dead. There were a few kine, but no Kindred. How many times could he mesmerize some mortal chick and then drain her dry? For real excitement, he needed other vampires. So he'd cruised over to Little Five Points. Pretty slow there too. He'd wandered into Nine Tails. Same old story. Loud goth music—moaning and machinery. *Can't anybody play a guitar anymore?* Rotty wondered. More mortal meat. No Kindred.

Until Thu waltzed through the door, that was. *And she ain't the Kindred I want to see,* Rotty knew right away. *The only thing worse than a chick with attitude, is a chick with attitude who can kick your ass.* Rotty had seen her in action before and didn't care to see any more.

There were enough black-clad goth types and multiple-body-pierced yahoos in the S&M club that Rotty was able to slide away from the front door. He didn't think Thu had noticed him. Yet. Maybe she was just hunting, scoping out some meat, but then again, being a permanently ragged-out bitch, maybe she was looking for trouble. He kept his head down and stayed near the bar—it wasn't normally a favorite hangout for Cainites. As he edged toward the back hall and the bathrooms, Rotty stayed away from the dancers who were gyrating the most spasmodically. He didn't need them attracting attention to him. One chick bumped into him and spilled her drink on him, but he let it slide. He didn't need a scene now either.

Rotty decided against the side door. Everybody tended to watch that exit more closely now, ever since Liza's and Aaron's messed-up bodies turned up in the alley a couple of months back. Down the back hall, and Rotty was safely out the back door. He breathed a sigh of pure relief.

Then the two-by-four smacked him in the back of the head. Rotty was face-down in the alley, his nose flattened against the grimy, cracked pavement. Swung by a lot of people, even a lot of Kindred, a two-by-four across the back of the head would have been no big deal. Whoever this was, it was not one of those people. That board was swung with some *oompa!*

Before Rotty's vision had cleared or the ringing in his ears had stopped, he was being lifted off the ground by strong hands grasping his shirt. "Nice of you to help me up," he muttered, wondering if the words were too slurred to make sense.

"What was that?" The voice very close to Rotty growled.

As his vision cleared, he could see another face inches away from his own—snarling mouth, flat nose, wide-set eyes, exaggerated Neanderthal brow. Xavier Kline, Rotty realized. *Crap*.

Kline held Rotty in the air, his feet dangling several inches above the ground. "What did you say?" Kline demanded again.

"Nothin'."

"Hmph." Kline, the huge, muscled Brujah, didn't seem to believe Rotty, but settled for violently shaking the smaller, airborne vampire. The rough motion set jolts of pain shooting from the back of Rotty's head to his temples. "You gettin' smart with me, gothboy?" Kline challenged him.

Gothboy? Despite his precarious situation, Rotty took exception to this. "Just because I hang out here, where the feedin' is easy—*Ah!*"

From behind, a chain whipped against Rotty's head just above the left ear, interrupting his retort. Welts rose almost instantly.

"You are what you eat," said a voice with a thick Vietnamese accent. Many Asian accents, to Rotty, sounded rather melodious. They created a syncopated rhythm almost lyrical in nature. Not this accent. Rotty recognized Thu's voice, and it grated like a butter knife over burnt toast.

Kline shook him again. Again the pain shot

through Rotty's head. "What you doing tonight?" Kline demanded.

"I thought I'd kick some Brujah ass," Rotty quipped. The chain tore into his flesh again, this time on the back of his neck. *Okay, smart guy,* he told himself, *shut your mouth. Always were a slow learner.*

Kline grinned. "Keep talkin', gothboy, and there won't be nothing left but a mess of bones and blood."

Rotty didn't doubt it. Kline and Thu were noted for their savagery, even among Kindred—not a sensitive, touchy-feely lot.

"You weren't at the gathering Tuesday night, were you, gothboy?" Kline asked. He didn't wait for a response. "You heard about the prince's decrees, right?" This time he shook Rotty, apparently wanting an answer. Rotty nodded, but either Kline didn't notice or that wasn't good enough. More violent shaking followed. "What'd you say?"

"I heard. I heard!" Everybody had heard, at the gathering or not. The prince was not only going to start enforcing the Traditions to the letter, he was also demanding that all Cainites in the city not belonging to a clan must join one, or face exile—or worse. The back of Rotty's head was throbbing. He knew he was bleeding from several wounds now. He wished his head would fall off, but then he decided he better be careful what he wished for with these two around.

"Good," said Kline. "I'm glad you're keeping up on current events." He showed no sign of tiring or of intending to put Rotty down anytime soon. "So, you decided what clan to join yet?"

"I was thinking about the KKK," Rotty said, against his better judgment. The chain bit into the right side of his head this time, striking hard enough to snap his head to the left. His vision began to blur again, or was that blood getting in his eyes? He was too woozy to be sure. All the blows to his head were taking their toll. Thu was silent except for the jingle of her chain.

"I hear good things about the Brujah," Kline suggested. "In fact, I highly recommend them. Wouldn't you like to work for me?" Rotty heard what he thought was Thu chuckling in the background.

Working for Kline. That sounded like hell to Rotty. Never mind that Thelonious was the Brujah primogen. He was more the upper-crust type, not the Brujah presence on the street like Kline. Prudence and physical pain finally having gotten the best of him, Rotty kept these details to himself. Elaborating the finer points of Brujah hierarchy would only earn him more of a beating.

Kline noticed this change of heart as well. "Nothing smart to say, gothboy?" Still getting no response, he threw Rotty to the pavement. "Remember, Brujah clan. You wouldn't want to go wrong." Kline laughed as he walked away. Thu kicked Rotty in the stomach for good measure, then followed Kline.

Rotty lay on the ground, not moving, just glad he was no longer being chain-whipped or beaten. He could hear the bass pounding from inside Nine Tails, or was the pounding inside his head? His eyes would not focus on the stars overhead. As badly as he hurt, he knew he was lucky. Kline and Thu could have done much worse. They could have drunk his blood, destroyed him, left his body so close to where Liza and Aaron had turned up dead. Among all the carnage of the curse, who would have cared? Still, that was small consolation with head wounds that, for a mortal, would have required fifty or sixty stitches at least. For Rotty, the injuries would require one or two mortals. The blood would do the healing.

He would recover, but Rotty decided he would have to be more careful in the future. With so few Kindred around these nights, those out in the open attracted a lot more notice. Would he join a clan? He didn't know yet. He would rather keep away from Kline than join the Brujah. That was certain. But if the prince was serious about this decree, Rotty didn't want to run into too much trouble on that front. He would have to ask around with the remaining anarchs, those who hadn't been laid low by the curse. Give in to the prince's demands, try to circumvent them, or fight back? Tough question.

At the moment, Rotty didn't feel like fighting anybody. He tried to sit up, but the racking pain convinced him that lying where he was for a while longer might not be a bad idea. Then he noticed something under his elbow. Trying not to move his head, Rotty reached under his arm to find the splintered half of a two-by-four. He started to laugh, but it hurt too much. *You wanted excitement*, he reminded himself. *You got it*.

Benison crouched on the roof of the shop behind Nine Tails, the best venue he had found from which to watch Kline's shenanigans. *A mindless brute*, the prince thought of Kline. *No, not mindless*, he corrected himself. *Predictable. Predictable but devious*.

The prince had charged Kline with finding the half dozen or so anarchs who had not attended the gathering of the Kindred two nights ago, at which Benison had delivered his New Year's Decrees, and making sure they received the news. Approved by the primogen, despite the narrow margin, the decrees carried the force of law. The first decree reclaimed control of the streets. The Traditions would be upheld without exception. There were too many dangers to the Masquerade without Kindred running amok, necessitating that Benison cover their tracks lest the mortal population discover their predators lurking in the night. The rights, too, of Domain, Progeny, and Hospitality were all too often abused. No longer.

The second decree would set the Kindred of Atlanta back in accordance with the ageless teachings, handed down through the eons from the scribes of the ancient First City. Cainite blood had grown weak. There were those most recently created in whom the strength of the Dark Father was so little that they were unable to create progeny. The scraps of *The Book of Nod*, which Benison had acquired over the years, had predicted that such a thinning of the blood would come to pass. Other predictions had borne truth as well—the Clanless running rampant, the ensuing chaos. If the Kindred of the Camarilla did not act, the Endtime would overtake them. The teaching spoke of that as well—physical and spiritual upheaval, the destruction of both Kindred and kine worlds as the eldest of the elders, the antediluvians, returned from their rest to reclaim all that they had directly or indirectly begotten.

Benison would not sit idly and watch that happen. Already, he had cleansed with flame the desecrated church, whence the unrecognized Daughter of Cacophony had conspired with demons to rain divine wrath down upon the city and to set all Kindred on the road to the Endtime.

Benison would not let it be so. With the force of his individual will, he would fight off Gehenna, or at the least he would enlist so much collective support as to forestall that end. His Atlanta would serve as a beacon of salvation to the rest of the world. This was his messianic crusade—to transform the city that had begun as Terminus to one known as Primus, the new First City, in thought and deed sanctified in its relation with the Lord, He who had handed such prominence to the Dark Father and all his race. The recasting of the city, Benison had come to believe, would be a conversion as miraculous as the transubstantiation of the bread and wine to the body and blood.

He realized that he was now standing atop the building, no longer crouching. His mind preoccupied, his body had attempted to parallel his thoughts on their exalted and transcendent path toward salvation. *Let them see me*, he decided, *a figure of righteous realignment, as they gaze toward the heavens*.

As it turned out, Kline and Thu did not notice him. They finished beating the anarch and left him to bleed in the alley. The attack on the anarch did not overly concern Benison. *Penance is good for the soul*, he felt, and unquestionably the anarch had much reason to repent, though Benison doubted that spiritual improvement was the motivating factor behind Kline's actions. The Neanderthal Brujah was doubtless a bit overzealous in carrying out his second charge—to remind all the anarchs that their indefinite status which had, to some extent, left them beyond the law of the Camarilla, was a thing of the past. Kline had combined with that task his own rather indelicate recruitment drive in an attempt to boost his status within the Brujah clan as well as in Kindred society as a whole. *Can't fault him for his initiative*, the prince conceded. Benison did not fancy a city full of young Brujah; it was a clan he could just as easily do without. But probably, he suspected, Kline's tactics would backfire. While intimidation could prove useful in temporarily persuading others to a particular course of action, it usually did little in the way of inspiring loyalty. Any Kindred might say whatever Kline wanted to hear if it meant avoiding being beaten to a bloody pulp, but that Kindred would also remember Kline's bullying. The aggrieved Cainite might fear and respect the decrees of the prince, but would grow to loathe the Brujah.

It did not surprise Benison in the least to see that Kline was mixing equal parts politics and intimidation with his official duties. The prince had been using Kline for some time now, in one capacity or another, and acting with subtlety upon discretionary orders was not the Brujah's strength. But better to keep an eye on him than not. *Easier an oxen under yoke than a bull in the field.* Benison remembered the saying from his mortal days.

The prince crouched again and watched from his concealed vantage point as the anarch lay unmoving on the pavement. There were at least a dozen or so unrecognized Kindred residing in Atlanta. There had been more, perhaps two or three times as many—they were so difficult to keep track of—before the curse. Benison's muscles tensed. The mere thought of the malady that had so afflicted his city was enough to stoke his temper, but he forced himself to maintain control. *From every tragedy there are lessons to be learned*, Benison reminded himself. *The Lord has visited my city with this damnable curse to challenge me, to spur me to greater triumphs. Primus.* He considered his new mantra. "Primus."

Eleanor had advised him not to go out this night. She had worried that he would appear to be dealing from a position of weakness. *Did she think I was going to scurry around and beg the anarchs to do as I wish?* Benison wondered. Surely she didn't account him so little credit as that. *She plays her Camarilla politics well, but that is not the same as leadership. The politicians manipulate. I build. I shore the foundations of my city.* How did she think that he could stay home? How did she think he could do nothing while his city crumbled? Benison knew that he was called to a higher purpose.

It was this new vision of immortality—glory and inspiration discovered within the depths of despair brought on by the curse—that kept Benison going. He was supremely confident that all his personal tragedy, his having to watch as the city he had helped build for over one hundred years unraveled at the seams, was the ransom demanded so that a greater good could emerge. His own childe had fallen prey to the madness of the curse. Madness, pain, death. Benison had locked that fact away deep within his own soul. He knew the tragedy, but he had not felt it. His city was his childe now, and there was no time to grieve. Only to persevere.

☥

If that isn't the darnedest thing, thought Dr. William Nen. *How could those bodies have been found there?* He set the files on his desk and began absently tugging on the corner of his thick mustache. It was a habit he had picked up as an undergraduate so many years ago, back before the mustache and his thick head of hair had been invaded by gray.

The files he was reading were the latest directed his way by the examiners. No one at the Center for Disease Control and Prevention quite knew what to make of these cases, so the enigmatic reports made their way to Nen's desk. He didn't know what to make of them either. Not yet.

He reached for his coffee mug, but instead of drinking, ran his tongue along the rim. That was another habit—one he had picked up in medical school. Each milestone in his career seemed to leave its own indelible mark, a personality quirk here, a peculiar mannerism there. *Symptoms of progress*, Nen called them. Leigh, his psychologist wife, had had plenty of suggestions regarding the significance of his "coffee mug fetish," as she called it, but William never had put much stock in Freudian analysis himself.

It had been early in his career, almost twenty years ago, after he had helped pinpoint the vectors of the ebola outbreak in the Sudan, that he had begun washing his hands so compulsively before and after every meal that he sometimes drew blood. His involvement in the Sudan had led to the containment of that outbreak—only thirty-four cases and twenty-two deaths. Three years before that, similar outbreaks there and in Zaire had left over three hundred dead.

He had been called upon again in 1995, when the Zairian strain of the virus had reappeared in Kikwit. Even in that city of four hundred thousand, an epidemic waiting to happen, timely quarantines and aggressive public information campaigns had kept casualties at a minimal level. Nen had returned from that trip to Africa with an occasional tic near the corner of his left eye. He could feel when it happened, but short of lying on the couch with a wet, steaming hot washcloth over his face, there was nothing he could do to stop it.

These latest cases that had so baffled the examiners were not ebola. At least not any strain that Nen had encountered before. There were some similarities, on a superficial level, that could conceivably be construed to indicate a hemorrhagic fever—uncontrolled bleeding, internal and external; absence of clotting; liver and kidney deterioration—but the bloodwork didn't bear out the symptoms, not according to the reports, at any rate. Nen wanted to follow that up on his own. Not that he didn't trust his colleagues in the lab, but when faced with contradictory data, his first inclination was to reexamine the data gathering. He had caught mistakes in the past, and considering that the consequences could include a hemorrhagic fever epidemic with fifty to ninety percent of cases proving fatal, double-checking some lab work seemed a small price to pay.

Nen set his coffee mug on his desk. The failure of the tests to corroborate the autopsy evidence was disturbing, but even more puzzling were the data concerning the bodies themselves. Looking down, Nen realized that he was wringing his hands, lightly but steadily, as if he had soap and water and were washing away the contagions he studied. He forced himself to stop and reached for the reports.

These particular bodies had been found here in the city, in Atlanta, in an alley by an active nightclub. The blood samples recovered had been relatively fresh, no more than several hours post mortem. The condition of the tissue samples, on the other hand, indicated that the individuals had been deceased for a number of *weeks*. The information was circled in red on the page before Nen. Someone else, *several someones, most likely*, thought Nen, had already been confounded by the same material, and no matter how many times Nen read over the report, the words were always the same, as was his conclusion. Impossible.

There were, he realized, some freakish possibilities. For whatever reason, fresh blood could have been left on the long-dead bodies. But some of the blood samples, in fact most of the samples, Nen noted, had been collected at the morgue, not on the street. Could someone have filled the body cavities with fresh blood? *Unlikely*. And besides, one of the two bodies had been nearly empty of blood. Nen tossed the files back onto his desk and started tugging on his mustache again. He had his work cut out for him.

For just a moment, the tic in his eye started up. He thought he faintly smelled the rot and the death that he had known in the Sudan. But these were the antiseptic offices and hallways of CDC. It must, he decided, have been the stale coffee he smelled.

Probably his mug could use a washing. William Nen shrugged and reached again for the reports.

Nicholas smelled the city from miles away. The highways stretched out in every direction from its black heart, arteries bearing the poison of human progress out through the last reaches of wilderness. Asphalt, exhaust, subdivisions—every time he left, he tried to forget how far they had spread, how much had been destroyed; and Atlanta was even a relatively green city, not like Chicago or Detroit or Indianapolis.

Months ago, he had come to the city simply to bring a message, a task that was a favor for the friend of a friend, and in exchange for another quite handsome favor. Had he known that the journey would bring a curse down upon his head, he would never have agreed to make it. No favor was worth that. To retrace the footsteps and choose a new path—if only that were possible. But the city had marked him, and now the curse ate away at him as surely as the mortals consumed the wilds.

Nicholas would not linger in the city. He would vent his rage, see justice served, and then return to the healing forests, the soothing plains. For one of these city Kindred had wronged Nicholas's lineage long ago. But what was *long* to the damned? It was an idea that belonged to the mortals. To the forest that grew and burned and grew and washed away and grew again, what was a *long* mortal life? And what was it to Nicholas?

He kept to the green places as he could, crossing the blacktopped automobile pathways only when he could not avoid them. He was well practiced, in his wolven form, at sniffing the route least tainted by mortals and their ways of progress. He had traveled much of two continents, and never had it been the allure of man-made wonders that had guided his steps. The closer he came to the city, however, the more arduous his task became. The property boundaries rose before him more frequently. Undeveloped tracts of land grew less plentiful.

With every mile traversed, his sensibilities were gradually losing ground to the rage that burned within him. Each obstacle delayed by seconds or by minutes the moment he would reach that walled estate, that false oasis of greenery within the cursed city. Each change of direction kept from him that much longer the instant when his claws and fangs would tear into the flesh of Owain Evans, and Nicholas would reclaim stolen Gangrel vitae.

As the outskirts of the city grew more dense around him, Nicholas veered less often from the most direct path toward his prey. Those few mortals he encountered at this hour of the night would likely be unaware of his passing. A passing motorist might see, if anything, a peripheral blur. A deer darting from the side of the road? A gust of wind from nowhere whipping through the weeds? As the farms and undisturbed stands of trees gave way to subdivisions and convenience marts, Nicholas felt the last of the wilderness-inspired peace evaporate from him. He cared less and less for keeping to the unspoiled places, for masking the signs of his passing. His attention grew more focused on his destination, more riveted to his goal.

Blood. He could smell blood. Already he could taste it, the blood of his ancestors. His wolven ears were laid back, his fangs bared, as his powerful muscles drove him forward with each unrelenting stride. Blighted suburbs remained undisturbed by his passing.

Nicholas had not fed this night. He had not wanted to stop, to divert the time from his progress. But mostly he had wanted to feel the hunger, not the curse-fueled pain that assailed him without fail when he drew sustenance. The emptiness was filled only by hate, insatiable except from one source.

The hours of darkness were passing rapidly it seemed, but Nicholas was certain that time enough remained. Closer now was the skyline, that great beacon, the silhouette of what on other nights he had almost been able to forget were merely lighted buildings, the sullying hand of man reaching upward into the once unblemished heavens, another paradise defenseless against corruption. Nicholas veered southward. Soon he was among the great houses, the monuments to mortal wealth, so close to, yet so separate from, the more prevalent urban squalor. The paths that he had taken before were familiar here, engraved into his mind as were perhaps each and every step he had taken in his wanderings over the decades. Each home was surrounded by acres of ivy and shrubs and trees, convenient routes to traverse with only the occasional stone wall or wrought-iron fence to hurdle. They were the most mannered of the mortals, those that lived in these dwellings, and Nicholas knew that it was their money that drove the ever-expanding pestilence, the bulldozers and concrete. Just as it had been Owain Evans, living secretly among these parasites, who had somehow visited the curse upon Nicholas. The night he had delivered the message had been the beginning of the bloodtaint, the beginning of the hunger and the pain. That was something else for which Evans would answer, something else for which Nicholas would make him pay, the price extracted in blood and flesh.

Over one last wall and down a tree-covered lane, and Nicholas had arrived. He stood before the estate of the Ventrue elder who had so woefully wronged Nicholas and his clan. Nicholas forced himself to pause, to reclaim the more human form that would most effectively serve him in the conflict to come. Even in this guise, Nicholas's ears retained a slight point, his eyes their wolven glare, and at his side he flexed the fingers and claws that would soon draw blood. He growled from deep within his throat, a sound no human should be able to make.

Slowly, Nicholas approached the outer wall of the estate. He had been here several times. First, delivering the message, later lying in wait and then following Evans to that broken-down church from which the disturbing music had emanated. This time there would be no introduction, no exchange of pleasantries. Nicholas would find Evans and then tear him apart.

As he leapt the wall, Nicholas felt his ancestors rising, felt the memories becoming more than that, taking control. He knew from before where the surveillance devices lay, what to look for, but he didn't care and made no effort to avoid them. His thirst for blood, for vengeance, drove him forward. Soon the braying of dogs marred the night. Nicholas was undeterred. He awaited their onslaught, welcomed it. He would have blood.

Blackfeather awoke, cradled within the earth's arms. He kept his eyes, which still burned with the afterimages of last night's star-chasing, tightly shut as if clinging to the remnant of his vision.

He stretched, his arms digging inverted furrows beneath the earth's surface. His hands instinctively sought out the moist, loosely packed topsoil. Scrabbling fingers worked like compass needles, searching out the only significant direction in this subterranean world—up.

There.

Blackfeather reached towards the surface, working the kinks out of his back and shoulders as he rose. He stifled an urge to yawn, a habit that not even decades of unlife had been able to break.

He felt the resistance suddenly give way as his hands broke the surface. This was always the anxious moment.

Blackfeather could never be entirely certain where the previous night's chase had released him. He had simply run until dawn overtook him, forcing him back into the earth's embrace. He knew all too well the chaos that might ensue if he should emerge to find that he was not alone.

Well, there was no help for it. Banishing nagging memories of the glare of oncoming headlights, the hooves of a panicked cattle herd, and that unfortunate tent revival, he planted his palms firmly on the upper surface of the ground and pushed himself skyward.

Silence.

It appeared that he was in a park, or at second glance, perhaps on some well-manicured estate.

Yes, he could pick out the line of stone wall to his right and that darker shape at the end of the colonnade of magnolias had the look of a manor house about it.

He scraped the dirt from his eyes and face, relieved that there did not seem to be anyone in the immediate vicinity. There was certainly some activity, a flurry of movement, in the direction of the house. A sense of apprehension passed over him.

There was something unsettling here. Blackfeather could feel a drumming in his chest. It took him only a second to realize that it could not possibly be his heartbeat. His blood swelled and ebbed in obedience to a different tide now.

No, the vibration in his chest had to be the reverberation of some other disturbance. Blackfeather's hands went to his ears, dislodging a layer of tightly packed dirt on the one hand and something that squirmed on the other.

There was now no mistaking the sounds coming from the vicinity of the house. Shouts, running feet, a bestial roar, glass shattering, wood cracking and giving way—a gunshot.

Blackfeather hit full stride before the retort echoed back off the stone wall.

He had covered the length of the colonnade before the hammer fell a second time. Just as he was clearing the trees, Blackfeather heard a noise behind him in the undergrowth and he checked his headlong rush. As he spun, he beheld an immense black sow with blood-red eyes. The beast held his stare briefly and then, disdainfully, returned to scavenging for acorns among the roots of a grove of tall oak trees.

Blackfeather shook his head sharply and the magnolias sprang back into focus as the oak grove vanished. The Veil between this realm and the next was thin here—a precarious situation at best and one that might soon prove to be far more than a distraction. He whispered a silent prayer that the moans of the dying emanating from up ahead would not attract any unwanted attention from beyond the Veil.

Turning the corner, his thoughts kept returning to the Black Sow. She was no direct threat, although the huge beast must have easily weighed over eight hundred pounds. No, she was no hunter, but rather a scavenger—a mere harbinger of death, a speaker of omens.

The third gunshot rang out like the voice of a prophet.

Blackfeather stepped out from beneath the shelter of the magnolias, fully alert, but utterly unprepared for the carnage erupting before him.

Almost at his feet lay a midnight black mastiff, its teeth gleaming up at him, wet and bright. Its neck was bent at an improbable angle. The animal was clearly still alive, although the only sure indication of this was the unearthly keening that arose from behind its clenched jaws.

Blackfeather's first thought was to end the beast's suffering. No, he admitted to himself, his first thought was a kind of revulsion, followed by a vague uneasiness at the disturbing geometry of the creature's broken spine. Only then did he get around to thinking that something should be done about the beast.

When it came right down to it, however, Blackfeather was somewhat at a loss as to how this might be accomplished. The mastiff had already lived through worse than any *coup de grâce* Blackfeather might hope to inflict upon it with his bare hands. He strongly suspected that nothing short of the sunrise would end this beast's unflaggingly loyal service.

He gave the poor creature a wide berth, taking no chances in the proximity of those preternaturally powerful jaws. As he stepped around the fallen mastiff, the outbuilding in front of him suddenly flattened.

Blackfeather flung himself aside and instinctively rolled away from the point of impact. He came up in a fighting crouch.

The building had folded in upon itself. A large cast-iron stove, indication that the structure had, in days past, housed the estate's kitchens, stood undisturbed at the center of the wreckage. The blackened stovepipe pointed a crooked, accusing finger toward the heavens.

But there was a blacker shape still among the tumult of toppled walls. Blackfeather did not so much see it as feel the wave of fury emanating from it. The intensity of that rage wrenched loose the overhanging stovepipe with a scream of metal on metal. Frustration tore at the pipe, twisting it into an implement of destruction, a great unhewn cudgel.

His wrath is like unto a hammer, an unhewn cudgel. He drives the lightning before him.

Blackfeather could hear, above the howling rage, the subtle but unmistakable sound of shadows gathering. The denizens of the realm beyond the Veil, drawn by the play of light and color streaming through the Rent into their twilight domain, began to circle cautiously closer.

Soon they would catch the scent of human emotion and lifeblood spilling through the torn Fabric and there would be no restraining them.

The pipe whistled as it cut its arc through the air and descended upon Blackfeather, giving him a fraction of a second's warning. He rolled aside, his body thrumming with the concussion as the iron cudgel buried itself half the height of a man into the earth.

The makeshift club quickly reversed direction, spraying tufts of carefully manicured lawn in all directions. Blackfeather flattened as the metal sang overhead, missing him by a mere handsbreadth. Then he was again on his feet, carefully giving ground as he backed toward the shattered outbuilding.

He nearly fell over the body of the guard. It was only the sharp sweet smell of the guard's precious lifeblood that caught Blackfeather's attention and saved him from stumbling over the body in the dark. The guard's uniform was soaked down to the waist in blood. It flowed still from the shattered remains of his forehead. The butt of a military-issue pistol protruded from the jagged break in his skull where the barrel of the gun had been slammed home.

There was also a stronger unmistakable smell— the heady, musky scent of vampiric vitae mingled with that of the guard's own blood. Blackfeather thought of the gunshots he had heard earlier and knew that at least one had found its mark.

The pipe end caught Blackfeather squarely in the stomach, doubling him over and knocking him backward into the ruined outbuilding. His flight was checked sharply by the cast iron stove and he could feel the hot rush of blood on the back of his head. Colors swam before his eyes and then, more disturbingly, tactile shades of black and gray as Those Beyond the Veil crowded over him.

Their tender ministries were suffocating. Dozens

of mothering hands poked and prodded him. The press of bodies blanketed him, blocking out the light and colors of his own world, sealing him in like the closing of a coffin's lid.

With a supreme effort of will, Blackfeather thrust his way through the clinging throng. He latched on to the sensation of cold metal along his badly torn back and climbed hand over hand along it, back into the waking world.

Immediately, he regretted it. The awareness of pain and bloodloss had patiently awaited his return. It now gripped him fully, monopolizing every ounce of his attention. He was vaguely aware of a high-pitched whistling noise cutting through the haze of his body's demands.

At the last possible instant, the screaming of his senses broke in upon him, and somehow his body managed to obey their warning.

Blackfeather did not so much dodge as fall heavily to one side. The resounding clang of the metal cudgel shattering against the side of the cast-iron stove burst windows in the nearby manor house. Blackfeather had the distinct impression that the concussion alone might well have knocked several teeth from his mouth. He was undoubtedly bleeding freely from the mouth and ears and had neither the time nor inclination to make a more complete inventory.

A flurry of claws and fangs descended upon him.

A bestial face pressed menacingly close to his own. Through the fog of pain, a realization—a shock of recognition—tried to force its way to the surface of Blackfeather's thoughts. But the blood-film closed like a visor before his eyes.

The Beast Within strained at its tether. The survival instinct seized Blackfeather, pushing aside the demands of screaming nerves, the haze of bloodloss. He lashed out with the all the ferocity of a cornered animal.

The two combatants thrashed and rolled among the ruins of the collapsed building. Debris pierced Blackfeather's back. Some distant part of his mind registered relief at each rusty nail or metal fitting that found its mark—grateful that it was not instead some jagged remnant of timbered walls or ceiling. At any moment his struggle might end, not with the hot ecstasy of his antagonist's fangs, but with the icy torpor of a makeshift stake through the heart.

Despite his injuries, Blackfeather held his own. He was running on instinct now. Each new offensive his opponent launched had a subtle note of the familiar about it. Blackfeather was surviving by anticipation. His shield was a mere fraction of a second in thickness, but he unerringly interposed it between himself and his attacker's claws.

With each increasingly familiar attack, feint, block, a word fought its way closer towards the surface of Blackfeather's awareness, a name. It was quite close now. All that remained was for it to slip past the jaws of the Beast Within, who stood like three-headed Cerberus, guardian of the gates of consciousness and oblivion.

"Nicholas."

The whispered name struck his opponent like a blow. The shadow of the Beast masking his features wavered, flickered.

It is Nicholas, Blackfeather thought. *But his blood is very near the surface and the Beast rides him.* Blackfeather scrambled backwards, regaining his feet, wary. He remembered their first meeting, mere weeks ago.

He had come upon Nicholas rampaging through the woods outside of town, deep in the grips of the Bloodrage. The younger Gangrel had been disoriented, confused, laying waste to everything around him—actually uprooting and shredding trees several years in girth.

"Tree-Render," Blackfeather said aloud. There was no hint of scorn or mockery in his voice. He spoke matter-of-factly, as if calling the other by his family name. Blackfeather's eyes never left those of his opponent. He could see the struggle there, the first hint of comprehension. Nicholas circled closer.

They had fought on that earlier occasion as well, Blackfeather recalled. Nicholas, deep within the clutches of the Beast, had fallen upon him immediately. But Blackfeather had bested him, using Nicholas's blinding rage against him.

This night, Blackfeather was not so certain of victory. There was something in Nicholas's aspect that Blackfeather was reluctant to meet head-on. The peerless hunter did not fail to recognize that look.

He had seen it many times in that most dangerous moment of the hunt, when the prey turns upon its pursuer. There is a certain abandon that courts the power of the Beast, drawing it as surely as mortal blood draws shadows. Blackfeather kept his distance.

Nicholas snarled back something that Blackfeather could not quite catch. But the words were heavy with age, distance, and meaning. They rang with a tone of reverence usually reserved for quoting scripture.

Blackfeather did not recognize the tongue, but he thought it wise to keep his opponent speaking.

"You remember, then, your battle with the trees?"

Nicholas barked a scornful laugh. Then he answered in that same alien musical tongue—words that rang with poetry, ritual, ancient challenge.

Blackfeather caught the word "Blaidd." Recollection pawed at him.

Blaidd. Nicholas's words came back to him from across the intervening nights. *Blaidd*, who was called, in the tongue of the Hillfolk, *the Wolf.*

"Blaidd. Yes, I know you, Nicholas childe of Jebediah, childe of Beauvais, childe of Ragnar, childe of Blaidd."

Nicholas drew back, his struggle for control plain on his face. Blackfeather pressed on, his words formal, prescribed by centuries of tradition.

"When last we met, you yielded to me. I carved my mark upon you. By what right do you challenge me again tonight?" Blackfeather pressed closer. "Have you brought the heads of our enemies taken in battle? Have you brought food to our starving children? Have you brought the words of power from high places?"

Blackfeather threw his arms wide and bared his throat to the stars. He spoke as if from a great distance:

"I am a stag: of seven tines;
"I am a flood: across the plain."

From the corner of his eye, Blackfeather could see the shades crowd closer in anticipation. The Reciting of Deeds was the most sacred of Gangrel traditions. The rite of challenge was more ancient than the Seven Traditions of the Camarilla and even more essential to the survival of the clan. It was a ritualized combat, a struggle to assert dominance. Its consequences were no less decisive or deadly.

Blackfeather hoped that Nicholas was not so far gone in the grips of the Bloodrage that he could not be reached. If he could divert the course of Nicholas's fury, it was still possible to satisfy honor without leaving one or more of their corpses to greet the sunrise.

Nicholas started to retort, stopped, and began again more deliberately. He forced his thoughts into ill-fitting English words with obvious resentment.

"At the Battle of the Trees, I was there. Each time Nicholas drew your blood, I was there. When the master of this house sent Blaidd to the Final Death, I was there.

"I am a storm: upon a deep lake;
"I am a tear: the sun lets fall."

The shades clustered tightly around Nicholas, almost blocking him from view. They drank deeply of his pride, his anger, his age-old vengeance. They began to grow bolder, testing the uncertain waters of the waking world. One had broken away already and reached the body of the guard.

"My blood runs deeper than your claws can follow," Blackfeather replied, meeting the other's gaze. "It was in this land when the moon was young. It was in this land when yours was adrift upon the sea. What is it to me if my blood returns to the land? Take care that your own is not scattered upon the waters and lost.

"I am a thorn: that pierces flesh;
"I am a hawk: above the cliff."

There was a nearly audible wail from the shades and they furiously set to smoothing over Nicholas's wounds—as if they were afraid even one drop of his precious vitae might escape them. Their hands grew ruddy with smeared blood and began to take on substance.

Nicholas, oblivious to their presence, pressed his challenge:

"I do not ride upon the waves, but travel a river of singing blood. What is your land to me? No more than your blood. If I wanted either, I would take them. Men call me *exile* for I am not of their lands. They call me *enemy* for I am not of their blood. But I am in their lands and I am in their blood. They hunt me, and hound me, but I drive them before me.

"I am a terror: upon the plain;
"Who but I sets the cool head aflame with smoke?"

The shade that had been feasting on the guard took two staggering steps forward. It reeled uncertainly, trying to find its balance, to relearn the unfamiliar weight of flesh and blood. Encouraged by its success, more shades struck out towards the guard, making their way hand-over-hand along the tenuous lifeline of his spilled blood.

Blackfeather advanced slowly, trying to keep both Nicholas and the Rent in the Veil in plain view. It seemed to have grown larger. Scores of hands clung to its jagged gray edges, all trying to fight their way through at once.

From the agitated state of those clogging the aperture, it was clear that their eagerness to pass through was motivated by more than simple hunger. Fear was plain on their faces. Something, on the far side of the Veil, was feeding upon that fear and driving them before it.

"You are, perhaps, a hunter among men," Blackfeather countered. "But I have not seen you— or the signs of your passing—along the paths of deepest night. Have you given chase to the questing beast, which bays with the voice of a hundred hounds? Have you tracked the white stag to the silent waters?

"I am a spear: quenched in blood;
"I am a salmon: in a still pool."

Blackfeather had already lost sight of the apparition that had shambled away from feasting upon the guard. The body itself had now vanished beneath the press of flickering shades. There was a loud retort as the gun came free of the shattered skull. Blackfeather saw the light catch the raised barrel as one of the gibbering dead triumphantly waved the dripping pistol overhead.

There was a growing illumination coming from the Rent. The shades clogging the aperture tried to flee, but succeeded only in stretching away like shadows at sunrise—shrieking into the dim distance.

Nicholas rose to his full height. The clinging spirits were wrapped tightly about him like a cloak. Although there was no wind, the garment seemed to flap in the breeze as the shades stretched away from the light streaming from the Rent.

"The pathways you describe, they are only twistings of the mind, labyrinths of thought. Your eyes are set backwards in your head. You see only internal landscapes, phantasms, delusions. How can you lead the people, you who stumble over shadows?

"I am a boar: ruthless and red;
"I am a breaker: threatening doom."

The mass of flickering shades upon the guard's body had grown more distinct. Individual blood-flushed hands and Cheshire-cat maws were clearly visible among the throng. A knot of shambling apparitions wove drunkenly towards the manor house. Their leader, still waving the pistol overhead, discharged it at random. Their roaring laughter was faintly audible, like the sound of the wind through dry leaves.

The Rent itself seemed to glow now. The light was bright enough that Blackfeather could not look directly at it and had to squint to make out Nicholas's silhouette.

The shades unfortunate enough not to have escaped the aperture seemed frozen in time, unmoving, captured like a photographic image. The light streamed through them, throwing into bold relief their expressions of pain and terror.

Time was growing short. Blackfeather harbored no romantic notions about sealing the Rent. Nor had he any heroic idea of banishing the rampaging shades. He certainly had no intention of facing the entity looming just beyond the opening. The task he set himself was a much more modest one. He needed to have himself and Nicholas away from here before the Other emerged from the Veil.

Blackfeather was maneuvering very carefully now. He chose each word with care. He was balanced precariously between the consequences of failing the rite of challenge and the threat of provoking Nicholas to renewed violence. He was very close now.

Blackfeather continued to give ground slowly.

"Perhaps there are no landscapes but the internal. Perhaps our people hunt only upon the mind-plains, war only upon the self-enemy, speak only with the thought-tongue.

"Perhaps our kindred are only shadows from beyond the Veil of Death, preying upon the warmth and passions of the living. Do you tell me you are somehow more real, more living, than our forebears? Or are you something less—blood grown thin through ages and generations—the mere shadow of a shadow?

"I am a light: from beyond the Veil;
"I am a barrow: where poets walk."

The light was blinding now. Blackfeather could no longer see the silhouette of Nicholas. He could not pick out the reeling shapes of the reveling dead. He could not even glance in the direction of the Rent. He moved towards where he thought Nicholas must be, following the sound of his voice.

Instead of being cowed, however, the voice was crowing now—sensing victory. "My blood, it is real. My rage is real. If we are but shadows, place yourself under my claws. They stretch out to you across the ages and the generations and when they mark you, you will know it with certainty. And your pain, that will also be real.

"Already you stagger like one half-dead. Come, let me finish it.

"I am a tide: that drags to death;

"Who but I peers from the unhewn dolmen arch?"

Blackfeather stumbled blindly forward. He could feel, rather than see, the light from the Rent. Pulsing. It threw distorted images past his tightly clenched eyelids, projecting them directly onto the inside of his skull.

"Yes," he managed to whisper, although his teeth ground together. "There are two worlds—one of light and one of shadow. The one you call real and the one you deride as dream. They are sides of a coin, waking and sleeping, spinning end over end, catching the light.

"But what you do not know is this: that the boundaries of the two kingdoms are not as fortified as either would hope. The great wall is a mere eyelid's thickness. And sometimes, the eyelid flutters.

"How will you lead the people when the fiery gaze of the Beyond fixes us with its wrath? How will you even warn them of the danger? How will you draw them forth again, alive and whole, from the far side of the forbidding dolmen arch?

"I am the blaze: on every hill;

"I am the womb: of every holt."

Blackfeather reached out. His hands closed upon Nicholas's arms, clasping him just above the elbows. The gesture was an embrace, an entreaty, an appeal.

He felt claws sink into his own biceps as Nicholas mirrored the gesture. The grip tightened as Nicholas bore down upon him, forcing him to his knees.

"You need not trouble yourself for my people any longer. My arm will lead them in battle. My voice will guide them in the hunt. At my word, they will brave the dark archway into that forbidden kingdom which is the Final Death. But I will hide them in the secret places of my heart—that no harm might come to them, unless it first proves my undoing.

"I am the shield: for every head;
"I am the tomb: of every hope."

Blackfeather felt a fist tighten in his hair, felt his head forced slowly back, exposing the arc of throat.

He did not resist. He did not speak. He did not squander his remaining energy in what was now needless struggle.

Concentrate.

Deliberately, Blackfeather drew a rasping breath.

It was not something he did often. Breathing was not particularly easy or even remotely comfortable

for him anymore—muscles atrophied through decades of disuse. It was still much more pleasant than
what he was about to do.

Blackfeather focused and drew another painful
breath, then another. He was no longer aware of
his surroundings. All of his concentration focused
on this one simple act—inhale, exhale—a task that
even a newborn baby can perform effortlessly.
Blackfeather threw every ounce of his will into
maintaining this most basic, fundamental motion
of life.

The tiny halting breath that was Blackfeather
was dimly aware of Nicholas's presence looming
over him. It lay heavy upon him, like a blanket
smothering flame. It pressed down upon him.

It has to be now.

Blackfeather drew breath as deeply as he could
and held it. One beat. Two. Three.

He felt the hot stab of fangs driving into his
throat.

Now.

With a sigh like a wall of snow tumbling off a
mountainside, Blackfeather's heart began to beat.

He could feel Nicholas jerk back in alarm, tearing free. Spray of blood. Rasping breath. Heartbeat.

With a twisting motion of one hand,
Blackfeather caught the trailing ends of those three
vital threads—blood, breath, heartbeat. His nails
dug into his palm, holding fast, a death grip. With

the same motion, he drove the heel of his palm upward with all his might, straight into the seat of his opponent's Chi.

The blow caught Nicholas just below the sternum. Had it been a physical blow, it would certainly have shattered his ribcage, driving shards of bone through his heart and lungs.

But there was nothing of the physical about it. Nicholas felt nothing more than a slight hiccup as Blackfeather rammed the life-energy deep into his chest. The entire weight of the blow fell squarely upon Nicholas's Chi, his spiritual energy.

There was an audible crack, like a latch giving way.

Blackfeather's hand still rested gently upon Nicholas's chest. He felt the younger Gangrel go rigid, jerk, pitch forward. Blackfeather bore him up.

Nicholas fought for balance. His eyes, wide and moon-bright, were fixed on something just beyond Blackfeather's shoulder. A chaotic jumble of images flowed from Nicholas into and over Blackfeather—as if the overloaded sensory signals were uncertain where one individual ended and the other began.

Nicholas's gaze flitted distractedly back and forth. It was as if his mind could find no purchase amidst the unfamiliar dreamscape. The grounds erupted with the cavorting dead. A translucent apparition raised high the severed head of the mastiff. With a howl of glee, he popped it down over his own features like a mask. The deadly jaws snapped experimentally, as if trying out the fit.

Three wavering figures danced around the old cast iron stove, stoking the blaze to bonfire height with shovel, poker and billows. Another shade worked furiously nearby, cobbling together like implements from available materials—human flesh and bone.

Shrieking corpses hurled themselves from upstairs windows, got to their feet again as best they could, and shambled back towards the house for another attempt.

Blackfeather could feel Nicholas slipping away, spiraling inward under the onslaught. He was not about to lose him now.

"Nicholas," his voice was sharp, urgent. "You will not fall here. Your death is no longer your own. You must live on to lead our people. You have sworn this thing, and it cannot be unsworn."

Nicholas's gaze lowered, fixed upon Blackfeather's own, anchored. Slowly, the young Gangrel drew himself back up from the depths. Taking Blackfeather by the arms, he raised the seer to his feet. "And you will live to guide them." Nicholas's voice was regal. All hint of the earlier menace had fled his countenance. "I have been…"

His voice died abruptly. His hands fell away.

Blackfeather felt the contact sever. It was as if

he had suddenly been blinded in one eye. Half of his range of vision was suddenly and irrevocably lost. He was never to know exactly what Nicholas saw emerging from the Rent.

The howl that came from Nicholas's lips had nothing of the human about it. It was a bestial cry of terror, pain and incomprehension. The outpouring of emotion unerringly drew the attention of the Other.

Blackfeather did not turn. He heard a sizzling sound, like a sustained arc of electricity, and then the ground rippled and flowed towards him under the concussion of what he took to be a monstrous footstep.

He threw his full weight against Nicholas, but the latter needed no urging. Together they fled, heedless and headlong, into the first hint of the sunrise.

CHAPTER THREE

Owain reclined in the plush seat and tried once again to make himself comfortable. This should have been simplicity itself. Everything about the tiny cabin suggested not only comfort, but opulence.

The Giovanni had spared no expense in outfitting this private jet—the pride of their line. It was a matter of great satisfaction to them that their unique clientele would tolerate nothing but the very best.

Owain thought they had perhaps gone a bit too far to put their guests at ease. The cozy, darkened compartment, curtained in red silk, was a bit too suggestive of the coffin for his tastes.

Gherbod Fleming

Every other detail, however, was "just so." The overall effect was that of a gentleman's library. The walls left and right were lined in rich, leather-bound volumes. The opposite wall was dominated by an antique map of the world that stretched from chair rail to vaulted ceiling. Owain brushed the controls recessed into the surface of the mahogany desk before him. The map seemed to fade, dissolving into a series of large projection television screens.

The only light in the room was a pale blue banker's lamp on the desk to Owain's left. With a tug at the delicate golden chain, he snuffed the light and thumbed the television to a public station he knew would be off the air by this hour. He let the cabin fill with soft static.

It was a soothing sound, a purely unorchestrated effort. There was no hint of artifice about it, no note of the self-conscious—no sense that it had been carefully arranged for his benefit.

It was a sound that might have been before man walked the earth. A primordial friction. An ever-expanding wave carrying the sound of stars being born. The music of the spheres.

Owain let tumultuous thoughts of what lay ahead—of Toledo, El Greco, the Sabbat—slip away from him and lose themselves among the intricacies of that grand, patternless music. At last, he closed his own eyes, surrendering himself to dreams.

It was not dreams that came for him, but visions.

A shadow seated itself across the mahogany desk from Owain. The surface of the desk had resolved itself into alternating squares of light and dark wood—a chessboard. The shadow crouched over its pieces. Owain could not follow its stealthy movements as it shifted the pieces around, shuffling them, subtly altering their starting positions.

The side of the board nearest to Owain was empty. Before him, there were thirteen black chessmen; there was no sign of their mates. Owain was not about to start any game at such a material disadvantage.

His opponent, however, seemed unconcerned. He began advancing his pieces in orderly ranks, closing inextricably on Owain's home row positions.

Owain hastily began slamming pieces onto the board, throwing up a defense. He checked suddenly, struck by a disturbing detail on the intricately carved figurine in his upraised hand. The dark king held an upraised cudgel—captured in the act of slamming it down upon the upraised face of a figure huddled at the piece's base.

Caine, the First Born, the Dark Father.

Owain set the piece down carefully. He picked up another and studied it closely, apprehensively. The black knight was depicted on his knees, in the act of gouging out his own eyes with a pin.

Oedipus, certainly. But why...?

The shadow spoke, tauntingly. It wore a voice that Owain had not forgotten all through the dim procession of centuries. It was his brother's voice. "Is something amiss, Kinslayer?" The word dripped with vitriol. It struck Owain like a blow. *"This is the Endtime. This is the fading of the blood."*

Owain felt the warm lifeblood trickling down his wrist. He stared in alarm at the figure of Oedipus, tightly clenched in his fist. He had the unmistakable impression that the piece bled from beneath its dark marble hands. Owain loosed his grip and the figure fell heavily to the desk. Only then did he realize that his white-knuckled grip had actually driven the knight deeply into his palm, drawing blood.

The adversary pressed his advantage. *"The shadow of Time is not so long that you might shelter beneath it. And by these signs, you shall know I speak the Truth which abides no darkness. I have seen the Isle of Angels trembling as if struck a great blow. Michael, most exalted of that Glorious Company—he that cast the Dark One from on high—is himself thrown to the Earth. Men look up without understanding at the darkened sky and the Children of Caine waken at dawn."*

The shadowed figure punctuated his words by advancing an exquisite white rook. Each fold of its toga stood out in bold relief. The figure was frozen in the act of drawing a concealed dagger.

Brutus.

Owain strained to catch a glimpse of the white king, to delve into the nature of his adversary, but his opponent kept the piece well hidden within the shadow of his billowing sleeves. Owain advanced a bishop into a position of vulnerability.

His opponent pounced. *"I have seen a Cross, steeped in the blood of our Lord, burst forth into new life. I have seen it ring itself in Holy Thorns, lest the impure approach and taste of that forbidden fruit. I have seen a great white Eagle perched in its branches. It opens its mouth and lo, it speaks with the hidden voice of mountains. Words of Undoing it speaks for the Children of Caine."*

The shadow swooped upon the exposed bishop with a contemptuous laugh, but as he extended his reach far across the table, Owain caught a glimpse of the forgotten white king.

Its head was bent disturbingly to one side. A noose coiled about its neck and a bag of coins lay at its feet.

Thirty talents of silver, Owain thought. *Betrayal.*

He retreated his queen to a more defensive position.

The shadow paused and cocked its head as if harkening to the sound of another's approach. *"And at its feet crouches a Lyon spitting flame and vitriol, its hide the color of blood. It lifts one great paw with the sound of all the Earth's tombs being broken asunder.*

Beneath that terrible claw there lies the Book. And I, Joseph the Lesser, beheld what was writ upon the face of the Lyon's book and I was sorely afraid. I called out to the Lord, but my voice was lost amidst the wailing of the afflicted. And as I watched, those wails took on substance, twisting upon themselves, and I beheld that they were a great and terrible road, stretching away before me into the dim recesses of night. And the road's name was called Gehenna, for it was paved with dying dreams."

Owain now found himself sorely pressed. He fumbled with a rook, as if trying to use it to check the unfolding of this strange revelation. As he reached out to lift the piece, however, he found he could not. As his hand came away, he saw not the cool gleam of his ebon castle, but a deeply veined red marble.

All of the pieces along the left edge of the board had suddenly taken on a similar aspect, as if a third party had joined their game. The shadow faltered, shaken by this latest turn of events. The red pieces seemed to threaten each of their delicately contrived positions.

The shadow's voice was halting, uncertain. *"I hid my face, and again the Eagle spoke. Its voice filled the Heavens and the Earth saying, 'Let it be thus. Thy will be done.'"*

The shadow swept its long flowing sleeve across the desktop, scattering black, red and white pieces to the floor. Owain lunged after them, trying to reconstruct some semblance of order, to divine some elusive pattern from their arcing flight. The pieces were hopelessly scattered, sliding away from Owain as he was pulled back to the world of flesh and blood.

He felt the hum of the landing gear as it deployed, and he felt the jostling of the plane as it dropped down through the cloud cover toward Madrid.

The stacks of books surrounded Eleanor, row after row, shelf after shelf. She was a woman slight of build and could easily have lost herself amidst this collection of mortal knowledge. How much they had discovered over the centuries, yet how little they knew. There were some Kindred, Eleanor knew, who had taken it upon themselves to gather the knowledge of the ages, to possess every tome produced in every language across the world. Eleanor had never met one of these quixotic beings personally, but she had heard firsthand accounts from those who had. The collectors had begun their task, and perhaps brought it close to fruition, long before Johann Gutenberg had made their unlives hell with his little toy. Some toiled on, refusing to acknowledge their defeat. They had an eternity to work, an eternity to waste, slaving in the darkness, a flickering candle flame and the musty scent of mildewed paper their only companions.

Everyone needs a hobby, Eleanor supposed.

The books meant something quite different to her. They were not the secret knowledge of ages so much as the key to liberation. She felt empowered as she surveyed the books in the Morris Brown library, this feeling heightened by the mingling of anticipation as she awaited her lover. Benjamin had responded to her epistle with a note of his own, and the words had brought her to this place once again. The written word had served her well, as it had many times over the years.

Books were the closest to having friends that Eleanor had ever come—companions to whom she could entrust her thoughts, allies she could utilize to get what she needed. She had excelled at reading and writing from her childhood days as a mortal. Steered away from the depravities of fiction, as well as the histories and political texts of the male world around her, she had sensed a higher calling, even in her voluminous consumption of the treatises on etiquette and natural history that were allowed her. When she had caught the eye of a wealthy planter, the articulate letters she had crafted, utterly proper yet beguiling nonetheless, made a mere formality of the courtship. Ten years later, when her husband, by that time a colonel in the Confederate army, had died in the early years of the War Between the States, Eleanor had ably administered the plantation holdings.

All that was before Baylor had Embraced her, before he had molded her as his protégée in the duplicitous world of Camarilla politics, and before he had subsequently, for all practical intents and purposes, disinherited if not disowned her when she had married Benison. It was also before she had met Benjamin, the lover whose presence she now awaited.

Eleanor had sent Sally, the delicate, pale serving girl, with the angry letter to Benjamin three nights earlier. First one night and then another passed with no response. Eleanor had wondered if she had been too harsh in expressing her thoughts. She had, after all, forgone her typical grace and tact in communicating her anger. Had Benjamin taken such offense, she had wondered, that he would not respond? But equally as strong as her anxiety had been her irritation at being ignored, her ire at being taken for granted. She vacillated between trepidation and aggravation, consoled only by the fact that Benison was busy elsewhere and not a complication in addition to her mood swings.

On the third night, much to her relief, a response from Benjamin had arrived. Sally, returning from errands, had delivered the note: *E, I have instructed Edgar to present this to you or your staff at the first possible opportunity. Please, the night after receiving this, meet me at the library. As always, Yours.*

Edgar, Benjamin's executive assistant ghoul—

though Eleanor doubted that was his actual job title—must have followed Sally when she had left the house and then slipped the note to her on the street when he was sure they were not being observed. The message itself Eleanor considered pure Benjamin, equal parts affection and caution. The opening "E" was lovingly familiar, yet at the same time protected Eleanor's identity. He formally referred to her "staff," but asked her to "please" meet with him, and his usual closing, which had so endeared him to Eleanor, was intensely personal without being explicitly passionate. Seeing the words lifted Eleanor's heart. This would not be the first time they had met at the library.

Thirty-odd years before, Eleanor had watched from a distance as the mortal Benjamin had parlayed his formidable legal skills into a successful law practice. She had watched, also, as he had abandoned that practice to offer his services instead to the activists of the civil rights movement. From the beginning, his sharp intellect had attracted Eleanor; that and the idealism that had governed him. Such principled actions were novel to Eleanor, steeped as she was in the politics of the Camarilla. She had followed him as he moved among the books. Then, as she was again this night, she had been one of the few non-African-Americans in the Morris Brown library, but Eleanor had a way of blending in when she wanted, as far as mortals were concerned.

After watching Benjamin for hours, Eleanor had spoken with him, and with the proximity, events had spiraled beyond her control. She had found herself unable to repress her desires any longer and had drunk of him there between the stacks. Leaving a body in the library would have been a messy affair, and she probably could not have brought herself to destroy the object of her infatuation regardless. But when Eleanor had attempted to remove from Benjamin's mind the memory of her feeding upon him, she was unable to do so. His will was too strong. The memory was permanent. Not content merely to enthrall such a brilliant mind as a ghoul, she had Embraced him. For more than three decades, her secret childe had proven her intellectual equal, and on the rare occasions that she had desired more physical stimulation—a nostalgic remembrance of mortal days more than any actual physical pleasure to her vampiric body—he had satisfied her in that capacity as well.

There was no denying, in Eleanor's mind, that their fates were intertwined, and his choice of this venue indicated to her that he felt similarly. She had ushered Benjamin into the world of the Kindred, and he had enriched her unlife beyond measure.

But where was he now? Eleanor had been waiting for three hours, since ten o'clock, and though wandering through the stacks had engendered memories of more pleasant times, her relief at having heard from him was beginning to give way to irritation at once again having been kept waiting. It would not have been difficult for him to have chosen a *time* to meet, Eleanor fumed.

Just as her mind turned to such bitter thoughts, however, he was there. Eleanor felt his presence before she saw him, standing stiffly in front of the collected volumes of jurisprudence, cardigan sweater unbuttoned, tie loosened. Again, Eleanor's heart lifted. All anxiety and aggravation were instantly banished from her soul. As she moved toward him, her long dress, the height of fashion in 1893, rustled against her ankles.

"Benjamin."

It seemed like forever since she had been able to speak to him thus, revealing the depth of emotion she held for him.

Benjamin remained where he was. He mechanically took Eleanor's hands in his and leaned down so that she could kiss him. His lips were cold against hers, and Eleanor sensed only the barest response from him. Her anxieties returned, sweeping over her, an avalanche of doubt and fear. She took a step back, wondering who this was in the form of her childe and lover?

"Eleanor." The way he spoke her name pained her. Gone were the thrill and anticipation of the past. The word formed upon his dead lips conveyed only custodial tolerance, not passion. "Eleanor." He attacked her by naming her again.

She withdrew her hands from his, not wanting to be confronted by the reality of his lifeless touch. "You've kept me waiting."

Sadness and pain were buried in Benjamin's eyes. This gave Eleanor hope, the knowledge that she still held some small power over him, but it also stoked the darkest of her fears. She looked away from his face.

"I'm sorry," he said.

Was he referring, Eleanor wondered, to his belated arrival or to more portentous matters? She turned her back to him. "We cannot continue this way," she whispered.

"I know," he said behind her.

Eleanor felt herself cringe, struck by the weight of resignation in his voice. He was quietly destroying them. With a half-dozen words, ambiguous in denotation alone, he had sealed the fate of over three decades of involvement. For a moment, she collected her thoughts. His mind was made up. That much was clear. But Eleanor had swayed princes and archons in her time. She would not make this easy for him. "Do you remember the first time we were together here?" she asked.

"How could I not?"

"What did you feel that first time I fed from you, those last hours of your mortal life?" she asked, her back still turned to him.

"Eleanor, you know…"

"What did you *feel?*" she demanded, spinning to face him. "What was going through your mind, through your heart?"

Benjamin bowed his head and sighed. "I felt the blood, the very life, draining out of me." His voice was tired. These were words he had spoken before many years ago. Hearing him, Eleanor was increasingly angered that although he answered her, though he followed the letter of her command, he was merely humoring her. But there was still a chance she could bring him back to her, and she would not give up that chance. "But I wasn't afraid," he continued. "I was curious. I knew somehow that I was being presented with an opportunity to learn more than I'd ever imagined possible. I knew you wouldn't kill me."

"How did you know?" she prodded.

Benjamin hesitated. His gaze met Eleanor's, then he looked away. "I don't know."

"What of the years since then, Benjamin?"

"Since then…" he answered, staring at his feet, "since then, you have introduced me to Cainite society. You have taught me those people I should know and those I should fear."

Eleanor allowed herself a gratified smile. Surely Benjamin realized that he would be nothing had it not been for her, nothing but a poor, aging lawyer engaged in social causes, the specter of retirement and a slow death looming in his future.

How much she had given him! She had opened the world to him, allowed him to use his natural abilities as well as his vampiric influence and powers to help his people. She hoped he wouldn't grovel before her. She would rather maintain a dignified relationship.

But Benjamin was not finished. "Since then, I have been forced to feed upon the blood of those still human around me in order to survive. I have become, in reality, the worst caricature of the legal profession." Benjamin met her gaze now. His voice took on the conviction it had lacked since his arrival. "Since then, I have learned on my own ten times, *a hundred times*, what you taught me. Though you would have preferred to have kept me in tow, I have taken what you showed me and recreated *myself*."

As Benjamin spoke, Eleanor stood dumbfounded. Only slowly did his words sink in, and even then, her realization of the incredible extent of his ingratitude was slow to form. Could he really be saying what she was hearing? "Benjamin, you would be nothing without me." She meant it honestly, not as a slap, not as a blow against him.

He glared at her from behind his steel-rimmed spectacles. "I would be my own man without you. A different man, yes, but my own. Never in these thirty years has my world revolved solely around you, as you seem to think. There have been nights that I haven't seen you, nights that I haven't *thought* of you. I would be more human without you, but I would still be my own man."

Eleanor could not believe that he would go to such great lengths to slight her, to offend her. As the depth of his rebellion grew apparent, a profound anger took hold of her. She hissed at Benjamin, baring her fangs. It took all her breeding and social graces to keep her from pouncing upon him and ripping his throat open, taking back the gift that so clearly had been spurned. "You forget, Benjamin, *I* am the master. *You* are the childe!"

"I am the childe, yes," he retorted, "but I am my own master. As I have always been, Eleanor. You want to know how I knew you wouldn't kill me that first night so long ago? I knew because I could feel your passion. It was later that I realized that passion was not for me as much as for the idea of *owning* me." His voice rose in volume. He was too incensed to care if mortals heard this argument. "I was your childe. I was your boy, or so you thought." Benjamin's own fangs were visible now. "*And I hated you for that.*"

Eleanor pressed her palms against her eyes. This insolence was too much to bear. She would reveal his treachery to Benison. She would see Benjamin destroyed, staked out for the morning sun to burn away the offending flesh that had once been hers to command. But when she lowered her hands to tell him this, he was gone. Trembling with rage, she stood alone among the stacks. Hundreds and thousands of volumes crowded around her, all staring, all laughing at her impotence in the face of her childe.

The two cars raced up to the front of the projects from different directions and screeched to a halt, front bumpers coming to rest only a few inches apart. The smell of burnt rubber filled the air. Mohammed al-Muthlim stepped out of one car into the night air. "This the place?"

His ghoul Rodney got out of the same car. Marvin emerged from the other car with an assault rifle, but before he could respond to his domitor's question, automatic weapon fire ripped into the cars and the ground all around them. Mohammed ducked behind his car. Marvin and Rodney jumped over the hoods to join him.

"I think it's the place," said Rodney.

Marvin was grimacing and flexing his left hand, which had a bullet hole clean through it. "*Damn!* That pisses me off!"

More bullets slammed into the cars. Windshields shattered. Air hissed out of punctured tires.

"Where's Kenny?" Mohammed asked.

"'Round back," Marvin answered, still flexing his hand. "He's there with Pancho and the others. We're here. Them's the only ways out, 'cept nobody's gettin' out."

Mohammed nodded grimly. He had never been impressed with Marvin, at least not before the gang war had broken into the open. Between the ravages of the curse through the ranks of Mohammed's underlings and the attrition brought on by the bloody hostilities, Marvin had first been ghouled, then thrust into a position of leadership within Crypt's Sons, and he had proven himself a tactical asset. So much so that Mohammed was considering Embracing the enormous ghoul and recruiting him for Mohammed's secret inner circle of Sabbat followers, who had been nearly annihilated by the curse. "Then go do it."

Marvin smiled. Forgotten was the pain from his hand. He took a cell phone from his baggy pockets and dialed. "Yeah, Pancho. It's a go. Right now." He replaced the phone and checked his rifle. Satisfied, he turned to Mohammed and Rodney. "Cover me?"

They nodded and checked their own weapons, two semi-automatic pistols. On three, they stood and returned fire at the apartment from which the sniper fire had come. Without hesitating, Marvin was out from behind the cars and running toward the front door, firing as he went.

Mohammed and Rodney dropped back down as more bullets tore into the cars. "Think he'll make it?" Rodney asked.

"We'll see." There was much still to be seen,

Mohammed knew. Turf skirmishes between Crypt's Sons and La Hermandad had always been a way of unlife in L.A., but since open warfare had broken out two weeks ago, the Cainites of Whittier and Covina had thrown in with La Hermandad, and though Mohammed was holding his own, maybe even gaining ground, the cost was high. His ranks already decimated by the curse, he was having ghouls and mortal flunkies blown away at every turn. Every ambush, every retribution, cost him one or two more people. There were always more to take their places. That was no problem. But leadership was a quality less easily replaced, and most of Mohammed's top men were already down. La Hermandad was undoubtedly suffering the same difficulties, but what concerned Mohammed was that his enemies were hanging on without their charismatic leader. If Salvador showed up in town, more L.A. Cainites would probably jump on the La Hermandad bandwagon, and that might just tip the balance. That was why Mohammed wanted to press his advantage as forcefully as he could, to win outright or at least to extract some favorable settlement from Jesus Ramirez, leader of La Hermandad during Salvador's absence.

More shots echoed inside the dingy apartment building. Stray bullets escaped into the night. Mohammed wanted this wrapped up soon. Although Compton was relatively free of interference from the local authorities, a protracted gun battle in the street was never wise. Plus, Ramirez had already had some success in buying off cops who had been in Mohammed's pocket, though probably the example Mohammed had made of one officer and his family would dissuade other potential turncoats.

Mohammed snuck a look around the car. He didn't see Marvin lying on the ground. The ghoul must have made it inside. Just as that thought crossed the mind of the leader of the Crypt's Sons, glass shattered and a screen was ripped from the building. From the fourth floor, a body came sailing through the window. Mohammed could tell at a glance that it was not Marvin. Too small. A loud thud reverberated throughout the courtyard as the body hit the concrete. Marvin grinned from the broken window above. He had taken care of the sniper. Then Marvin's smile faded.

Mohammed was suddenly aware of another automobile speeding toward him. *Police?* was his first thought, but what he saw as he turned was worse. A small pickup truck was bearing down on him, two Hispanics in the back pointing sub-machine guns at him.

Mohammed jumped the car as bullets slammed into the less shot-up side of the vehicle. Marvin returned fire from the window, but the truck sped on and was gone.

Mohammed stood and brushed himself off. The

indignity of being attacked in his own territory riled him more than anything. He hoped that one of his patrols would stop that truck, and that at least one of those La Hermandad members would be captured alive. *Just one*.

Then Mohammed noticed Rodney lying on the ground. He hadn't made it out of the way, and at least one bullet had caught him square in the face. Most of the back of his head was scattered over fifteen or twenty feet of pavement. Mohammed stared after the truck.

From the opposite rooftop, the violence looked almost staged—an impromptu drama performed for an audience of one. Kli Kodesh impassively surveyed the carnage below.

Although he gave no outward sign of concern, he calculated furiously. With great care he plotted the trajectory of each stray bullet. He was acutely aware of the exact time and distance a body would plummet before impacting the pavement below. He apprehended the precise angle of each shard of bone exploding from the splintered skull.

It was always the same. The individual acts of violence, the specific deaths, were unimportant. It was the larger pattern that held his interest.

The wind tore at Kli Kodesh in vain, failing to displace a single strand of his long white hair, or rustle the least fold of his robe. He stood like a pillar, a statue carved of marble. He was a colossus perched precariously at the very edge of the world.

Those below would not see him. Not because he concealed himself, for he did not. They would not see him because their world had no place for beings such as he. Their thoughts could find no purchase upon him. Their minds could not hope to encompass the thousands of miles he had walked, the hundreds of thousands of violent acts he had endured through the ages.

The words of the ancient prophecy were slight solace in the face of this procession of death and betrayal: *They also serve who stand and wait.*

But his waiting was drawing to a close. A great reckoning was at hand. He looked down upon the City of Angels, surveying the great expanse of asphalt and neon for the last time.

Already it had begun to recede. For a long time afterward, Kli Kodesh clung to the distant echo of the city's cries—the mechanical wailings of the great machine winding down, devouring itself. The haunting sound comforted him, whispering that release was at hand.

But he recognized in the city's parting promise, the cry of a newborn who would not live through the night.

Sally knocked at the parlor door. "Miss Eleanor, the gentleman you asked me to find, Pierre, I've brought him back."

Eleanor looked up from her journal. "Where is he?"

"I showed him into the living room." Sally was a slight girl, two or three inches taller than her mistress but gaunt and frail. Like Eleanor, her skin was pale, her long, dark hair kept up in a bun. The ghoul was everything Eleanor wanted in a serving girl, all deference and dependability, and though Sally appeared fragile, she was one of only two of Eleanor and Benison's five ghouls not to fall victim to the curse.

"Very good," said Eleanor. "Tell him I'll be down shortly."

"Yes, ma'am."

Eleanor heard Sally's light steps receding down the stairs. Eleanor's journal still lay open before her on the writing table. For the better part of three nights, she had collected and organized her thoughts in light of her disturbing meeting with Benjamin. She had considered what he had said, tried to make sense of it, attempted to see the past years from his perspective—attempted and failed. The more often she reconstructed their argument, the more convinced she was that he had fallen victim to the delusional ravings of the curse. She had witnessed with her own eyes as Benison's childe

Roger had succumbed to the insanity and then perished shortly thereafter. That seemed to be the way of things. Across the nation, across the world if the stories were to be believed, Kindred were suffering similar fates. Obviously Benjamin's usually impeccable mental faculties had given over to the madness. Could death be far behind?

She had, over the past nights, regretfully resigned herself to that inevitability. Even so, she had difficulty so callously abandoning her prodigal childe. The possibility did exist, however slight, that he was not, in fact, affected by the maleficence of the curse but had instead arrived at his baseless conclusions on his own.

Eleanor closed her journal, not meaning to slam it, but the oil lantern on the table rattled alarmingly. *If he hasn't been driven mad by the curse*, she wondered, *how could he have been swayed by such wrong-headed ideas?* The ideas that had led him to renounce her love could not, Eleanor felt, be the result of his normally precise thinking. Someone had influenced him unduly and, with very little effort, Eleanor had divined the identity of the culprit:

Owain Evans.

This realization was actually confirmation of suspicions she had held for some time now. It all fit together too well for coincidence. Evans had blackmailed Benjamin over some inconsequential legal matter months ago. The information that would have so compromised Benjamin had it been made common knowledge: his involvement with Eleanor, the prince's wife. There was also the possibility, though Eleanor considered it incredibly remote, that Evans was aware of the specific nature of Eleanor and Benjamin's relationship, that Benjamin was secretly her childe as well as her love.

Eleanor could easily reconstruct Benjamin's line of reasoning. The only way to ensure that their active relationship was not found out was to end it. They had been cautious enough that past actions would almost certainly prove impossible to uncover, and so if no additional rendezvous occurred, they were beyond reproach. This would leave Benjamin free to battle any future blackmail attempts with complete confidence and nothing tangible to hide.

Seen in that light, Eleanor knew that Benjamin had done it all for her. He was trying to protect her, to shield her from possible harm. He realized that any aspersions cast publicly against them with even the slightest substantiation would be far more damaging to her, considering her rather significant social standing. So idealistic was he in his motivations and in his desire to protect her, he was pretending to actually break off their relationship rather than risk trying to work secretly with her to negotiate these perilous waters. *The darling*. It was all so clear to her now upon reflection.

Of course he wouldn't risk hurting her feelings

unless it were to safeguard the long-term stability of their love. That was where she could help. Owain Evans was the only individual who had revealed his knowledge of that which he should not know. Quite possibly, he received information, rumor or fact, from spies. It would be helpful if Eleanor could find out who those spies were, so they could be dealt with properly. That would be ideal, to eliminate the leak at the source. At the very least, however, if Evans were removed from the picture, there would be no one in a position of influence who could threaten her and Benjamin.

So the past nights of soul-searching had not been without success. Eleanor had constructed three alternative scenarios to explain the uncomfortable situation in which she found herself. First, that Benjamin had fallen prey to the curse, his insanity and rejection of her derived therefrom, in which case he would soon be dead. Second, that Benjamin was misguidedly attempting to protect her from the recriminations of Owain Evans's extortion, in which case her removing Evans from the scene would alleviate the problem and Benjamin would be hers again. Third, that Benjamin did actually, through some twisted delusion of his own inception, want to bring an end to their involvement. If that were somehow the case, it would become apparent if Evans were dispatched and Benjamin refused to resume contact with Eleanor. If that happened, Eleanor would make sure that Benjamin did indeed wish that he had fallen to the curse rather than to the revenge she would arrange for him.

None of that, she knew, would happen if all she did was sit in her parlor night after night writing in her journal. Eleanor methodically straightened the book on her writing table, along with her pen, ink well, and lamp. She was careful not to dribble any of the ink on the white doily. She had learned long ago that, even in a fit of pique, a lady conducted herself in a composed and calm manner. It was a standard up to which Eleanor did not always measure, but one to which few even aspired these modern nights. Only after smoothing her dress and attending to her hair did she venture from the parlor.

The first night after her altercation with Benjamin, Eleanor had barely left her room, so consumed by despair had she been. Her firm resolve to carry on had been achieved only through reflection and self-examination over the next evenings. Two nights ago, on Tuesday, having largely decided upon a course of action, she had sent Sally out to contact Robert Gillus, a younger Ventrue whom Eleanor had always treated kindly. Unfortunately, Gillus had taken insane and expired several weeks ago. Twice more Eleanor had sent Sally in search of junior Ventrue who likewise turned out to have been victims of the curse. Only then did Eleanor truly realize how completely the curse had devastated the ranks of even the recognized vampires of the city. It was not a malady reserved for the anarchs and unestablished, though they seemed to have borne the brunt of it initially.

And so Eleanor made her way into the living room and greeted Pierre the Toreador, he to whom she was turning for lack of any viable alternative. "Eleanor!" He was pleased to see her and rose as she entered the room, stepping forward as if to take her hand, but then hastily stepping back as if afraid to be too forward with one of Eleanor's standing. Pierre's thin frame was topped with listless black hair trimmed on the sides to long, narrow sideburns. As Eleanor did take his hand and smile, she could see distinctly the bones in his hand, wrist, and forearm. She imagined that if she jerked too hard, his arm would pull out from the socket, but such Kindred of seeming frailty as Pierre were the only available tools of the trade in desperate times.

"Pierre, how kind of you to join me with such short notice," she said graciously.

The Toreador placed his other hand over hers, as a grandmother might do to a child. "No trouble at all, Eleanor. No trouble at all for our friend, the wife of the prince."

Eleanor nodded. "You are too kind." She took her seat on the armchair and watched as Pierre perched daintily upon the edge of the couch. "I trust you are doing well?"

"As well as can be expected," Pierre sighed. "So much uncertainty in these…well…uncertain times." He looked at her solemnly, as if he had imparted a most profound wisdom. He spoke with his hands, gesturing with each word. Only, there seemed to be a short lag time after he finished speaking, when his hands continued moving until realizing there were no more words to accompany.

"You are so right," said Eleanor. She had never cared for the Toreador as a clan—gossips and arthouse dandies for the most part—and generally found that she cared for them as individuals even less. Marlene, the leader of the clan in Atlanta, was a prime example, affecting pretensions as a sculptor while spending most of her time maintaining the strip joints lining Cheshire Bridge Road. On top of that, Marlene had claimed illness last Saturday and, along with Hannah, had missed the weekly bridge game, leaving Eleanor alone to entertain the senile Aunt Bedelia, Benison's sire.

Eleanor regarded Pierre in his black boots and Renaissance-style blouse, measuring him against the task she had in mind. There were just so few accessible Kindred in the city these nights. Most of those who had not succumbed to the curse avoided all other Cainites like the plague for fear of being stricken. Eleanor believed that her own moral fortitude protected her.

"Pierre," she began, "I have an important favor

that I must ask of you." He sat bolt upright on the couch, attentive, a little soldier ready for command. "It is a matter that requires a modicum of discretion."

"I see." He nodded vigorously. Eleanor feared he might strain his neck.

"It is not a matter with which I wish to trouble the prince," she explained, "so I will ask you to report exclusively to me." Eleanor was a little worried by the degree of eagerness with which Pierre was approaching his task, not yet even knowing what that task was to be. The Toreador, as a rule, were schemers. Not as devious as the Tremere or as unpredictable as the Malkavians, but conniving nonetheless. Pierre, being a Toreador of no great standing, could be genuinely excited to serve the wife of the prince and by extension, one would assume, the prince himself. Pierre could, then again, be interested in furthering his status within his own clan in particular, perhaps by double-crossing Eleanor in some way. That would make him, with his obvious enthusiasm, quite the bungler. Such transparency was unlikely, but Eleanor was not yet ready to rule out complete ineptitude. Also possible was the scenario in which Pierre was the skilled infiltrator intentionally projecting the disarming manner of the fool. This, from what little she knew of him, Eleanor doubted.

"I need you to keep track of a certain vampire

in the city," she explained. "There is nothing too complicated about it. Follow his movements. Record whom he sees. I prefer that he not realize he is being watched, but should you be discovered, neither my name nor the prince's enter into the matter. Understood?"

Pierre's smile was a bit more nervous now. His hands began their motion anticipating his response. "It sounds as if there is 'nothing too complicated,' but the complications could arise from the identity of he who is followed."

"You are quite right," Eleanor agreed. "I must first ask that, even should you decide not to undertake this favor, which would be quite disappointing to the prince and myself but which is still a valid choice, this conversation remain confidential, no word spoken of it to anyone. May I have your word on that point?"

Pierre swallowed, feeling that he was somehow getting himself in deeper before he knew all the details, but Eleanor's request seemed innocent enough. "You have my word."

"Many thanks." Eleanor smiled warmly. "The Kindred in question is Owain Evans. Do you know him?"

Pierre thought for a moment. "Ventrue?" Eleanor nodded. "Young looking, fairly stodgy?" Again Eleanor nodded. "I know *of* him," said Pierre, "but we've never been formally introduced."

Eleanor waited until Pierre's hands completed their gyrations and were still. "I'm afraid I don't have a great deal of time for you to think about your answer," she pressed him slightly. "I was thinking, in return, that I might be able to arrange an exhibit of your work, of your…"

"Paintings," he prompted her.

"Yes, your paintings. Perhaps at the High Museum?" Then Eleanor shrugged her shoulders. "But if you are not able to help me, I'll have to find someone else…"

"I don't think that will be necessary," Pierre interrupted, almost before he knew what he was saying. Even his own hands were caught off guard by his sudden answer, and rushed to catch up. "I think I should be able to help you."

Eleanor smiled warmly. "Wonderful." She had known that the possibility of a showing at the museum, aside from any other motivations Pierre might have brought with him, would be a difficult temptation for the young Toreador to resist. She still didn't trust him. There was always the possibility that he would run straight to Marlene with this information, but frankly Eleanor saw no great harm in that. What could Marlene, the Toreador whore, do with the knowledge? Besides, if Pierre crossed Eleanor, she would merely fabricate some story for Benison, and he would have Xavier Kline dispatch the little Toreador.

Pierre seemed only slightly less nervous now that he had made his decision. His fingers twiddled constantly in his lap.

"Wonderful, Pierre," Eleanor said again. "I know you've made the right choice."

The spray-can rattled like knucklebones in Blackfeather's hand. He popped the top and fired off a few short bursts at the underside of the bridge. Satisfied the nozzle was working properly, he returned to where Nicholas sat cross-legged on the concrete.

Even before Blackfeather had turned his back on the hastily rendered sigil, he began rationalizing. After all, he seriously doubted that anyone would be able to pick out the arcane cipher amidst the scrawl of graffiti. And even if someone did make it out, there were only a dozen people on this continent that might recognize the spidery rune as a symbol from the (thankfully) long-forgotten language of the Howling Priests of Mu. And there were maybe three beings on the planet that might attempt a rough translation of the cryptic rune, which would be most closely rendered, "Don't look now, but there's an Elder God in your beer."

Blackfeather often felt that his best efforts went unappreciated.

Nicholas was watching him expectantly. As

Blackfeather approached, he was again struck by the visible changes that had been wrought upon the young Gangrel. It had been no more than a week since their encounter at the Veil and although each of them was once more whole in body, the signs of the struggle were still all too clear in Nicholas's bearing and visage.

His figure was stooped as if under a great weight of age or responsibility. Blackfeather could not quite shake the image of Nicholas at the manse, standing defiant despite the horde of shades clawing and clamoring over him. The comparison was not a flattering one. Although Nicholas had never bent under that burden, it was clear that the spirits had left a more lasting mark upon him.

Any encounter with the powers beyond the Veil, Blackfeather reflected, was like placing oneself at the mercy of a rather clumsy sculptor. The shapers of spirit are unused to working with such ephemeral materials as flesh and blood.

Nicholas had been in the grips of power before Blackfeather came upon him at the mansion. Judging from the carnage, it was not a gentle power. Blackfeather knew full well that the dark spirit that rode Nicholas would never have released him of its own accord.

Over the years, Blackfeather had seen similar forces at work in those who had lost themselves irrevocably to the ravenings of the beast. More recently, Blackfeather had witnessed such baleful spirits perched upon the shoulders of those touched by the blood curse. Even the clan's Wailing Women had been unable to drive off the predatory spirits.

The Fading of the Blood, the Women would whisper, making the sign against evil. *Dark crows among the ripening corn.*

Blackfeather had been too long among the spirit paths to disregard such obvious trailsigns. Surely some great reckoning was at hand—not only for his clan, but for all of his kind. *A Winnowing*, he thought, *a separation of the wheat from the chaff.*

These thoughts did not comfort Blackfeather. They did, however, steady him and give him a strong focal point for his will. If a judgment were at hand, the challenge before him was clear—to go among the Fallen, to identify those who still managed to cling to the true, the beautiful, the compassionate, the sacred—and to make them endure.

Blackfeather circled three times, laying down a wide terracotta-colored ring of paint as he went. A perfect circle.

He was taking no chances. Last week's mayhem was still fresh in his mind. There was no telling what creatures from beyond the Veil might still be abroad, having weathered out the days in the manor's wine cellars or family crypt. Some of the apparitions, fortified by blood and suffering, might even have had the strength to pass among the waking.

But Blackfeather and Nicholas would be safe here. The circle was inviolate. The trick was not, as some suspected, the Patterner's magic of perfect Platonic forms. Nor the Gnostic wonders of realized Euclidean dreams. Blackfeather's circle drew on a more humble enchantment—the everyday miracle of flawless craftsmanship, of the job impeccably done. The circle itself was just a ready-to-hand expression of this mundane enchantment. Blackfeather would have been equally impervious to all harm in the eclectic little house he had constructed with his own hands, the car he had saved from scrap and rebuilt, the night-blooming garden he tended.

In that garden, the clan's Rootweavers had slowly nursed Nicholas back to health. When the pair had fled the disturbance at the manse, Nicholas was barely aware of himself or his surroundings. He had been ridden and discarded by the dark power; he was little better than cast-off clay thrown from the potter's wheel.

It was all Blackfeather could do to drag the incoherent Nicholas as far as Piedmont Park. The latter kept involuntarily sinking ankle-deep into the earth, his body obeying a primal need to flee the first hints of the sunrise. Blackfeather struggled to put as much distance as possible between them and any pursuit.

The Dreamstalkers found them at sundown. A

layer of earth barely six inches deep was all that had lain between the pair and the deadly rays of the sun. Both were broken in body from their struggle as well as being severely burned from exposure. The Dreamstalkers carried them back to the rest of the clan in the mountains to the north.

It was a full three days before Nicholas showed any signs of awareness. Each day he would walk in the garden, shuffling forward, eyes staring fixedly into the middle distance. When the clan pressed Blackfeather with questions about the newcomer, he would answer them only, "We must have him back."

On the third day, one of the Rootweavers came running to Blackfeather to report that their young charge had awakened briefly, still in the grips of delirium, and then fallen back into his somnambulism.

"What did the young lord say?" Blackfeather asked.

The Rootweaver was taken aback, puzzled by this turn of question. "He raved only, Guardian."

"Can you remember what he said in his ravings?"

"Yes, Guardian. He said to summon his people. Do you know who his people are? I think he was afraid. He said something about a nightmare—a nightmare, carved in marble, walking dripping from the sea."

"Do not leave him," Blackfeather replied, "either

by day or night. You are accountable for his blood. You are his people."

Blackfeather sat down inside the protective circle, facing Nicholas across the low pile of debris they had collected. When they had painstakingly cleared the area that the circle would occupy, Blackfeather insisted that all of the moldy leaves, Coke cans, odd scraps of clothing, fast food wrappers, etc., be gathered in the center. Not one cigarette butt was lost or wasted.

Blackfeather reached into a hip pocket and pulled out a turquoise-studded silver Zippo.

"*Wa-Kan-Kan Ya-Wa-On-We,*" he recited. The traditional words rang with about the same sense of reverence that a paratrooper invokes in yelling, "Geronimo." The lighter snapped open, sparked. A turquoise-blue flame, two feet in length, leapt out.

Nicholas drew back with a start in the face of the adversary—for fire and sunlight are the two most ancient and respected enemies of the Gangrel. He quickly checked himself; he hoped Blackfeather had not noticed.

The pile of wet debris roared inexplicably to life. Nicholas could feel the heat of the sudden blaze stretching taut the skin of his face. It was not a pleasant sensation. He was acutely aware that his face, neck, and arms were still badly cracked from his headlong flight into the sunrise.

It was strange to be back in the city. Details of that night at the estate were still hazy in his mind. It was the fever again—the blood curse that ravaged this God-forsaken city. Not for the first time, Nicholas found himself cursing the city, cursing that dilettante Evans, cursing the damned Nosferatu, Ellison, who had first put the idea of Atlanta into his mind and that ominous message tube into his hand.

But thoughts of vengeance slipped from him, finding no purchase. With resignation, Nicholas admitted that it was unlikely he would live long enough to avenge this wrong. The attacks were growing more frequent now.

Each time the ancestor-memories returned they gripped him more fiercely and were more reluctant to loosen their hold upon him. At first they were merely memories—ghost images, stray thoughts, snatches of conversation. Soon, however, the scenes began to take on detail and substance.

Nicholas was no longer recalling events, he was reliving them, acting out scenes of ancient violence—the heritage and legacy of his bloodline. And always there was the hunger. The pangs of the blood-longing were overwhelming, banishing thought and awakening the ravening beast.

Dazed by fever and hunger, Nicholas found himself slipping again and again across the narrow divide between the two worlds. The transition was as easy and seamless for him as the shift of perspective achieved by alternately closing first one eye and then the other.

Last week, at the estate, the situation had taken a dramatic turn for the worse. He felt as if he were sleepwalking, viewing both realities—the past and present—at once. Nicholas was overwhelmed by the impressions streaming in from two distinct sets of senses. It was like looking both forward and backward in the same instant.

The immersion had been complete and nearly irrevocable; Nicholas had lost all sense of self in the grip of the past. He had no idea whether he could have emerged from it of his own volition, without Blackfeather's help. Nicholas did know that he had very nearly killed his friend.

Nicholas looked across the fire, but did not meet Blackfeather's eyes. This was the second time that Blackfeather had come upon Nicholas fighting with phantasms, tilting at windmills. Each time, his friend had called him back from the brink of berserk abandon at great personal risk.

Nicholas knew that the curse he carried in his veins was a threat not only to himself, but to all those around him. He resolved that he would slip away from Blackfeather at the first opportunity.

If Blackfeather were aware of the nature of the struggle within Nicholas, he gave no sign. He patiently studied the younger Gangrel and waited.

Nicholas broke the silence. "I'm going after him."

Blackfeather continued to regard him without expression.

"I'm going back to the mansion," Nicholas hurried on. "I'm going to find this Evans, or whatever he's calling himself nowadays. I'm going to get some answers."

Blackfeather shook his head. "It will do no good. He is gone."

"Then I'll find him. I know him and I know his kind."

"Nicholas, this vendetta of yours, it will be the..." he broke off.

"The death of me?" Nicholas could not keep the hint of bitterness from his voice. "No, my friend, you can't deny the evidence of your eyes. I'm dying now. You've seen the victims of this plague in the city, dead of hunger, face down in pools of their own blood."

"And you wish to hasten this end?" Blackfeather's voice was guarded. "Here is the flame. Give me your hand."

Without waiting for him to respond, Blackfeather reached out and clasped Nicholas by the wrist. Nicholas did not pull away from him. Blackfeather drew Nicholas's clenched fist into the fire. Nicholas stiffened, locked his jaws around a rising howl of pain, and held firm.

His eyes were locked on Blackfeather's, boring

into him. Blackfeather could read the rising agony and fury there. Nicholas's features contracted into an animal snarl.

With a whoomph of bright white ignition, Blackfeather's hand caught flame, burning like a torch within the larger bonfire. Slowly, he raised his hand from the fire until Nicholas's fist broke the plane of their locked gazes.

The fist dripped with liquid shadow. It trickled down his forearm, black and viscous. In its wake, the flesh of his hand gleamed, unburned and unblemished.

Blackfeather released his grip and hastily extinguished his own hand. Nicholas stared in dumb amazement at his fist. He clutched it to his chest. He stroked it absently with the other hand. He was silent for some time.

"You *saw* that night," Blackfeather said, gingerly wrapping a bandage around his own badly charred appendage. "I do not know if you remember it and it is probably best that some things remain unremembered. What did you see when you drew your hand from the flame?"

Nicholas did not answer at first. "It was wrapped in shadow, living shadow. The shadow interposed itself between me and the flames."

Blackfeather was suddenly intent. "But where did the shadow come from?"

Nicholas was puzzled. Of course there had been

no shadow in the heart of the fire. It was ridiculous. He couldn't image why he would have said such a thing. It was just the fever again—another spell brought about by the pain.

"I don't know," Nicholas stammered. "I'm sorry. It will pass. The delirium, the hunger. I'm, I'm not myself."

"But where did the shadow come from?"

Nicholas had the overwhelming urge to break away. He felt the silly spray-painted circle closing in on him like the walls of the city rising on all sides.

Blackfeather caught the cornered glances. He reached to his belt with his good hand and drew a long bone-handled hunting knife. He held it by the wicked-looking blade and gestured towards Nicholas with the hilt.

"Would you like to see the source of the shadow? Take the knife."

Nicholas looked at the ground; he did not reach out for the knife.

Blackfeather's voice came to him from very close by, as if his friend were behind him, bent over him, and whispering.

"Nicholas, the curse is in your blood. The shadow courses through your veins. The fury races up and down your bloodline. The rage pulses just beneath the surface of your skin. If I drew this blade," Nicholas felt the whisper of cool steel just below his ear, "downward, blood and shadow would spill together. Your vengeance, your ancient hatreds, they are consuming you."

Nicholas raised his head and, unconcerned, turned into the knife. Its edge was cradled in the folds of his throat, but it did not bite. He looked steadily at Blackfeather.

"I would know why I have been brought here, across continents and oceans, to bring a message to a man, a creature, who killed my ancestor-self. If it is by his device that I have been lured here to my death, I will put an end to his foul lineage before this curse overtakes me."

The knife fell away, and his tone softened, "Don't fear for me, old friend. Wait here and I'll return to you. By tomorrow evening."

Nicholas rose, clapping his friend on the back and, without a backward glance, walked from the shelter of the circle.

CHAPTER FOUR

Antoinette smiled again at Maxwell Ldescu, who sat at the table. They had been waiting in the conference room in the Academy of the Arts for very close to an hour, and still there was no sign of either Wilhelm or Gustav. Maxwell nodded politely in response to Antoinette's smile, then returned to his own private contemplation. He was there as a representative of the western primogen, but more importantly was one of the few Kindred in Berlin whom both Wilhelm and Gustav accorded some degree of respect.

Antoinette was acting as mediator to some degree. At Wilhelm's request, she had secured this meeting place in the Tiergarten district. Though the Toreador clan was avowedly neutral in the conflict between Wilhelm and Gustav, Antoinette's predilection for Wilhelm was fairly common knowledge. Still, Gustav did not reject the location of the meeting.

The sound of footsteps in the corridor was a relief to Antoinette. Though she admired Ldescu and his company was not unpleasant, there was a great deal of pressure involved with having arranged this conference, and she was anxious for it to be underway.

Peter Kleist, Wilhelm's bodyguard opened the door and surveyed the room. He disappeared back into the corridor briefly, then opened the door for Wilhelm, who entered. He, Maxwell, and Antoinette exchanged polite greetings. Antoinette was amazed by how calm and relaxed Wilhelm seemed. Gustav had repeatedly sworn to destroy Wilhelm and reassert undisputed control over the city, while Wilhelm had vowed upon his unlife to keep that from happening. This face-to-face meeting between the two would be the first in many years. If Gustav attended. There was the distinct possibility that he would utilize the knowledge of Wilhelm's whereabouts to stage some sort of attack, a scenario for which Kleist was not unprepared. He had examined the entire Academy building hours ago, and was again scrutinizing every cranny of the conference room. No doubt, Antoinette realized,

Peter and Wilhelm had arrived late in order to avoid providing Wilhelm as a stationary target for any longer than necessary. Still, if that was indeed their strategy, Gustav had disrupted it by being even later.

Kleist completed his inspection of the conference room. "I will wait in the corridor, Wilhelm." The recognized prince of the western portion of the city nodded his assent.

Ldescu retook his seat, deep wrinkles crossing a face that otherwise appeared fairly young. Wilhelm, his blue eyes friendly and at ease as he began to walk slowly around the table, smiled warmly at Antoinette. "Thank you so much for arranging this meeting."

"I am glad to have been of service," she answered formally.

Wilhelm extended no further pleasantries, and Maxwell seemed disinclined to offer any, so they waited in silence, Antoinette standing patiently, Wilhelm slowly pacing, Ldescu leaning with chin on hand, index finger crossing his lips.

Antoinette was relieved that they did not have to wait long before Kleist returned. "Gustav is here. And de Lutrius. No others."

He sounded so sure that Gustav and de Lutrius were alone. How, Antoinette wondered, could he be certain there weren't others lying in wait?

Ldescu rose as Gustav and Thomas de Lutrius

entered the room. Gustav halted just inside the door. He glared at Wilhelm. How long it had been since these two enemies last stood so close to one another, Antoinette did not know. They faced each other across the table, neither offering a hand or word of greeting. Gustav, with his solid, square build and severely short gray hair, gave the impression of being an immovable boulder, a force of nature. Wilhelm was not intimidated, Antoinette noticed. Even though more slight of stature, he more than held his own in the presence of his former friend.

Thomas de Lutrius, standing next to Gustav, wore matching black turtleneck and slacks. His strong jaw could have been a younger, more handsome version of Gustav's imposing jowls. Unlike everyone else in the room, de Lutrius wore a broad grin across his face.

The very sight of her Toreador rival was enough to grate on Antoinette's already strained nerves, but she attempted to ignore her own discomfort and proceed with the task of mediating this rarest of meetings. She could see her efforts would be required, for neither claimant to the title "Prince of Berlin" had moved or spoken since Gustav entered the room. They remained immobile, glaring at one another. The three or four feet that separated them was undoubtedly the closest they had come in decades. Antoinette would have been far from surprised had one, or each, lunged for the other's throat. Such hatred burned in the room. *And they hope to come to some agreement?* She was bewildered. But dear Wilhelm had asked her, as a favor to him, to arrange the meeting, so she would do her part.

"Gentlemen." Her words seemed very small, dwarfed by the vehement animosity between prince of eastern Berlin and prince of western Berlin. "We are here tonight to speak in a civilized manner. I believe no introductions are necessary."

Neither prince responded.

"Perhaps, Fräulein Mediator," Thomas de Lutrius interrupted, still with his mocking smile, "you could introduce yourself and explain how a *neutral* meeting site can be procured by one so decidedly unneutral?"

In an instant, Antoinette's train of thought escaped her. Not only flustered, she was angered that the miscreant poseur was so easily able to distract her. Obviously, it was why Gustav had brought Thomas, to upset her, to keep her from aiding Wilhelm in any way. Like the two claimant princes within clan Ventrue, Thomas and Antoinette maintained a bitter rivalry of long standing. Antoinette was the titular leader of the Toreador in Berlin, but Thomas made a regular practice of defaming her and her chosen artistic medium— film—whenever opportunity presented itself. For her part, Antoinette did not hesitate to savage what she referred to as Thomas's "attempts" with charcoal.

Strangely enough, it was Maxwell Ldescu who came to Antoinette's defense. "Thomas, certainly there are enough points of contention to be discussed already?" scolded the normally mild-mannered Tremere.

De Lutrius turned his sly grin that direction. "How can *she*," he gestured derisively toward Antoinette, "claim any status except that of partisan?"

"To evaluate or classify Antoinette was not the reason this meeting was deemed necessary," Ldescu reminded. His words were soft-spoken, but for just a moment his eyes glowed angrily red. "You and I are here to advise. Not to complicate."

Thomas's confidence visibly withered in the face of this unspoken challenge. He began to reply but, words escaping him, contented himself with stroking his chin.

Instead it was Gustav who finally spoke. "Yes. Exactly correct, Maxwell." The menacing tone of Berlin's former Kindred ruler belied his agreeable words. He had shifted neither his stance nor his gaze. Barely acknowledging the presence of anyone else in the room, he stared directly at Wilhelm. "Why is this meeting deemed necessary? I am a reasonable man. I am here to talk."

Wilhelm, also, had not looked away from his opponent. From his expression of studied concentration emerged a smile, slight and politic. "I thank you for agreeing to this meeting, Gustav. I have always known you to be a wise man, and it is wisdom that our city needs at present." Wilhelm relaxed somewhat as he spoke. Gustav retained his rigid stance.

"I thank you, Antoinette," Wilhelm nodded in her direction and even shifted his gaze from Gustav momentarily, "for arranging this meeting, and I thank you, Maxwell and Thomas, for attending as well." Maxwell nodded his acknowledgment. Thomas looked at no one.

"And the purpose of this meeting?" Gustav asked again, though Antoinette had communicated that information to him on repeated occasions before he had agreed to participate.

Having satisfied the dictates of protocol, Wilhelm turned earnestly to Gustav. "Berlin is ravaged, as is the rest of Europe, as is the world, by a curse of unknown origin. What is needed, if any of our kind are to survive, is cooperation. Maxwell and his brethren have made great strides in combating this threat, but there is much more work to be done. We cannot be distracted by…" he gestured dismissively, "by personal squabbles. We must set aside, for now, disagreements that are political in nature, that are divisive. We must focus our energies and our resources and aid the Tremere in their endeavors if any of us are to survive."

Gustav, having listened patiently, shrugged. "I am a cooperative man. What do you propose?"

"I propose," Wilhelm responded immediately, "a truce."

Antoinette could feel the intensity with which he spoke. She knew how he had wracked his brain and combed the city as the fatalities had mounted over the past months, searching for any clue as to the cause of the curse. But always, as the Kindred of Berlin wasted away, there was Gustav to deal with, to watch for, to guard against. Wilhelm had been unable at any time to devote his full attention to aiding Ldescu.

"A truce," Gustav repeated noncommittally. The words seemed to hang in the air, pregnant with possibility.

"I propose," Wilhelm continued intently, "that we both turn our attention to aiding the Tremere. I believe they are our best hope in determining the cause of this curse and in stopping it. Let me speak frankly."

"Oh, please do," said Gustav.

"The Cold War of the mortals has ended. But between you and me it carries on. There is a more pressing need at hand than either of our individual goals. This curse is more immediate and more deadly than either of our grievances. We must find a way to bring it to an end. We will find a way, and then both east and west in our city will be healed." A fire burned in Wilhelm's bright blue eyes. He was fully committed to that which he believed was the only sane course of action.

Gustav remained silent. He crossed his arms.

Antoinette realized that they had launched into negotiations without so much as sitting down. Maxwell looked on with interest. Thomas still nursed his wounded pride. Peter Kleist kept close to Wilhelm, lest any trouble should erupt.

"You place a great deal of faith in the Tremere," said Gustav. "No offense meant to Herr Ldescu, but I am not sure that I share your confidence that what you hold out as the best interests of all Kindred are actually the best interest of the Tremere."

Wilhelm was prepared for this contention. "I have been quite explicit with Maxwell and with his superiors that attempting to extract some sort of political leverage from the dire need of their fellow Kindred would be a certain way to alienate the Tremere from every other clan and to bring their chantries down in flames and ruin across the world. Though I am positive that they would never resort to such duplicity and opportunism, I have assured them that if they did, I would lead the charge against them. I will work beside the Tremere. I will not hand them the city. This is Berlin, not Vienna."

Gustav still appeared skeptical.

"This is so," added Ldescu in way of reassurance.

Gustav, his ire suddenly raised, ignored the

Tremere and spoke to Wilhelm. "You spoke with his superiors? With Schrekt? I will not have him in my city!"

Antoinette flinched at Gustav's outburst. She had always felt that he was merely such an outburst away from attacking anyone in his presence. She had also heard rumors of the fateful confrontation between Gustav and Schrekt centuries ago. Kleist, alerted as well, edged closer to Wilhelm.

Wilhelm was taken aback by this sudden turn of the conversation, but he quickly recovered. "We cannot order about the Tremere Justicar as if he were a chamber maid," Wilhelm smiled and spoke in reassuring, reasonable tones, "but Maxwell and I can do what we are able to see that he does not enter the city."

Gustav cast a sidelong glance at Wilhelm, and then at Maxwell. "You will keep Schrekt out of the city?"

Ldescu nodded. "We will do our best."

Gustav snorted. He seemed satisfied with this concession. "Very well. A truce it will be, and I will not disrupt your working with the Tremere to counteract this curse."

A moment of amazed silence followed. Antoinette could not believe what she was hearing, that Gustav and Wilhelm would agree to anything. Wilhelm and Maxwell looked surprised, but expressions of pure shock registered on the faces of both Thomas de Lutrius and Peter Kleist.

"And in exchange for this truce," Gustav added, "you will, of course, publicly acknowledge me prince of Berlin. You will renounce your claim, and you will leave the city, never to return. I am a gracious victor, Wilhelm. I will allow you your life."

Wilhelm's optimism instantly deflated. His brief hope for sanity came to an abrupt end, while Thomas's smug grin, Antoinette noticed, was restored. *How could any of us have thought Gustav would be reasonable?* she wondered.

"Gustav," said Wilhelm, not yet ready to give up, "I am not proposing that we definitively resolve our situation. We are too far apart. It is possible that our differences will never be reconciled, but let us, at the least, defer them to another night so that we might, for now, combat the curse."

"You have heard my price," Gustav snapped. "If it is too high, then you are not serious in your desire to save the city."

Wilhelm stifled a derisive laugh. "Be reasonable, Gustav."

The implication of unreasonableness brought color to Gustav's cheeks. His gray eyes darkened. "Reasonable? Reasonable! You!" He pointed with quivering finger at Wilhelm. "You manipulate. You stroke egos. You betray. You do these things because you want to rule, because that is the way you are. I…" he pounded his own chest with the flat of his palm, "I have a passion for this city. It is a *possession* to you, something to be lorded over. For me, it is my *child*. I have made it what it is! And I have seen it stolen from me, handed over to foreigners, violated." Gustav spewed vitriol. Every word was formed in the forges of his hate. "And you would have me aid you? You, who turned on me and took my beloved city? Why? So that you may turn it over to the foreigners, to the Tremere? Their word is worth nearly as little as yours!"

As Gustav's tirade progressed, and Antoinette saw any hope of reaching an accord rapidly slipping away, Wilhelm grew increasingly calm. He had heard all this before—recriminations, veiled threats. He could not end this war by himself. Kleist, expecting this harangue to break into open violence, watched Gustav and Thomas closely.

Gustav stood before them, his face flushed, a semi-permanent snarl creasing his features. "*That* is my proposal." They stood silently facing one another, Gustav's eyes burning with hatred, Wilhelm's face showing only pity and resignation. "Just as I thought," Gustav said eventually. "You care that Berlin is yours, but you do not care about Berlin." With this, he turned on his heels and strode to the door, but stopped before he left the room. "And, oh yes, Wilhelm…" Gustav's expression softening to a facsimile of concern, "my condolences regarding your childe's recent difficulties."

Wilhelm stiffened. His normally pale cheeks blanched solid white. Antoinette couldn't help but gasp. Weeks prior, Wilhelm had sent, via his beautiful young childe Henriette, a message to Gustav requesting just such a meeting as this. The choice of messenger had been deliberate, a show of good faith on Wilhelm's part in hopes of establishing the basis for cooperation. Also quite deliberate had been the manner in which Gustav had ravaged Henriette. Beyond mere physical injury, he had blood-bound her, and sent her back to attack her sire. Gustav had covered his tracks, with the help of some renegade eastern Tremere no doubt, Antoinette suspected. There was no definite proof linking Gustav to Henriette's attack on Wilhelm, but, Antoinette knew, there could be no other explanation.

For Gustav to refer to the affair in such a diplomatic setting, for him to gloat so blithely before Wilhelm, was the mark of highest cruelty. Laughter danced in Gustav's eyes as he left the room. "I would destroy anyone who harmed *my* childe," he said with a nod.

Childe or child? Antoinette wondered about his meaning. Progeny or the city that was his self-avowed child? Although for Gustav there was likely no distinction.

Wilhelm was completely still. He did not move; he did not speak. Antoinette marveled at the rage he must be suppressing. Thomas, absolutely beaming now as he followed Gustav out, winked at Antoinette and then closed the door.

Pierre rapped at the door of Rhodes Hall. It had been only two nights since Eleanor had charged him with his mission, but he felt she should be informed of the unusual visitor to Owain Evans's estate. Peachtree Street was fairly quiet. Some mortals drove by every now and then, but there was no sign of other Kindred about. Pierre was one of four recognized Toreador in the city, and there were rumors floating about that Marlene, the primogen, was not in the best of health. Ominous news for such uncertain times.

Sally, Eleanor's serving ghoul, opened the door at last. She did not invite Pierre inside and checked back over her shoulder before greeting him. "Pierre. What brings you here this evening?"

Pierre was surprised not to be asked in, and took some umbrage at the affront. His was not to speak with minor retainers. "I must see Miss Eleanor," he informed Sally rather coolly.

Sally looked behind her again, uncertainty clouding her actions. Pierre could hear voices from the living room. "I'm afraid Miss Eleanor has company at the moment," she said. "May I deliver a message?"

This was not at all what Pierre had been expecting. He was undertaking a personal favor for the prince's wife, a matter of some delicacy. To be turned away at the door, and by a serving wench, no less, was unacceptable. "I must deliver this message in person, I'm afraid." Sally was clearly troubled now, not comfortable standing and talking in the open doorway, but unwilling to ask Pierre in. He decided to press his advantage. "If you do not tell Miss Eleanor that I am here, I will stay here on the doorstep and pound on the door until she comes."

This terrorized Sally. She stared at Pierre aghast, as if he might force his way past her and barge into Rhodes Hall. A third time she checked over her shoulder as high-pitched, twittery laughter resounded from the living room. She frowned at Pierre. "Stay there please." Then she quietly closed the door, but Pierre was certain she would not abandon him to pound upon the door.

Sure enough, after a few moments, the door opened again, and this time Pierre faced Eleanor. She greeted him with a chillingly polite smile. "Yes, Pierre? Back so soon?"

This was more what Pierre had expected. Perhaps she would offer him some refreshment. They had been trying nights, sneaking around outside the Evans estate, secretly observing the beastly Gangrel that had shown up. She and he could even discuss some of his pieces that might be most appropriate for an exhibit at the High Museum. "So sorry to disturb you, Miss Eleanor. I have some important news."

"Important news about Evans in only two nights?"

He could imagine that she was quite impressed, but then he realized that he had not actually laid eyes on Evans himself as of yet, but that was inconsequential. "Not about Evans himself, not directly," Pierre explained. "But important news nonetheless. If I may have just a small amount of your time, perhaps a half-hour…"

"I'm afraid I don't have that luxury at the moment," Eleanor interrupted him. "I have company."

Wafting from the living room, Pierre heard a voice that could be mistaken for no other save Aunt Bedelia, Prince Benison's sire. "Eleanor? Eleanor, where have you gone? Who is there?" This was a high society gathering, indeed, Pierre realized. If only he had the opportunity to show them some of his paintings…

"It's a message from Marlene," Eleanor called back to Bedelia. "She won't be able to join us again, I'm afraid." Eleanor faced Pierre impatiently. "What do you need to tell me?" she asked quietly but insistently.

Pierre was appalled by the indignity, but what else could he do but answer? "There has been a

Gangrel, not a resident Kindred of Atlanta, trespassing at the Evans estate," Pierre informed her.

"Why?" Eleanor asked.

"Pardon me?"

"Why?" she repeated. "What is the Gangrel doing there? And where does it go after?"

"I...I..." Pierre had, of course, wondered similarly, but he had not followed that line of inquiry any further. "I don't know."

Eleanor placed her hands on her hips. "Why do you bring me partial information?" she asked pointedly. "Why do you interrupt me with worthless news?" Pierre was speechless. This was so far from the warm, respectful reception he had expected. "You have much work to do," Eleanor pointed out. "And if that Gangrel returns, follow it. Find out why in the world it's interested in Evans."

This charge caught Pierre quite off guard. "A Gangrel?" he asked, assuming that he must have heard her incorrectly. "You want *me* to follow a *Gangrel?*"

Eleanor stared at him as if he were merely confirming a grocery list. "Of course," she said. "Now go do it, and don't bother me with inconsequential bits of nothing."

Before the dumbfounded Pierre could summon a reply, the door was closed, and he was again alone on the street. *Follow a Gangrel.* Why not spit on the prince, or take up sunbathing? *Follow a Gangrel.*

What, Pierre wondered, had he gotten himself into? What indeed?

The hunger was gnawing at Rebecca. It had been a couple of nights since she had fed, but she couldn't help wondering every time she was hungry...not after seeing what had happened to Tonya. Rebecca shook herself and tried not to think about it. *A girl's gotta eat.* Curse or no curse. "Greg, let's go out."

Gregory was where she knew he would be—on the couch in the living room of the cramped apartment, chain-smoking and watching TV, *America's Funniest Home Videos*, no less. Rebecca hated the show. "Watch this, hon," Gregory called. Against her better judgment, Rebecca watched as a man on the screen leaned over the railing of a boat. He leaned a little farther, and a little farther, then he flipped over the railing and fell off the boat. Gregory howled uncontrollably with laughter.

"How can you watch this shit?" Rebecca asked. Gregory hadn't stopped laughing yet when a small child with a plastic bat hit his father in the crotch. Gregory doubled over, pointing at the screen and laughing. "At least hit the mute button, so we don't have to listen to what's-his-ass, the idiot host," Rebecca suggested. Disgusted, she went to the bathroom and began brushing her dark hair. She was going out, with or without Gregory. He could stay and smoke and watch TV if he wanted. *Serve him right if he fell over laughing, knocked over the ashtray, and set the couch and himself on fire*, she thought. *That'd make a hell of a video.*

Over the sound of the TV, Rebecca heard knocking at the door. She also heard Gregory, instead of answering it, turn up the volume on the TV and pretend not to hear the knocking. *Great. Probably the neighbors complaining about Gregory being so loud again.* Of course, Rebecca realized, if they fed on neighbors and then removed the memory from their minds, it wouldn't be the first time. Maybe Gregory's noise was easier than hunting. *But he could at least get off his lazy butt and answer the door.*

More knocking, and louder to be heard over the TV. Rebecca stomped to the door. "No, no. Don't worry. I'll get the damn door." Gregory ignored her. "And get dressed. We're going out. I'm hungry."

"Just order pizza," Gregory suggested. "You always like the pizza boy."

Rebecca was debating the merits of food that came to her, rather than the other way around, as she unlocked the door. As soon as she turned the knob, the door crashed open into her face. She stumbled back and fell, nose bloodied and broken.

Xavier Kline stepped into the apartment, axe in hand, his buddy Ron right behind him. Without a second thought, Gregory made a break for the sliding door to the balcony. He threw it open and ran headlong into Thu, Kline's other Brujah helper. She smacked Gregory across the face with a chain and shoved him back into the apartment. He landed roughly on the couch, knocking over the overflowing ashtray.

"Nice of you to check on your girlfriend before you leave, Greg," said Kline. He closed the door behind him. Rebecca sat on the floor, both hands clasped to her face. Gregory looked back and forth anxiously between Kline and Thu. "You people know you're supposed to choose a clan, to be respectable vampires like me and my friends." Ron bowed. "And you really should have done it before now." Kline shook his head like a parent disappointed with a child. "We will have to discuss this." He reached for one of the cigarettes that was smoldering on the couch. The tip glowed red. For a moment, Kline smiled contentedly, then his expression went blank as he approached Gregory. "Thu, turn up the TV. We don't want to disturb the neighbors."

Pierre hugged the shadows as the Gangrel he had been following loped off into the night. Perhaps Pierre should follow, but he wanted to see what the Gangrel had found so interesting amidst the ruins of the burned church. Besides, Pierre still was not convinced that following a Gangrel was the wisest of activities. In fact, he was convinced of the exact opposite. Few activities could be more foolish. Or more suicidal. So if the Gangrel happened to slip away while Pierre was examining this important scene, that would be just too bad. If Eleanor thought the Gangrel was so important, *she* could follow it. *That's what I should have told her,* he decided. "Now go do it," he mimicked her aloud. "Some appreciation I get."

After his humiliation on Eleanor's doorstep, Pierre had returned to his hiding place across the street from the estate of Owain Evans. Hoping for an uneventful evening, devoid specifically of Gangrel, Pierre had been singularly dismayed when he saw the wolf figure appear before the estate and lithely leap the brick wall. Shortly thereafter, the Gangrel had leapt back out, this time in its more human form, able to pass as kine among the uninitiated. To Pierre and anyone with even passing knowledge of the Kindred, however, the Gangrel's true nature was obvious; the curve and hidden point of the ears, the slight hint of wolfish snout gave the secret away.

The Gangrel had seemed agitated, constantly pausing to scrape at the earth or sniff the air. When the creature had begun to wander away from the estate, Pierre, still stinging from Eleanor's rebuke, had, against his better judgment, followed. He'd been surprised by how easily he'd kept up. The Gangrel had maintained a steady but nondemanding pace, leading Pierre through section after section of the city. Eventually they had made their way to Reynoldstown, where the Gangrel had busied itself amidst the rubble of the burned church. Pierre had watched from the shadows and observed the one area of the debris that attracted the Gangrel's particular interest. By the time the creature appeared ready to move on, Pierre had had his fill of traipsing around the city. He had also decided that every step he followed the Gangrel provided another chance to be discovered, and he judiciously chose not to push his luck.

Pierre waited long enough to be sure that the Gangrel had moved far along. Not only did members of that clan smell like kennels, they nursed testy dispositions. *Always steer a wide berth around a Gangrel*, was one of Pierre's primary rules of survival. "And here I am following one," he sighed, not believing it himself.

There was not a great deal left of the old church. It looked to have burned fairly recently, Pierre thought, maybe in the past few weeks. As he picked his way through the debris, he tried to miss the dirtier parts. *No need to track ash and filth all over everything for the rest of the night.* Not all of the steeple had burned. One portion was even, with a little imagination, fairly intact. Pierre tentatively climbed over to where the Gangrel had spent the most time. It took him several minutes to manage, searching for clean handholds and sturdy footing.

What would a Gangrel find so fascinating here? Pierre wondered. He looked around carefully. *Dirt. Filth. Par for the course for a Gangrel.* Otherwise there was nothing of note. Perhaps the Gangrel had been curious about what had started the fire, or maybe it had smelled something peculiar, though Pierre couldn't smell anything except ash. Gangrel were funny that way. *Or maybe it was just scraping around in the dirt.* Gangrel were funny that way too. Nothing. Nothing of any interest.

Just as Pierre was turning to escape the disgusting pile of rubble, however, the glint of metal in a crevice between the pieces of a split floorboard caught his eye. Whatever was there was almost completely covered with ash and soot. *Imagine my surprise.* Pierre took a silk handkerchief from his pocket. He looked around for anything else to use but, to his great chagrin, found nothing. Finally, he reached down with the handkerchief to protect his skin from the filth. To his surprise, he retrieved a dagger from the shadows. He held it by the very tip of the point so as to sully his handkerchief as little as possible. A small area of steel showed through, and on the pommel a tiny glint of gold was visible. His handkerchief already in need of a washing, he wiped a bit more of the dagger. There appeared not to be a substantial amount of gold, just gilding, but even so, the workmanship, what little Pierre could see through the grime, impressed him.

His attention focused on the dagger, Pierre nearly lost his balance, and in catching himself was forced to rub against a particularly sooty section of wall. This surviving portion of the steeple was tilted, so there was no level footing to be found, and his black platform boots were designed for style, not traction. There was no reason, Pierre decided, that he must remain balanced precariously amidst the rubble to inspect his find. As much as possible, he wrapped the dagger with the soiled handkerchief, then slipped it into his jacket pocket.

Carefully he turned, and found himself face to face with the crouching Gangrel.

Pierre screamed and jumped back. He lost his balance on the unlevel footing and tumbled backward, landing in a heap. He remained there for a moment, eyes closed, arms covering his head, expecting the Gangrel to tear into him any instant. But that did not happen. Eventually, Pierre dared to peak.

The Gangrel still crouched, coiled to spring, Pierre imagined. Its nose twitched, sniffing at the cloud of ash that marked Pierre's fall. Long, unruly hair framed a face that belonged in the primeval forest, not in civilized Atlanta. The Gangrel curled its lip and snarled. Pierre covered his face again, but still the attack did not come.

"You followed me," the Gangrel growled, a statement of fact, not a question. It did not ask why. Pierre supposed it didn't care. Wasn't it enough to know that the hare followed the wolf, without wondering why?

As the Gangrel remained perched atop the rubble, Pierre slowly recovered from his shock, if not his fear. His mind was racing, seemingly hundreds of thoughts demanding immediate attention. He could invoke the protection of the prince. He was, after all, practically serving Benison. But hadn't Eleanor said something about not revealing his purpose? The details grew so hazy in the heat of danger. Any means to keep this beast from ripping his throat out were warranted.

"You did not present yourself to Prince Benison," said Pierre, wishing his voice had not cracked midsentence. His thoughts had not wandered far from the protection he wanted desperately to derive from the prince, or at least from invoking the prince's name. Pierre did not know if the statement was true, but the accusation might give the Gangrel pause, might provide a few moments for Pierre to scheme.

The Gangrel did not reply. Whether he considered or even heard Pierre's words, the Toreador could not be sure. The Gangrel remained incredibly still, all its attention and concentration focused on Pierre, who was quite uncomfortable beneath such predatory scrutiny. Finally, the Gangrel spoke: "Do not follow me again." And then it leapt. Straight for Pierre.

When Pierre again opened his eyes, the Gangrel was gone. He hadn't even felt the breeze of its passing, but it must have come within inches of him. The realization sinking in that he was still bodily intact, Pierre looked around frantically. The Gangrel was indeed gone.

Pierre scrambled to his feet and stumbled as quickly as he could out of the rubble. He did not pause to brush the soot from his hands or clothes or face. He did not fret over or even notice the rip in the knee of his pants. All he did was run. And keep running. Away from the ruins of the church, and more importantly, away, he hoped, from the Gangrel.

☥

William Nen washed his hands for the fifth time. He scrubbed as thoroughly as if he had just left a plague-stricken village in the Sudan rather than the CDC cafeteria. Some of his colleagues would say that there was little difference between the two, but then a cafeteria at a center studying infectious diseases was bound to take a certain amount of undeserved criticism. He patted his hands dry with a fresh white towel—always a fresh white towel—then applied the lotion that kept his skin from drying and cracking as it was prone to do in the winter from all the washings.

As he returned to his desk, he knew there was something he was supposed to remember. He began tugging at the corner of his mustache. That always helped him think, or maybe thinking always started him tugging at it. He wasn't sure. As he pondered that vital chicken and egg relationship, his gaze fell across the file atop the stack on his desk. He might as well stamp a giant question mark on the folder. Over the past two days, he had personally double-checked the labwork on cases JKL14337 and JKL14338, running again the tests on both the blood and the tissue samples, and what he had found was not helpful.

Not only had he confirmed the contradictory information from the earlier reports, fresh blood in weeks-dead bodies, he had discovered through his probing another quandary. The blood in JKL14337 was listed as O-positive. With his first run of tests, Nen came up with A-positive. Strange but not impossible. He ran the tests again: A-negative. Two more tests resulted in A-negative and O-positive. There seemed to be three blood types from this one body, which led Nen to believe that some error had occurred in sample collection. Either that or some strange ritual had taken place that involved mixing large amounts of blood from different people. Nen had found two different blood types in JKL14338, the body that had been almost completely drained of blood.

He rubbed his face then resumed tugging at his mustache.

Call Leigh! he suddenly remembered. That was what he was supposed to do. He needed to let her know that he would be late getting home this evening, later than usual. These cases bore further scrutiny. There was the possibility of some localized cult ritual, or it could be a case of incredibly poor sample collection. It happened occasionally.

Either way, Nen had more research to do, and he could see this stretching late into the night, a fact that he wasn't any happier about than he knew his wife would be. It was a struggle, at times, just to keep his eyes open. He had not been sleeping well recently. That morning in particular, he had awakened anything but rested. His dreams were populated by the faces of those he had failed to save—Sudanese, Zairians, and now countless Americans who might be struck down if he failed. They accused him of not trying, of not caring for their diseased infants crying in distress, fevered bodies radiating heat. William tried to plead his case, but they could not understand his words, or would not listen. The specifics varied, but never with his impassioned pleas had he succeeded in more than waking Leigh next to him. He worried about disturbing her rest so often.

But perhaps this investigation would save thousands of lives. Perhaps it would put the shades to rest, and then Nen's beleaguered wife would be able to rest as well. And William.

Thelonious, in his dark business suit and tie, strolled along Euclid Avenue amidst the nightlife of Little Five Points. Some of the New Age shops were closed. All of the tattoo parlors and sex shops were open to the throngs of mortals who slinked from club to club. Normally, a fair number of Kindred would be mixed in with the mortals; normally, this was not an errand Thelonious would be attending to in person. Since the onslaught of the blood curse, however, Cainites, especially the anarchs who had frequented this part of the city, were few and far between.

For the longest time, Thelonious had been the only recognized Brujah in Atlanta. Neither Prince Benison nor Eleanor were fond of the clan, and though there had been underground Brujah occupants in the city, Thelonious had been alone in his task of pressing for social change while, at the same time, not aggravating the anti-Brujah prejudice of the ruling Ventrue elite. He had used stealth and cunning and patience. Secret messages encoded in the personal ads in the back of the *Journal-Constitution* and *Creative Loafing,* both newspapers that he controlled, had instructed his Brujah and their anarch counterparts in what needed to be done.

The curse, though, had struck hard among the anarchs. They were largely the first wave to be wiped out, though every week proved that the curse had not yet run its course, and increasingly it was reaching into the higher strata of Kindred society for its victims. Perhaps it only seemed that way because there were so few anarchs left, relatively speaking. Before the curse, there had been almost fifty unrecognized Cainites in the city, a gross overpopulation on top of the forty or so recognized Kindred. Thelonious didn't think that most of his kind realized exactly how many anarchs there had been. Benison and his type had never bothered to keep track. But Thelonious, he had known by name every downtrodden anarch, every ancillae looked down at and spit upon by the powerful of the city. Many of them had trusted him, and many of them had perished, claimed by the curse.

Perhaps, as Benison claimed, the curse was a form of divine retribution, but Thelonious was not convinced. He had known Benison too long to believe that the prince had exclusive insights into divine will. More likely, Benison chose to believe what he did because it was politically expedient. How convenient for both the Almighty and the Dark

Father to be angry with those not following the prince's rules.

As Thelonious approached Moreland Avenue, he looked around for the anarchs he was supposed to meet outside the Little Five Points Pub. It was a very public spot, and Thelonious in his suit should have stood out among the punk and goth crowd, but no one seemed to take notice of him. After a moment, he saw Elliott and moved toward him.

The scrawny goth, with his pierced nose and eyebrows and his green hair, jumped when Thelonious touched his shoulder but was relieved when he recognized the Brujah primogen. "You about scared the piss out of me," Elliott sighed. "I didn't think anybody could sneak up on me anymore."

"I didn't mean to startle you." Thelonious's calm, quiet voice was out of place amidst the raucous crowd, but Elliott heard him with no problem, and still no one seemed to notice them. "Where is Didi?"

Elliott wilted at the question. He took a deep breath but was not able to form words.

Thelonious needed no more of an answer. It was a story played out over and over again throughout the city these past months. He placed his hand on Elliott's shoulder. "I am sorry."

Elliott nodded.

Thelonious took a piece of paper from his pocket

and handed it to Elliott. "This is the name and address of a friend in Athens. Stay with him. I will let you know when anything has changed."

Elliott nodded again and took the slip of paper. As much damage as the curse had caused, it was Benison's decrees and his persecution of the anarchs that was driving them away from the city. Thelonious had been tempted to lead a nonviolent resistance to the New Year Decrees, but whereas the mortal world could be swayed through the media and public opinion, the Kindred were a singularly bloodthirsty lot, in every sense of the word. Granted, an open display of defiance and an extremely violent reaction from the prince might draw Camarilla attention, but that was less likely now, with the curse raging across the nation and the world, than it would normally have been. There was trouble everywhere among the Cainites. The Inner Circle of the Camarilla would most likely be unable to respond to civil unrest in Atlanta, and so Thelonious would be setting his followers up for beatings and final death with no hope of producing change.

Perhaps it was a lack of courage that stayed his hand. He doubted himself constantly on this matter. But for now, he waited and watched and tried to help those he could to escape the persecution.

Elliott was gone, slipped away into the night. There was no guarantee that he would even make it to Thelonious's friend in Athens. Outside the city, the lupines held sway, and they seemed to be able to smell Kindred passing through their territory, even Kindred speeding through in an automobile along the highway. More than once, a Cainite's wrecked car had been found out there with no sign of driver or passenger. Only the roving Gangrel and the rich who could fly traveled with any real degree of safety.

To Elliott, Thelonious wished luck. He had done all he could for now.

CHAPTER FIVE

The plane touched down roughly. One moment the world was all night-time cloud cover and darkness, the next instant the plane was awash in runway lights. The landing gear tires took hold of the hardtop, reclaiming contact with the earth possessively, as pleased to be reunited with solid ground as was Owain. Air travel was a concept with which he had never quite come to terms. From his earliest days as a mortal, flight had been the province of birds, arrows, and gods. How disturbing that mere mortals had mastered the magic as well, and in such giant, glistening monstrosities of metal.

Owain had experienced a similar skepticism years earlier as the construction of ships had evolved. A wooden ship, part of his life since his youth as a mortal, made sense. But metal ships that floated? He supposed that the step from metal armor and plating to a ship completely made of metal was a small one, and though he had eventually devoted time to study and understand the dynamics of water displacement and weight distribution, the notion remained in his mind that, although wood would float, metal should not.

The first airplanes, at least, had been crude affairs, tinkerer's quilts of canvas and metal rods, the pilots both bending the wind and the sky to their will, and at the same time hoping not to attract the notice of the elements which still reigned supreme. Owain had not noticed for several decades as change had again asserted its furious chaos, and suddenly there were metal monstrosities streaking through the sky. Though he had come to accept it, he never really believed, and every time he heard reports of a plane bearing tens or hundreds of people plummeting to earth and disintegrating in a mile-long cascade of bodies and wreckage, he silently noted that the mastery of mortals over the elements was never truly complete.

Not cheerful thoughts to contemplate as he crossed the Atlantic in the private Giovanni jet. Neither did the disturbing visions serve to improve his mood. The dreams he had come to associate with the slaughtered siren had mingled with his inadequacies as a chess strategist to form images of truly ominous portent. Gone were the images of the living tree that reached out for his blood, and the hilltop chapel that crumbled around him, replaced by the shadowed chess master and the invisible interloper, who turned pieces of both white and black to bloody scarlet. *The shadow of Time is not so long that you might shelter beneath it.* Owain pushed the words and images back into the depths of his mind. They concealed something that was vaguely familiar but that he did not want uncovered. More immediate concerns called for his attention: Spain, El Greco, the Sabbat. Distractions could prove deadly. A dark brooding had taken hold of Owain by the time the plane broke into the glare of the runway lights in Madrid, a fatalism that he was being carried along both by the mechanical creature to which he now played Jonah, and by the events of the past weeks.

The descent reminded him of a ship having risen atop a great wave, now with no escape except to crash to the trough below. Even as the wheels touched down, he expected the entire contraption to smash into a fiery mass, spreading his blood and flesh across the earth that had already claimed his friends and ancestors.

Owain joined Kendall Jackson in the rear cabin, where she unconcernedly worked crossword puzzles. She wore a stylish gray suit concealing her shoulder holster and weapon that, thanks to the Giovanni and their transportation network, would not need to pass through customs.

Miguel had gone up to the cockpit as the plane had approached Madrid, no doubt to give the pilot some vital instruction or to otherwise assert his ostensible control over the situation. Owain was just as happy not to have to look at Miguel. From the day they had met, they had hated one another, and Owain only wished that he could have started hating Miguel sooner.

The jostling of the landing seemed to last for several minutes, but at the conclusion, much to Owain's sardonic surprise, both he and the aircraft remained structurally intact. They had not yet come to a complete stop when Miguel entered the cabin from the cockpit. "The other plane is waiting. We will change over in just a minute."

"The other plane?" Owain asked. "Toledo is not so far from Madrid."

"We do not proceed directly to Toledo," explained Miguel.

"Where *do* we proceed?"

Miguel's grin revealed his crooked teeth. He thrived on control, on parceling out information as he saw fit. "We will arrive in Toledo, *mi hermano*, but not by a direct route. There are too many eyes that might see you here and see you there and put two and two together. We will confuse them."

"When will we reach Toledo?" Owain asked tersely.

"A few nights."

"Just a moment." Owain sighed. At least he had removed that idiotic smile from Miguel's face. "It is urgent that I reach Toledo as soon as possible, but we're going to waltz around for days first?"

"It is urgent," Miguel clarified, "that you reach Toledo *undetected*. It was important that we left the United States quickly, because this process takes time." Miguel's smile returned, his unspoken *I told you so*.

Owain argued no further. Clearly, Miguel had worked this routine out with El Greco, and Owain did not wish to provide Miguel the opportunity to demonstrate how clever he was by explaining his plan. Instead, Owain proceeded without comment when they had come to a stop and Miguel indicated that the next plane was ready. Kendall walked a step or two behind Owain as they crossed the short stretch of runway, her eyes constantly scanning their surroundings for signs of any threat. Miguel, too, was vigilant ahead of Owain. The Sabbat lackey, Owain knew, would take pride in his charge reaching Toledo safely. Despite all of Miguel's flaws, he served his master.

Within a few minutes, the party of three was on the next plane. Miguel confirmed the identity of the pilot, and before twenty minutes had passed from their touchdown, they were once again airborne. Only then did Owain inquire as to their current destination.

"Barcelona," Miguel answered.

Owain was dumbfounded. They were within fifty miles of Toledo, yet very shortly they would be several hundred miles away. All in the name of secrecy. The situation in Spain must be volatile indeed. Owain, in his lethargy over the past decades, had not kept well-informed of the Cainite goings-on across the Atlantic from his new home. Aside from occasionally passing on bits of information he acquired regarding Camarilla activities, generally involving the contested area around Miami, he had had little interaction with the Sabbat for many years. That was how he liked it. Within the Camarilla, he was more easily able to keep to himself, to avoid entangling alliances that dragged him into conflicts not of his choosing. There was more constant maneuvering within the Sabbat, less subtlety. Ironic, he supposed, that the Sabbat, a sect formed on the principle of absolute freedom, would be the more cumbersome of the Cainite factions. Or had been, at least. That was not holding true currently, as both the Camarilla and the Sabbat seemed to have caught up with him with a vengeance.

"Miguel," Owain decided to pry, "I am flattered that you value my safety so greatly, but what exactly are you protecting me from?"

Miguel laughed at the question. "You were always the sly one, *mi hermano.* Do you not think there is value in secrecy when an elder of the Camarilla visits a priscus of the Sabbat?"

"But Spain is Sabbat territory, for the most part. Do we have so much to fear? Must our precautions be so extreme as to fly across the country?"

Miguel shook his head but was no longer laughing. "I have my orders to bring you to Toledo, and no one must know. Anything else, you must hear from El Greco."

That was all Miguel would say, no matter how much Owain pressed the point, and much to Owain's dismay, he had many opportunities to do so, for he soon discovered just how extreme Miguel's precautions were. Within a few hours, the plane had landed in Barcelona. A black Mercedes was waiting to whisk them away from El Prat de Llobregat. As the airport fell away behind them, Owain could see the gray outline of mountains to the west, but the smell of the nearby Mediterranean was inescapable as well. He and Ms. Jackson were in the back seat. Miguel, who seemed slightly more at ease as Barcelona receded in the distance, shared the front with the driver.

They continued south, hugging the coast, deep into the night, not stopping until several hours before dawn at a *rancho* north of Tortosa. The *ranchero*, after briefly conferring with Miguel, retreated into a part of the house from which he did not emerge. There was no need for him to see his guest that morning and, in fact, all were safer if he did not. Owain, Kendall, and Miguel rested throughout the day in an underground room that was comfortable and conspicuously devoid of windows to the outside. The driver, Miguel explained, would wait upstairs, ensuring that neither the *ranchero* nor his wife left the premises. When dusk had passed to evening, the travelers were again on their way.

They spent the next days and nights in much the same manner. Much of the night they were on the road, not traveling directly to Toledo. If so, the journey would not have been excessively long. Instead, the driver took them along routes that, to Owain, seemed to wind without pattern and even to double back on the way they had come. Their time was split between the coastal plain and the more mountainous inlands, stopping during the night only for more *gasolina*.

The shelter they took during the day seemed as random as their routes through the countryside. One day they spent in an abandoned hut in the foothills, the next in a lavish hotel room in Valencia. All were safe houses of one sort or another, maintained by Miguel and El Greco for just such necessities.

Lacking knowledge of the specific danger from

which Miguel was protecting him, Owain assumed an attitude of perturbed indignation. The inconvenience and constancy of the travel, combined with his pre-existing dislike of Miguel, were more than enough to justify his surliness, if in fact he had required justification. He allowed Ms. Jackson to coordinate all communication with Miguel and refused to speak to El Greco's messenger except in the tersest of grunts.

The Spanish countryside was not unfamiliar to Owain, though much had changed in the seventy-odd years since he had relocated to the New World. Humanity, sprawling development, had spread to every inhabitable cranny of the peninsula. There were still small, poverty-stricken villages which had seen little progress since the Great War, but even here, the obtrusive Coca Cola advertisement or the occasional satellite dish were reminders of the modern age. As the nights of travel blended one into another, Owain peered out the tinted windows of the Mercedes less and less often. He had spent most of his existence attempting either to recapture or to escape his past. This land was a part of his past, and he did not wish to be reminded of it. He had moved to Spain, to Toledo, in 1375 after debacles in Wales and in France had proven the value of migration. The Spanish hills had become his residence but never his home. Not until several years after he had awakened from his extended torpor had he realized that he had resided in Spain longer than he had in his native Wales. On that night, another part of him had died.

He refused to allow the nostalgia, the memories, to take hold. This might be the same land, but the mortal inhabitants were a different people. Even Señor and Señora Rodriguez, whom Owain had taken with him to Atlanta less than a century ago, were people of a different age. The world changed. It changed more quickly than he did, and he could not permit himself the luxury of thinking otherwise.

More immediate concerns demanded attention, and Owain willingly turned his thoughts to them. El Greco had been a friend in the past. It had been his idealism and enthusiasm that had led Owain to join the Sabbat shortly after his emergence from torpor in the eighteenth century. El Greco had preached a doctrine of total freedom, and his words had echoed the call that Owain had always heard welling up from his soul. *Libertad. Lealtad. Inmortal para siempre.* But like any group to which allegiance was pledged, Owain had found that the Sabbat had made unwarranted demands upon him. It could be no different with a king, an archbishop, or a prince. El Greco had helped Owain almost a century ago, but what could Owain expect now? Years had ways of twisting friendships. Affection too often beget a desire to control, and that Owain could not, would not, accept. He had been called to Toledo against his will. Did El Greco not recognize the immensity of the imposition, or was his need so great? Owain would reserve judgment.

He would not reserve judgment, however, for Benison, the Camarilla prince of Atlanta. It was strange, Owain realized, that already he thought so distantly of Benison. For years, with no significant connection to the Sabbat, Owain had come to think of himself, by default, as a Camarilla vampire. He was never an ardent supporter of the sect, but he had identified himself with it nonetheless. Now, with this reassertion of his older ties with the Sabbat, he already was thinking of Benison as being part of *them*. It was another grip that the Sabbat held on Owain, a hold that he preferred to be free of from any quarter.

Regardless of the relative merits of either the Camarilla or the Sabbat, Owain realized, Benison had become a detriment and must be dealt with. Generally in the past, Benison had been a fairly unobtrusive, if temperamental, prince. He made his demands, as did any prince, but aside from expecting his *subjects*—and how Owain hated that word applied to himself—to attend infrequent prayer meetings or exhibits and the like, he had conducted himself fairly benevolently. With the onset of the blood curse and the prince's attempts to counter it, however, he had egregiously wounded Owain.

Many times during the nights in the Mercedes, traveling across Spain, over hills and coastland, countryside and city, Owain was lost in reverie. He heard not the sound of the engine, but the magical song of the siren. It carried him back to his mortal life in Wales, to his family, to his one true love. Like his previous life, the memory of the song was all that was left to him. Thanks to Benison. Thanks to the prince's reactionary response to what he did not understand. Benison hawked Marlene's abominable "art" at the High Museum, yet he destroyed offhand the greatest beauty to touch Owain in centuries. Owain had found some small link to his lost humanity, and had had it ripped away.

Benison had sullied that joy, and another as well. He had put to death poor, harmless Albert. Albert, who had committed no crime more than Owain had. At least not until his final words. *What would Angharad think?* Owain fumed that the name of his only love should be invoked from the executioner's stand, tossed before the masses like a pearl before swine. It was less the loss of one Malkavian that pained Owain than the fact that Albert, with his utterance, had indelibly linked her name with the tragedy of his death, in which Owain was complicit. In one brief moment, Albert had managed to dirty the name that Owain had carried closer to his heart than any other for so many centuries. That was Albert's true crime in Owain's mind, and one that could never be erased, not by the Malkavian's execution or by the passage of time. Albert and Benison, the childer of insanity, were both guilty, and only Albert had thus far paid the penalty.

Owain had emerged from a world of emotional bankruptcy into an unlife full and rich with hatred. That was the gift that, in the end, both the siren and Albert had given him, and in both cases, Benison was the accomplice. Owain resolved that, when he returned to Atlanta, he would not see these crimes go unpunished. He would see Benison brought low; he would see the prince disgraced, humiliated. His city would cast him out. Whether or not Owain would take his place required more thought. Owain had tasted leadership, he had paid the price to rule and found it too high. Could he ever retrace those steps to power? That he did not know.

Though Owain spoke barely a word through the nights of driving, his mind was full of hate, his heart overflowing with vengeance. It was with this disposition that he greeted the city of Toledo, almost eighty years after he had left it last. Because of the twisting route that the driver had chosen to reach the city, they approached from the north. They passed the Puerta de Bisagra and were within the old wall of the city. The buildings of stone and sun-dried brick that lined the narrow, twisting streets were largely unchanged over several centuries. The peacefully juxtaposed Moorish arches and Gothic flying buttresses were understated reminders of the religious and social turmoil the city had seen. The roads were roughly adapted to, but not designed for, modern automobiles. Horses and carts had still been plentiful when Owain had left, and even then the patchwork streets and blind corners had been treacherous.

The driver of the Mercedes gave little thought for other motorists or pedestrians, however. He thrust the car forward as quickly as he ever had in the open countryside. Aside from the gunning of the engine, the city was quiet this night. The austere facades of the buildings revealed nothing of their inhabitants, and Owain felt the familiar sensation that somewhere out of view, behind closed doors, the city was abuzz with life and activity.

The car raced through intersections and past blind alleyways. Ahead loomed El Alcazar. The great fortress that had been destroyed and rebuilt more times than Owain could remember, most recently during his absence in the Spanish Civil War. The building, with its corner towers, dominated the skyline.

Owain and Kendall in the back seat were jostled as the driver jerked the wheel and the car lurched to the south. Not far ahead was the cathedral. Modest by European standards, the sole completed tower with its pointed, slate-covered cruet and spiked crowns seemed to duck in and out from behind the surrounding tall buildings. Fortunately, the cathedral was not the Mercedes's destination. Owain had had quite enough of churches recently. Instead, the car darted into a series of alleys, speeding along as if on the German Autobahn, when there was not even sufficient room for two cars to pass. In fact in several spots, there was some question as to whether there was room for one car to pass between the overhanging buildings. Miraculously, the driver navigated the maze of streets without so much as overturning a garbage can or disturbing a stray dog. Without warning, he whipped the car into an opening in a building that, as a door slid shut behind them, Owain realized was a garage.

As he stepped out of the air-conditioned automobile into the just-closed garage, the rich smells of the city swept over Owain. Not far away was the Plaza de Zocodover and the odor of the various animals sold in that market during the day. Noticeable in a different way were the lingering scents of food prepared earlier in the day in shops and kitchens all around—peppers, saffron, artichokes, seafood, sweet marzipan. The surroundings were more assertive, more demanding of attention, than in Atlanta where Owain had easily hidden himself away from the world. The sights and smells were all so familiar. He'd been gone not even for a century, Owain reasoned. If he ever returned to his beloved Wales, he wondered, would the surroundings be as familiar? Would it be so much like stepping back in time, back closer to his mortal days, to his family and his love?

"This way." Miguel opened a door into the house, leaving no time for Owain to contemplate this painful question.

He and Kendall were led to a sitting room and left to wait as Miguel conferred with servants in the other room. The house itself was rather modest, not the grandeur that Owain might have expected from El Greco, his long-ago friend who had such a taste for the finer comforts. Perhaps this was just another in the series of safe houses, Owain guessed. After a journey of nearly a week to get from Madrid to Toledo, he would be surprised by very little.

Shortly Miguel, visibly annoyed, returned to the sitting room. "He is not here," he said tersely.

Ms. Jackson responded, used to, by now, acting as go-between for her master and Miguel, even when they were in the same small room. "El Greco? Is he supposed to be here?" She too had guessed that this might merely be the most recent in the progression of safe houses.

"Of course he's supposed to be here," Miguel snapped. "This is his haven." His dismissive tone hinted that Kendall should have known that somehow. "He was called away last night. We missed him by one night. Your dallying in Atlanta has cost us, *mi hermano.*" He glared at Owain.

Owain restrained his urge to stand and strike Miguel. Kendall did not restrain her tongue. "Perhaps one less night touring the Spanish countryside would have made a difference."

Miguel tensed at the suggestion that the poor timing was his fault. "I would remind you," he said to Kendall, "that ghouls are not thought of so highly among the Sabbat."

Now Owain did rise. He walked very close to Miguel, and in a low voice spoke to El Greco's lieutenant for the first time in several nights. "And I would remind *you* that Ms. Jackson is my personal retainer, and as such, a guest in this, the household of my friend. I will consider slights to her slights to myself."

Owain and Miguel stood staring at one another for several moments, until finally Miguel, without a word, turned and left the room.

The pounding at the front door was quite insistent. Eleanor heard it clearly, even from the parlor. The sound reminded her of the fateful night that Roger, Benison's only childe, had shown up on the steps of Rhodes Hall carrying his poor, departed, mortal mother. Roger, delirious in the grip of the curse, had believed that he was Benison, and after a brief altercation with the prince, had collapsed and finally succumbed to the curse.

That night had changed Benison. Though he expressed little emotion at Roger's loss, Benison had been affected. Eleanor knew him well enough to see. In her mind, the death of Roger was representative of the greater grief her husband was suffering as his city unraveled about him. It had been shortly after Roger's parting that Benison had hit upon his current strategy to reclaim divine favor, to transform Atlanta into a model of spiritual propriety in order to circumvent the curse. Since then, he had barely spoken to her, except in passing. She had heard him muttering to himself about transcendence. He kept repeating the name *Primus*, whatever that meant, with great urgency. His nights were full of prowling the city. Seldom did he spend an evening with her at home. She understood his responsibilities as prince, his commitment to the city above all else, but she wished he would allow her to aid him, to lift some of the weight from his shoulders. But such were not his ways. So her nights were spent in isolation, without her husband, without Benjamin. But that would not last forever.

The pounding at the door continued. With Benison away, and Vermeil attending to the prince or some errand, only Eleanor and Sally were in the house. Eleanor imagined another crazed Cainite trying to get inside. Probably she should lend support to little Sally, who tended to be easily overwhelmed by occurrences out of the ordinary.

Eleanor descended the stairs as Sally opened the front door. A familiar voice, impatient and impertinent, carried into the foyer. "I absolutely *must* speak with your mistress. This is a matter of the utmost importance."

"Show him in, Sally," Eleanor instructed as she reached the bottom step. Sally appeared relieved not to have to deal with this bothersome Cainite. She opened the door fully, and Pierre entered. He seemed somewhat unnerved to see Eleanor standing there waiting for him, as if perhaps he had been prepared for more of an argument from the gatekeeper. "Do come in, Pierre." Eleanor gestured toward the living room. "That will be all, Sally."

Within the living room, Pierre did not sit. Instead, he engaged in truncated pacing, a step this way, then that, until Eleanor sat. He did not wait for her to invite him to speak. "I'm afraid I have done what I can. I can do no more." He wrung his hands and avoided meeting Eleanor's gaze. He seemed to realize how rudely he was treating the prince's wife. The thought caused him some discomfort, but he pressed forward. "I performed my duties faithfully, but I cannot continue. I mean no disrespect." He glanced nervously at her.

Eleanor regarded him not too harshly, but with curiosity. He had run into something. That much was certain. For this ingratiating social-climber to disregard common courtesy with someone of Eleanor's standing, he must be upset indeed. She felt a small amount of pity for him. She had, after all, sent a Toreador to do a man's job. "I see," she said flatly, conveying neither disappointment nor tolerance.

Pierre, almost as an afterthought, reached into his jacket pocket and withdrew something wrapped in a dirty silk handkerchief. "Here." He placed the bundled object onto the coffee table, obviously trying to displace as little of the grime from the handkerchief as possible. "I followed the Gangrel," Pierre failed to suppress a shudder, "and found this at a burned church in Reynoldstown." That was apparently all he had to say, as if it explained anything. He took a step toward the door, but then suddenly remembered his manners once again and stopped.

"I see," Eleanor said again. Pierre's usefulness to her was at an end. "I thank you for your service."

Without further elaboration, or even inquiring about his reward, Pierre nodded nervously and then showed himself to the door.

How odd, thought Eleanor. He had been more intent upon terminating their agreement than on pursuing any compensation. *Not interested in an ex-*

hibit? How unlike a Toreador. But Pierre's actions themselves, including his churlish behavior this evening, were inconsequential, except in what Eleanor might be able to infer from them. Pierre had been scared away. That was apparent. Only fear would induce that degree of crudity in one such as himself. The explanation might, Eleanor realized, be as simple as his having been frightened away from the trail by the Gangrel. Such had happened to more stalwart a Cainite. If that were the case, was the Gangrel in the employ of Owain Evans? Eleanor had put out other feelers, hoping to discover as much as she could about this fellow Ventrue who, for so many years, had done virtually nothing to make waves in the Kindred community. Usually faced with more pressing matters, Eleanor had spared little attention for him. Until now; until he had driven her beloved Benjamin away.

But no one seemed to know much about Owain Evans, and no one had seen him since the gathering just over a week ago when Benison had delivered his decrees. Evans's absence was more frustrating than unusual. The number of questions mounted more rapidly than did the answers. What connection did this Gangrel have to Evans, and why was it at the burned church in Reynoldstown? It was undoubtedly the church where Benison had rooted out the interloper, the violated church that later the devout prince had had burned.

Eleanor's gaze fell upon the bundle that Pierre had left on the table. Gently, she pulled back the edges of the soiled handkerchief. Within it rested a dagger, partially covered with…soot? From the burned church. That made sense. Much of the weapon had been rubbed clean by the handkerchief. There was gilding visible, on the pommel and hilt, but even so, this was a functional dagger, not an ornamental piece.

Eleanor pondered her discovery, the meaning of which was unclear at the moment. The presence of the dagger and of the Gangrel at the church were somehow connected, she felt. Because, however, questioning the Gangrel without Benison's aid, which would potentially alert the prince to her mission against Evans and its underlying motivations, was largely impossible, it only followed that she should investigate the dagger further. Oftentimes, where one avenue of inquiry was closed, a parallel avenue might achieve the same destination.

Five more nights passed without sign or word of El Greco. Owain questioned Miguel repeatedly, but he was unshakably obstinate. He would reveal nothing of why or to where El Greco had been called away, though Owain sensed that Miguel had been unpleasantly surprised by his superior's departure. The two human servants, Maria and Ferdinand, proved equally uncommunicative, and Miguel warned both Owain and Kendall against questioning them.

El Greco's absence forced upon Miguel the duties of host, a role he most certainly would have preferred to avoid. He accounted for his guests' most basic needs—safe haven during the day; he even brought a young Toledoan debutante for Owain to feed upon, though Owain was not particularly hungry and had not requested a meal. Over the centuries, Owain had fed less and less frequently, and he could not remember the last time he had actually found pleasure in the deed. Otherwise, Miguel stayed as far away as he could from Owain and Kendall.

They grudgingly respected his instructions not to leave the house. As Owain paced the corridors and examined the rooms that were not locked, he was nagged by a constant inconsistency. The decor was uniformly modest—tasteful but not expensive throw rugs, conservative modern furniture, paintings that might have been found in any respectable hotel. That, really, was the feeling that Owain got from his surroundings—that he was staying in a rental cottage, its furnishings bland enough to offend no one. Such restraint was not like the El Greco that Owain knew…or had known. This comfortable but tiny dwelling was a far cry from the sprawling chambers beneath El Alcazar that El Greco had occupied when Owain had first met him back in the fourteenth century. El Greco had surrounded himself with priceless artwork. He had ostentatiously fed upon the wives of the most powerful men in the city, leaving neither their memories nor their honor intact. Could it be the same Cainite who had taken up residence in such a cozy-to-the-point-of-cramped abode? Aside from the personal quarters of Maria and Ferdinand and one other locked room on the second floor, Owain inspected every room in the house. He even discreetly poked about the cellar searching for tunnels or hidden rooms—tricks that El Greco had used to great effect in the past. Owain found nothing extraordinary, and by the end of the third night, his thoughts were drawn increasingly to what might be behind the locked door upstairs.

Miguel did not reside in the house. Apparently he maintained a separate haven elsewhere in the city. Each evening, early and again late, he stopped by to inform Owain that there was no new word, and to remind the guests not to leave the premises. In Atlanta, Owain had often spent months without leaving his estate, but there he had a veritable mansion and acres of gardens and woods in which to wander. Staying in the house, especially after a week of being confined to the inside of planes and the Mercedes, was fairly maddening.

Kendall spent her time reading, meditating, or exercising. Owain had never taken notice before of how her every waking moment was dedicated to keeping herself, body and mind, ready to serve him. She did not rely solely on the vampiric vitae he fed her for her abilities. Owain had always preferred brooding to meditating. He wondered if the yoga helped his ghoul maintain her unflappably calm efficiency. Regardless, he felt fortunate to have found her.

Each of the nights that Owain spent in El Greco's house, there came a brief period early in the morning, just after four, when Maria and Ferdinand retired but before Miguel made his second visit, when Owain and Kendall were for all practical purposes alone. The second night during this time, Owain's thoughts briefly turned to the locked door upstairs. The third night, he seriously considered pursuing the matter, but his manners got the best of him. Though he had been summoned across the Atlantic against his will, he was still a guest in El Greco's house. The fourth night, he stood for half an hour outside the locked door, bored by the sterile confines of the small house, curious about why he had suddenly been brought back to Spain after so many years.

The fifth night, shortly after Maria and Ferdinand withdrew to their own quarters, Owain quietly summoned Kendall. "Keep watch at the top of the stairs. If the servants stir or Miguel arrives early, alert me." She nodded, not needing to ask what he would be doing.

Owain had never had much trouble with simple locks, not since his introduction into the world of the unliving, at any rate. He was pleasantly surprised to discover that his concern El Greco might have an elaborate security system proved unfounded. With little more than a gesture of his hand, the bolt clicked free, and Owain entered the forbidden room.

Seeing the simple furnishings through the darkness, Owain again wondered if this house actually belonged to El Greco—El Greco, who had lived so extravagantly and flamboyantly, who had thrilled at the touch of finely crafted furniture or sculpture more than a glutton at the finest feast. The room was quite plainly adorned. A sturdy but unremarkable rolltop desk was flanked by a flat desk and an end table supporting a common store-bought chess set. The arrangement of the pieces was unfamiliar. Evidently, El Greco had begun another game, for this was not the situation of the death knells of the game in which he had so recently bested Owain. Perhaps, like Miguel, El Greco kept a haven elsewhere in the city, and when he returned, Owain would be summoned to the luxurious chambers beneath El Alcazar. In the game currently before Owain, white was backed to a corner, every piece save the king and three pawns captured. White's position had undoubtedly been hopeless for many a turn.

It was the rolltop desk, however, that held more immediate interest for Owain. Another lock. More complex, and trapped, no doubt. But to Owain's amazement, that was not the case. Another wave of his hand, and he was free to inspect the contents. This small area, beneath the rolltop, was more in keeping with the El Greco that Owain had known. Stacks of papers were spread across the desk. Many were rough sketches of people or of landscapes. Even the financial documents, lying haphazardly askew, had drawings in the margins and encroaching over the text. There were bits of poetry, heavily marked and edited, some on scraps of paper that had obviously been balled up and then smoothed out again.

Owain looked through the papers, trying to disturb them as little as possible. *No need for El Greco to know I was inspecting his belongings.* He opened the small drawers which contained a hodgepodge of pens, paper clips, and stamps—all quite mundane. He closed the drawers and began to inspect the wood paneling within the rolltop and shortly found what he sought—a concealed compartment. It was not laboriously hidden, just inconspicuous enough to go unnoticed at first glance. Owain would have been disappointed in El Greco if something of this type had been lacking. The stationery in the drawer was familiar to Owain. He removed it and saw that it was the same bone color and finely crafted style that he preferred. In fact, as he inspected the contents of the letter, Owain realized that the handwriting was his own.

El Greco,

My luck is holding in matters more weighty even than chess, so do not condemn your own abilities overly much. While Cainites the world over tremble behind closed doors, fearing to venture out into the night even to feed, lest they fall victim to the blood curse, I have discovered the true cause of the curse, and I believe that you will be keenly interested.

Owain looked more closely at the words. The script, every idiosyncratic, technically imperfect stroke, was unmistakably his own. Even the paper and the irregular distribution of ink from his antique dip pen were a perfect match.

But Owain had never written these words.

Not able to believe his own eyes, he read on:

I believe you have, on one or two occasions, made the acquaintance of one Carlos, bishop of Madrid. Would it not be unfortunate for him if those in positions of authority above him were to learn that he was responsible for the outbreak of the curse which has so dramatically pruned our forces these past weeks? I'm sure nothing would be further from your mind than to wish ill luck upon a comrade.

Perhaps this will not, after all, interest you. Perhaps it comes as no surprise to you to learn that Carlos is a Cainite of exceedingly healthy ambition, as are so many of our colleagues. It has come to my attention that certain of his underlings were, at Carlos's instruction, conducting experiments upon Cainite vitae—magical experiments, bringing their dark arts to bear in an attempt to transform the blood, to strengthen it. Why might this be of interest to them? you may ask. There is a certain correspondence among our kind between age and power, is there not? Generally, the older of us are of a generation closer to the original source of our power, the Dark Father. The older the vitae, the more potent. Increase the potency of a Cainite's blood, and that Cainite is more powerful. That is what Carlos was attempting to achieve through his "Project Angharad."

Owain's every muscle tensed. *Angharad.* Here was her name again! His love, her memory evoked by the siren first, then her name profaned by Albert, and now this. Owain sat at the desk. He felt lightheaded, sick. The mists were swirling about him, the visions again encroaching upon his conscious mind—the living tree, the tower—but he fought them off. He forced himself to continue with the letter:

That is what Carlos was attempting to achieve through his "Project Angharad." Perhaps merely to further strengthen our sect. But are there not other possibilities?

If younger Cainites suddenly become more powerful, especially lacking as they do the seasoned wisdom of those of us from distant times, who is threatened? Are we not at greatest risk? Are not you? Is not the archbishop? If Carlos is the conveyor of this power, does he not stand to gain a great deal?

Luckily, he has not achieved his goal. The curse is our proof. But how long until he does succeed?

How do I know all this? Because the curse was unleashed in my own Atlanta. An underling of Carlos's, another ambitious Cainite, a certain Grimsdale, made off with a vial of the experimental blood, not yet perfected. He wished to sell the secrets of the blood in the New World. Is it not the land of opportunity, mi amigo? But other of Carlos's retainers tracked down poor Grimsdale, who as the pursuit closed in, drank the blood him-

self, no doubt hoping to utilize the power of the blood to preserve his own existence. He did not succeed. And as his blood was stolen by those who pursued him, the curse was spread.

I need not elaborate upon the repercussions for those of us—

"Greetings, Owain."

Startled by the voice behind him, Owain spun in the chair toward the door. There stood El Greco, in one arm the limp form of Kendall Jackson. His eyes gleamed red even in the darkness. The hollowed recesses of his face held shadows far darker than the night.

Nicholas returned to the underpass early the next evening but Blackfeather was nowhere to be seen. The spray-painted circle was still clearly visible on the damp concrete. Nicholas fidgeted, cleared away some debris that had drifted across the circle, and settled down to wait.

It was hard not to think about the gnawing hunger. It scratched at his insides as if impatient to be let out. He half regretted not killing that miserable Toreador who had been following him.

No doubt the fop had already made full and obsequious report to Prince Benison of Nicholas's presence and activities in the city. The prince was not a patient man and he was given to fits of outrage at the slightest perceived insult.

He took a special interest in unannounced visitors who did not formally present themselves at court. If Nicholas stayed in the city much longer, he could certainly expect a summons to the royal presence to account for his breach of etiquette.

Nicholas was no better off now than when he and Blackfeather had parted yesterday. He had found no trace of Evans. The mansion showed none of the telltale signs of habitation and no hint that the master would return anytime soon.

Nicholas had had high hopes that he might pick up the trail at the abandoned church, but that had also proved a dead end. Judging from the condition of the place, it had seen some kind of struggle and not entertained many visitors since. True, the dagger had smelled of Evans, but the scent was weeks old.

The trail had grown cold and Nicholas had returned, no closer to either the answers or the vengeance he sought. He was, however, one evening nearer to the unpleasant end that he carried within his veins.

"If love is blind, then hatred is stone deaf," said a familiar voice directly behind him. Nicholas fought the instinctive urge to whirl and lash out. He even managed to suppress the heated retort and words of challenge that rose to his lips.

Nicholas was madder at himself for being taken unawares than at the gently mocking tone in the other's voice. He mastered himself and rose to greet his friend.

"He is gone," Nicholas said simply. "And it is long past time for me to be gone as well. The prince put an agent on my trail. After the disturbance at the mansion, no doubt. I'm surprised they haven't been…" He trailed off.

"They have," Blackfeather answered his unasked question. "They took a long look at me and the circle and the fire and fell back to regroup. If there is one of power among them, he will come tonight. If there is not," Blackfeather shrugged, "then many of them will come tonight."

Nicholas scanned the surrounding shadows, kicking himself for his earlier inattention. "Then we need to get away from here. Not far, just beyond the sprawl of the suburbs. They won't follow us further."

"But where would you go?" Blackfeather looked at him appraisingly.

Nicholas did not answer right away. Blackfeather's presence made him cautious, cagey. He was not at all convinced that it was a benign influence.

"After Evans," he said at last. "Either way, it ends with Evans."

Blackfeather was not sure what "either way"

meant. He could see nothing but death and vengeance along that road.

But he heard the finality in Nicholas's words. No amount of arguing was likely to shake the young Gangrel's conviction.

"And how will you find him?" Blackfeather replied, pushing aside Nicholas's carefully marshaled arguments. "By your own admission, there is no sign of him anywhere in the city."

At this, Nicholas smiled broadly. "You will find him for me."

For the first time, Nicholas noted with satisfaction, he had taken Blackfeather aback. Blackfeather muttered something dismissive, turned his back on Nicholas, and walked to the very edge of the circle. He stopped there as if held by some unseen force, his toes just touching the ring.

Nicholas spoke softly, almost apologetically. "Of course. I understand. If this thing is beyond your abilities, I will just have to find myself another hunter, or perhaps a seer…"

Blackfeather did not rise to the taunt. "You ask me to speed you to your death. You even try to make the choice more appealing." Here he turned and smiled. "But I want you to think further than yourself," he continued more solemnly. "Further than your bloodline and the demands of honor it binds you with. I want you to think of our clan, of our people. I speak with their voice.

"Ten nights ago, you were willing to fight to the death to prove your claim to lead. Tonight, you ask my help so that you might turn your back upon them and pursue a personal vendetta. There is no honor in this.

"Come with me back to the wilds. There is solace there, among the pines, beneath the stars, within the unbroken circle of the clan."

Nicholas glowered, stood firm. "Would you have me go like a dark wind among them, a pestilence, a shadow of death? No, I am fit company for neither man nor beast. Release me. Send me on my way."

Blackfeather studied him for some time. He knew Nicholas was right; he could never return. The curse that roiled the city had taken hold within Nicholas, was irrevocably enmeshed with the shadow rising within him. "Come," Blackfeather said. "We will ask for guidance."

He led Nicholas back to their accustomed place near the remains of last night's fire. Blackfeather took a cold blackened stick from the fire and, pulling Nicholas's hair back from his forehead, marked a cryptic symbol there—Urdun, the ox. Not altogether flattering, perhaps, but those with eyes to see would know to steer well clear of Nicholas's path. The ox was impossible to turn from its appointed course, and none too concerned with who or what might be trampled underfoot.

Blackfeather then took soot and blacked all of his own exposed skin except for his hands.

"Clear away the remains of the fire."

As Nicholas busied himself with this task, Blackfeather untied a tooled leather satchel at his waist and laid it between them, where the fire had been. The pouch was striking, covered with some intricate design or pictures that Nicholas could not pick out in the dim light. It occurred to him that he had never seen Blackfeather open this particular pouch before.

Blackfeather undid the clasp and began extracting a curious array of objects.

He recited the inventory quietly to himself as he removed each piece. To Nicholas, this little ritual took on the aspect of a chant—an arcane formula recited by rote: *Bus tokens, theatre stubs, American Express card; Tarot cards, keys from a twice-stolen car; Kennedy half-dollar, Camel unfiltereds; Straight razor, floppy disk, phillips-head screws; Spent tube of superglue, walkman, a rolex; Double-A batteries, surgical gloves; Boarding pass, dental floss, thirteen matched chessmen; Shotgun shells, snapshots, a cellular phone...*

Blackfeather drew forth each new treasure as if it might well contain next week's winning lottery number. He paused over certain objects, rolling them over in his hand, savoring their feel, their proximity.

He noticed that Nicholas was still standing nearby, staring in wonder and incomprehension. Blackfeather gestured him back to his seat. Then he spoke.

His words had that same mystic, singsong quality, but he was definitely addressing Nicholas now. He was patiently trying to explain something. *"These things and more have I gathered and carried Like feathers and bearteeth, symbols to conjure Memories and stories. I weave them around me. I cloak myself in them; I wear them as armor. I eat them for courage; I cast them for omens."*

Nicholas waited anxiously for Blackfeather to reveal the secrets hidden in the jumble of oddments. His mind tried in vain to draw meaning from the objects, or from the things he associated with the symbols, or from the relations of distance, proximity or overlap between them. It was no good.

He simply did not speak this obscure language of signs, premonitions and divination. Blackfeather, however, seemed to expect something of him. Hesitantly, he shifted some of the objects around.

He picked up the straight razor, started to open it, checked himself and hurriedly returned it to its place. Blackfeather watched him impassively.

"But I don't..." Nicholas began.

Blackfeather reached out slowly and picked up the Camels. Nicholas was almost too startled to catch the pack when Blackfeather tossed it to him.

"You need to relax," Blackfeather said. "You're trying way too hard." The turquoise-studded Zippo snapped open and flared.

Nicholas stared at the flame for a moment, thinking of the test of the night before. Then, he suddenly seemed to remember himself. He fumbled open the Camels, stuck one in his mouth and passed another to Blackfeather.

Nicholas couldn't remember the last time he had smoked a cigarette. He wasn't even sure he could manage the trick anymore. Breathing itself was a chore and he always felt as if people were staring when he tried it.

Blue flame danced before his eyes and receded, leaving the smell of burning tobacco in its wake. Nicholas drew slowly, feeling the steadying proximity of the tiny flame. Now there was something he could understand.

"Better," said Blackfeather and forged ahead: "*I lay them before you, That after our parting Their power be yours and Their story, your story, And that in the dark hours, You may find them familiar.*"

Nicholas still did not understand. But he was, at least, no longer struggling. Decisively, he wrested his gaze from the jumble of objects and looked squarely at Blackfeather. "Well, where is he?"

Blackfeather laughed and began tucking the objects back into his satchel. For a long while, Nicholas thought he was going to refuse to answer him.

Blackfeather reached the end of his scattered pile. "Car keys. Amex. Boarding pass." Blackfeather slapped each object down in rapid succession in front of Nicholas.

"The car's parked across the street. The boat leaves from Savannah tomorrow night. Evans will be in Madrid by the time you embark."

Nicholas pocketed Blackfeather's gifts. He rose, heaving a great sigh. "I'll leave the car where you can find her again, outside of town."

Blackfeather stood and refastened the satchel about his waist. "Nicholas," he started and fell silent again. After a long while he said, "It doesn't have to end in blood."

Nicholas didn't know if Blackfeather was talking about the confrontation with Evans or the curse or some greater struggle.

Nicholas did not know of any other ending. It all began in blood, it would have to end in blood. He did not give voice to these thoughts.

Blackfeather stared after him for some time— long after he had heard the engine roar to life and then recede into the distance. He lit another cigarette, watched the smoke rise lazily skyward, and let his thoughts drift toward home.

Kli Kodesh rode a maelstrom of violence, betrayal and terror. He was vaguely aware that he was moving eastward at a breakneck pace—away from the City of Angels and out into the vast American wasteland.

The maddeningly regular progression of city, suburbs, city, suburbs, that flashed past him left no lasting impression. To his eyes, it was all one vast unbroken desert—rolling dunes of asphalt, concrete and prefab houses receding toward the horizon.

There were, however, some details that he could not shut out. The irritation of a flickering fluorescent light on a bared knifeblade. The retort of gunshots along a subway platform. The delicate tracery of red lifeblood spiraling down a pristine porcelain washbasin.

Kli Kodesh was moving quickly and could not quite put a placename to each of the atrocities and bloodrites that intruded upon his consciousness. They came upon him suddenly and irresistibly—flashes of lightning through the storm that carried him forward.

He imagined each act of violence as a single drop of blood amidst the raging downpour. The words of the ancient Cainite prophecy rose unbidden to his mind:

At his word, the sky opens, raining blood upon the furrows he has prepared. His children raise expectant faces to the Heavens, but they are choked and drowned in the torrent of spilling life. Such is the price of their hungers.

The words from the *Book of Enoch* rolled around like thunder through the quiet corridors of his mind. The book, one of the Kindred's oldest and darkest legacies, older perhaps than the *Book of Nod*—though who could know such things for certain?—was an eclectic assortment of prophecy, saga and lore that revolved around the great reckoning to come—the Endtime.

The father calling down a rain of blood upon his childer was certainly a reference to Caine, the Dark Father. But this particular passage might just as easily be read as history rather than prediction.

Other passages were less ambiguous, speaking directly of a Winnowing that was to come. Kli Kodesh lost himself in tracing the labyrinthine paths of tangled verses. He sorted and sifted cryptic shards of prophecy, weighing each one carefully, arranging them into careful piles, testing their fit. He soon lost himself in his systematic preconstruction of the future.

It was some time before he realized that he was no longer being assailed by the storm of violent acts that buffeted him. He thought he must have left the Eastern Seaboard behind him and was now well out to sea.

There was a solace in the oceans that Kli Kodesh could find nowhere else—a freedom from the constant demands of the hideous crimes of others—a prefiguration of his final release.

Kli Kodesh allowed himself to drift off towards oblivion. He softy repeated to himself the mantra of his newest acquisition—the shard of truth he had so recently sifted from the treacherous sands of prophecy, oracle and lore:

Only then shall Caine unyoke his red-eyed ox, whose name is called Gehenna, for none may abide its countenance, and loose it to graze upon the Plain of Mediggo.

CHAPTER SIX

The people around Little Five Points this night were definitely not the type William Nen was accustomed to—punkers with hair of various neon shades; second generation hippies in falling-apart clothes; homeless types who might live on any bench; young women in tight shirts who had forsaken brassieres. Nen could not help but wonder about the infection rate of the body piercings which were so numerous and obtrusive. Loud music poured from the clubs sprinkled along Moreland Avenue, one of which in particular attracted Nen's interest. He tugged on his mustache as he looked at the address scrawled on the scrap of paper in his hand. Nine Tails was one of the loudest and liveliest of the clubs, and it was in the adjacent alley that cases JKL14337 and JKL14338 had been found.

Let it go. That's what Nen's superior, Dr. Maureen Blake, had said. Nen found it strange that at first Maureen had been intrigued by the case, but then later had practically ordered him to drop the investigation. But more important, in Nen's mind, was the necessity that a potential epidemic be averted. He had seen all too personally what an unfettered hemorrhagic fever could do to a population center. So, since Dr. Blake had *practically* but not *actually* ordered him to drop the investigation, he was continuing with it.

That was what brought him here to the alley beside Nine Tails. As he moved out of the light of the main street into the shadow of the alley, Nen considered for the first time that poking around in a dark alley in a somewhat seedy part of the city might not be the most sensible course of action. Who knew what could be lurking there? But it was so hard to get away from the office during the day, and though it was not completely rational, after having survived highly saturated contagion zones in Africa on several occasions, Nen had trouble believing that a common mugger was much of a threat. As he moved more deeply into the alley and the shadows thickened, however, he conceded to that little voice warning him away that a mugger would probably not be particularly interested in the fact that Nen had survived highly saturated contagion zones in Africa.

The muscle by Nen's left eye began to tic. He could hear the pounding bass from the music inside Nine Tails. *The patrons must all be half deaf by now*, Nen thought. Halfway into the alley, he stopped. He turned and looked back to Moreland Avenue. He could see clearly the people walking past. In the other direction, the alley led to another street with houses and apartments. Probably throughout the day this alley was a well-used lane of foot traffic for the people living there. There was little chance, he felt, that two bodies could lie here undetected for several weeks, which is what would've had to have happened for the tissue to have been as deteriorated as it was. There was still the possibility that someone could have dumped the bodies in the alley, but why dump them and then pour fresh blood onto them? Nen didn't have these answers, but he had learned what he could from seeing the alley. He at least had a picture in his mind as he continued to try to reconstruct what had happened.

As Dr. Nen retraced his steps back out of the alley, he did not notice the figure standing against the wall to his right. He should have noticed, considering how conservatively the individual was dressed in contrast to most everyone else around

Little Five Points—a business suit and tie; neat, short hair; wire-rimmed glasses. But the individual whom Nen did not see was Thelonious, Brujah primogen of the Kindred of Atlanta, and he had a way of going unnoticed by mortals when he wanted. He stood silently and watched as Nen walked past, out of the alley, and back to his car.

El Greco stood in the doorway, his silhouette bathed in shadow. Owain could make out only the gleam of his old friend's eyes. El Greco was tall, but a bit more stooped than Owain remembered. Without turning his back, Owain casually slid the letter back onto the desk. El Greco did not move. He stood completely still, watching the guest he had come upon rummaging through the host's personal effects. After a moment passed, Owain could discern more of the gaunt, almost frail, features. El Greco's eyes and cheeks were sunken deeply, intensifying the depth of the shadows across his face.

Without preamble, El Greco dropped Kendall Jackson's inert form to the floor. She landed hard. "I believe this is yours," said El Greco.

Owain could read neither El Greco's tone nor expression—anger, amusement? "El Greco," said Owain, "meet Kendall Jackson. I will have to introduce you to her later."

"I am afraid so," replied El Greco. He stepped

over Kendall and moved to a table in the corner where he lit an oil lamp.

The struck match cast eerie red light and dancing shadows across El Greco's nearly skeletal face. For an instant, Owain thought he was looking at the visage of the devil himself—narrow jaw, hollowed cheeks, pointed chin, thin mustache, and eyes as piercing as death. In fact, El Greco had called Owain here like Satan settling accounts with one who had sold his soul.

"It has been a long while," said El Greco, moving slowly toward the desk. He carefully pulled back the second chair and sat. "I was called away unexpectedly. You know how business can be."

"Indeed," Owain responded. "One night, all is normal. The next, old favors are called due."

"A favor is one matter," El Greco disagreed. "A *duty* is quite another. Don't you agree?"

Owain's tone remained noncommittal. "The distinctions are slight."

"I quite disagree." The two aged Cainites faced one another, gazes locked, both probing, yet revealing nothing. Finally, El Greco sighed mightily. "I appreciate you and *la señorita* helping Miguel look after the place," he said cordially, "though sorting the mail is hardly necessary."

"I do so miss my own tedious chores," said Owain dryly. Never mind that he had not opened his own mail for over forty years.

"*Chores,*" repeated El Greco. "How American of you, Owain."

Again the two sat and stared at one another. Owain had to concede that, six hundred years before, the two had been friends. Toward the end of the fourteenth century, he had wandered to Spain. Banished at that point for less than a century from his native Wales, having finished his play with the Templars in France, Owain had been devoid of purpose, questioning whether or not he even wanted to continue with his hellish existence, his damnation on earth. It was El Greco's energy and lust for all things living that had invigorated Owain and kept him going for seventy-five years, until the death of his long-time ghoul and companion Gwilym at the hands of the Inquisition had propelled Owain into despair, and he fell into torpor.

When he had rejoined the world of the living more than two hundred years later, that world was quite a different place. The Sabbat had been formed by those that would not give up the struggle when the Camarilla put an end to the Great Anarch Revolt, and El Greco was in the fore of that movement, one of the few Toreador to take a direct interest in the conflict. His enthusiasm, his passion, had been a magnet to Owain, who had had so little fire of his own by then. All the talk of freedom, *libertad*, had been intoxicating, and Owain had joined the Sabbat.

That had been long ago, however, and Owain had greatly distanced himself from the group over nearly three hundred years. But now he sat across from El Greco, one of the few living or unliving beings who knew of Owain's affiliation with the group El Greco had played such a fundamental part in founding. Owain had made certain promises, had sworn oaths of blood, and though over time they had come to mean next to nothing to him, that was certainly not the case with El Greco. El Greco would hold Owain to his word. Of that, Owain could be sure, but of little else.

El Greco had obviously changed over the past hundred years. The pallor that hung over him was that of the grave. Even for a Cainite, normally drawn and pale, he looked bad. It happened sometimes, even with the undead. The years caught up. The deterioration could be mental, or physical, or spiritual. As Owain looked at El Greco, he saw a tired, withering man, shoulders stooped, back tired. But the eyes…trapped within the decaying form, his eyes still held that same fire. They were aware of the failings of their physical prison. Undead was not the same as immortal.

"You look well," said El Greco on cue, as if he had been reading Owain's thoughts. His words, however, were a mere observation, not a compliment, not evidence of caring. El Greco spoke abruptly, his words as cool as his previous comment.

"We must speak now, Owain, for tomorrow evening you must leave me, and none may know of our relationship."

Owain was caught off guard by this. He had traveled across the Atlantic at El Greco's request, and now he was being sent away? He wanted to ask, why the bother? Why uproot him and risk discovery in the first place? But he kept his questions to himself. "Miguel will be heartbroken."

El Greco laughed. It was a cold, hollow sound, a weak seed of humor strangled among the weeds of decay. "You and Miguel were always fond of one another, weren't you?" His smile lingered, but was anything but warm. "He, at least, is loyal." The words bit as deeply as any dagger.

"You say we must speak," said Owain, irritated by the implied aspersion, true or not. He had not come all this way to be the target of innuendo. "Speak, then."

El Greco laughed quietly as he ran his fingers across the top of his desk. "The years have taught you the value of neither patience nor respect, have they?" He closed his eyes and laid his head back. "Ah, friendship is so like a fine wine, isn't it, *mi amigo*? With the years it can grow richer and fuller," he opened his eyes again, "or it can turn to vinegar."

Owain did not speak. He could learn more by listening than by feeding El Greco's rising ire…for the time being.

El Greco, his eyebrows raised by Owain's self-restraint, nodded at his old friend. "Speak, then, I shall. As I said, I was called away several nights ago. Otherwise, I would have been here for your arrival as I had planned to be. I was called to a meeting by Monçada." El Greco paused. "I realize that you have not kept abreast of goings-on within the Sabbat, but you do know who Monçada is, I presume?"

Owain nodded. He knew of the Sabbat archbishop of Madrid, Ambrosio Luis Monçada, who at one time centuries ago had pulled the strings that had manipulated so much of western Europe.

"Good." El Greco was pleased. "I traveled to Madrid to meet with him. I was quite pleased by the honor Monçada did me, until I learned that Carlos had been summoned to meet with Monçada as well. I know you are aware of my...*feelings* toward Carlos."

Before reading the mysterious letter moments before, Owain had never heard of Carlos. Now he knew him only as El Greco's rival, but that was all Owain had to go on. Again, he nodded.

"Monçada, too, is aware of my feelings toward Carlos," El Greco explained, "as well as Carlos's toward me, especially since several supporters of Carlos's who had been encroaching upon my territory, Toledo, met unfortunate ends."

Owain had little trouble imagining this. He well

remembered what El Greco had done to those who had crossed him back in the eighteenth century.

"Monçada demanded that we cease our bickering." Without warning, El Greco slammed his fist upon the desk. "Bickering!" His face screwed into a fierce snarl. Saliva sprayed past his bared fangs. "Can you believe it? Calling it bickering when that treacherous jackal from Madrid is moving in on my territory!" For several moments, he seethed. Owain did not disturb him. It was not impossible for El Greco to whip himself into a killing frenzy, and Owain had no great desire to test just how far the old Toreador had deteriorated. After a few minutes, El Greco had regained his composure. "Ironic, is it not," he asked, again in a conversational tone, "for Monçada to deliver such a pronouncement so soon after I receive your letter?"

"Indeed." Owain had no way of knowing exactly when El Greco had received the false epistle, but it had to have been at least in the past few weeks, since the curse had swept through the Cainite world.

"Did it surprise you that Miguel did not participate in the Vaulderie, that he did not share the blood, when he first arrived in Atlanta?" El Greco asked, abruptly switching topics.

Owain pondered this for a moment. "It hadn't crossed my mind, actually. It has been so long since I've performed the rites, nearly a century…"

"So, neither are you surprised that I have not offered you the blood. '*Libertad. Lealtad. Inmortal para siempre.*'"

"No."

El Greco, suddenly seeming quite tired and old, laughed half-heartedly, as if the gesture were too taxing and required his full concentration. "Ah, Owain, you have been away for too long. I left you to yourself for too many years."

"I rather fancy the opposite is true," quipped Owain.

El Greco's weak smile vanished. With his anger returned his strength. "You weary me Owain. I will put up with only so much."

Owain stiffened. It had been years and years since anyone had spoken to him so condescendingly. Benison, at least, had always been respectful. Owain could think of a very few individuals who had *ever* spoken to him thus, and they had all shared a similar fate. But by a supreme effort of will, he held his tongue.

"The blood curse, Owain," said El Greco. "It has been hard for the Camarilla, but it has *devastated* the Sabbat. Half, in some places three quarters, of our forces have wasted away or fallen into maddened bestial frenzy." His stare was incredibly intense. His rheumy eyes bulged against their sockets. "Only the strong survive. *As it should be.*"

El Greco, his fingers digging into the desk, leaned

close to Owain, but the emphasis of the brutally Darwinian statement was lost upon the Ventrue. Something about El Greco's words struck a chord within Owain, causing his thoughts to shift back hundreds of years, long even before he had come to live in this ancient city.

Only the strong survive.

In that earlier time, in another place, Owain had spoken those very same words and more. *Only the strong survive. Only the strongest rule.* He had spoken to his nephew Morgan. His nephew and his ghoul. Owain had been old enough to have lived three mortal lifetimes, but young enough still to have believed himself invincible. He had spoken those words, and then he had sent poor Morgan to his death.

Owain shuddered. His mind snapped back to the present as he realized that El Greco, a sly grin on his face, was staring at him. Owain was speechless, his concentration completely broken by the onslaught of the unbidden memory from Wales seven hundred years past.

El Greco was not speechless. "The years have not left you untouched, have they, Owain?" The stooped Toreador took smug satisfaction from this. "You may appear not a day older than when you were Embraced, but one does not survive through century after century without scars, eh? Some scars are merely more visible."

The two vampires sat facing one another in El Greco's study. In the corner, the oil lamp's flame danced contentedly, oblivious to the conversation it bathed in living light and shadow. Owain could see in El Greco the remnants of the passion that had once been so attractive. In El Greco's mocking smile Owain also sensed cruelty; he had been blind to it six hundred years earlier. Since then, Owain had become well-practiced at recognizing cruelty. He could see it in himself as well as in others. Cruelty was an outward manifestation of control, of power. Owain had spent too long fostering his own autonomy. Since his days as a mortal, he had balked at complying with a will other than his own. As he became actively involved once again in the world of the Cainites, he was faced anew with the challenge of those who would exercise control over him. He would not yield control to Prince Benison in Atlanta. He would not yield control to El Greco in Toledo. He would see them destroyed first. He would see himself destroyed first.

Owain did not care for this scrutiny under which El Greco was placing him. What did it matter, Owain wondered, if his mind wandered at times? Who, mortal or undead, could truly claim that the passage of time had not inflicted upon him or her certain regrets and sorrows? Was El Greco any different? "You were speaking of the Vaulderie?"

El Greco chuckled politely, fully aware that Owain was shifting the focus of the conversation and at the same time implying that it was El Greco's mind that was slipping, that it was the Toreador who was leaving thoughts unfinished. He dipped his head as if to say *touché*. "I was indeed speaking of the Vaulderie. I have instructed my followers not to engage in the rites while the blood curse persists."

"You speak as if you think the curse will pass," said Owain.

"All things pass."

"Perhaps it is the time of the Cainites that has passed."

"The Endtime?" El Greco's eyebrows rose, but then he laughed dismissively. "There are vampires on every street corner preaching that, Owain. And do you know what they all have in common? They are the have-nots. They have nothing to lose and everything to gain from the end of the world. They may be correct, but if so, then there is little I or anyone else can do, so I will proceed under the assumption that they are not correct." He leaned back in his chair. "But about the Vaulderie—you see, you distract me again—I have instructed my followers to forgo the rites."

"Because…?"

"Because, as you stated in your letter, the curse is magical in nature, and only the most powerful of magics are permanent."

The letter. Owain thought about what he had read, what he had supposedly *written*. He had played along with that misconception thus far and would need time to think before being willing to admit that he was, in fact, not the author. He had not been able to finish the entire letter before El Greco had appeared, so Owain needed to tread lightly. He could not afford to ask a question that might be answered in "his own" letter. Otherwise, he would have voiced exceptions to El Greco's reasoning. Perhaps the curse was somehow self-sustaining. Perhaps it fed on the blood of every vampire it touched. There was no way to be sure. How could El Greco proceed based upon such a shaky premise?

"This will pass," El Greco reiterated. "There is a power, an energy, in the transference of vitae. We've all felt it, Owain—during the Embrace, during the Vaulderie. I believe it is that power that fuels the curse." El Greco looked perplexed. "From your hints in the letter, I thought you had surmised the same?"

Owain's throat tightened. He offered no response. His mind was racing, assembling every fact and rumor he had heard about the curse in case El Greco asked a more pointed question.

El Greco shrugged. "But as you suggested, I am somewhat intrigued by your notion that Carlos, thrice damn his soul, is responsible for the curse. You know that I cannot merely present hearsay to

Monçada and expect him to act. Tell me how you propose to secure proof of this allegation of yours?"

Proof. Owain tried to reconstruct what he had read. *Proof that Carlos inadvertently set loose the curse. Project Angharad. Grimsdale. Increasing the potency of vitae. Proof!* Owain had been aware of the curse, but he had not paid Prince Benison's ravings much heed. Owain had been more concerned with personal matters—the siren, his reawakening desires—but they had all been touched by the madness of the curse. Caused by it even? He didn't know enough. How could he answer? El Greco sat waiting expectantly. "I have heard…" said Owain speaking very deliberately, assembling the words into some cohesive order as they crawled off his tongue, "that…some of those cursed all but starved…even though they fed regularly…and their bodies were full of blood."

"Yes?" El Greco obviously knew this already and did not see where Owain was going with this explanation.

Unfortunately for Owain, neither did he. How could he hope to prove anything about this curse when hordes of sorcerous Tremere had failed to uncover anything? He was coming up with nothing. "Others…" he kept stalling, "went insane… more quickly."

"Yes?" El Greco was leaning forward in his chair. "And your plan?"

From the doorway, Kendall Jackson let out a low moan where she lay on the floor. Owain latched onto that sound. Trying not to be too obvious in his relief, he walked around the desk and knelt by Kendall. With each step, he tried to devise a plan, something that he could toss to El Greco to keep him content for now, at least until Owain could decide what to do about this entire matter. Gently, he supported Kendall's head and neck as he raised her to a sitting position. "Ms. Jackson, are you all right?"

She raised a hand to her head, and then her eyelids fluttered open. She moaned again, confused as her eyes focused on Owain. Almost instantly, however, she was scrambling to her feet, alert for danger, reaching for the .45 magnum tucked in her waistline. She froze as she saw El Greco sitting not ten feet away, scowling slightly but not posing any obvious threat at the moment.

"Ms. Jackson," said Owain formally, "allow me to introduce El Greco, Priscus of the Sabbat, master of Toledo."

"Sir, I…" Again she was confused.

"Would you be so kind, Ms. Jackson," El Greco asked, "as to wait downstairs?"

Owain nodded his assent and Kendall, all the while keeping her gaze locked on El Greco, eased her way out of the room. Owain watched her depart, his back turned to El Greco and sorting out what to say next. The supposed author of the letter had hastily settled on a plan that would have to do for now.

"She's admirably obedient, Owain," said El Greco, referring to Kendall, "and not unattractive."

For the second time in the space of an hour, Owain's thoughts were jolted back to the distant past. *Blodwen is not an unattractive woman.* Owain had spoken these words also to Morgan, shortly before Morgan had killed his own brother, before Morgan had become king of Rhufoniog. This time, Owain snapped out of the sudden reverie more quickly. He still had his back to El Greco, so perhaps his host did not realize that Owain had again lost his grounding in time for a moment. Was the old Toreador doing this on purpose, or could it just be coincidence? Were their pasts so linked that every phrase was a gateway to memories better forgotten?

"As for your plan, Owain…?"

Owain turned slowly. "As you said," he spoke as if he had devised his plan weeks ago rather than minutes, "Archbishop Monçada will want proof. He will not act against Carlos based on hearsay or rumors."

While Owain explained, El Greco stiffly, even painfully, rose from the chair and made his way around the desk to his rightful seat. How had he bested Ms. Jackson, Owain wondered, without her even having time to make a sound? But there was little time to ponder this question, with El Greco waiting somewhat less than patiently.

"And circumstantial evidence will matter little to the archbishop in such a weighty affair," Owain continued. "Even if you had the vial of tainted blood that Grimsdale had taken…" Owain paused, suddenly positive that he had misremembered the name from the letter, but El Greco did not noticeably react, "that would not be proof enough. You must find the laboratory where Carlos's underlings conducted the magical experiments. You must find it, and you must be able to reveal it to the archbishop."

El Greco thought solemnly for a moment, then nodded slowly. "You are correct. You are absolutely *correct!*" His sudden burst of enthusiasm quickly died away. "I had thought as much myself. But, of course, with this latest advisement from *his holiness*, the archbishop," El Greco spat the honorific like vinegared wine, "my hands are somewhat bound. And regardless, I could no more enter Carlos's domain than Hitler could stroll through Jerusalem."

"You do have servants," Owain reminded him.

This brought a genuine smile to El Greco's sunken, ashen features. "Indeed, I do." El Greco smiled a bit too purposefully for Owain's comfort.

Owain could guess where this was leading, and he could see why El Greco had invited him to

Spain. Owain smiled pleasantly. "I'm so glad I could help you with that matter." He drew his pocket watch from his vest and glanced at the hands that had not functioned in over three decades. "I'm afraid I'll have to be going. There's so much to keep up with back in Atlanta." He had not taken even half a step out of the room before El Greco called his half-hearted bluff.

"Owain," El Greco indicated the chair that he had recently vacated, "please sit."

Owain felt himself bound by old loyalties, oaths sworn back when he was less completely jaded. Whether he wanted to be or not, he was Sabbat, and El Greco was his *master*, the individual who inducted him into the sect. How that galled Owain. As he crossed the room to the offered chair, his mind was aswirl with scenarios by which he could free himself from his responsibilities to El Greco and to the Sabbat. This was a matter, he realized, that would require much thought, for El Greco, having left Owain to his own for the better part of two hundred fifty years, was now calling promises due. El Greco would not forget. And so Owain must find a way to sever the binds that held him.

As Owain sat, he noticed again how old and tired his former friend looked. The bags under El Greco's eyes were large and dark; his narrow face seemed fragile in the flickering lamplight.

"Dawn approaches," said El Greco, "so I will

speak plainly. You will find that laboratory, and whatever other proof is necessary to convince Monçada that Carlos is to blame for the curse that has annihilated much of the Sabbat. You will begin this evening. Miguel will be here shortly. He can tell you what you will need to know. Your connection to me, of course, must remain secret, and should you fail, I shall deny knowledge of both your presence in Spain and your task."

It was as Owain had suspected. "And if I refuse?" he asked as if in jest.

El Greco found no humor in the question. "Then I will reveal your ties to the Sabbat to your Camarilla brethren, and for every night of your unlife henceforth, both war party and justicar will hunt you as a traitor, and the only peace you will know will be after you are staked out for the morning sun."

Owain slowly stood. "I see." *So much for the ties of friendship*, he thought. *Threats are much more compelling*. He left the room without again looking at or speaking to El Greco. There was no doubt in Owain's mind that he would be free of this burdensome Cainite. The only questions were when and how.

CHAPTER SEVEN

The biting wind whipped through the streets of
Kreuzberg, but to Wilhelm it was little more than
a summer breeze. He wore only a light jacket over
his turtleneck. On his arm, Henriette in her thin,
clinging sweater attracted the stares of passersby as
she and her sire exited the Berlin Museum.
Wilhelm did not begrudge the bystanders their roving glances. His childe was a creature of beauty. Her
physical perfection along with the deep soulfulness
of her pale blue eyes had attracted him initially,
and he had come to enjoy the envy she evoked
from others. It was an almost tangible reminder of
his success, of the status and prestige that he had
achieved. Amidst dealing with the ravages of the

blood curse upon his city, there had been few occasions recently when he had derived satisfaction of any sort from his position.

In the museum, Wilhelm had been showing Henriette the scaled models of Berlin as it had grown and changed over the years, from the modest *stadt* of the 1500s to the international center of the present. Wilhelm remembered the city from even earlier, and he had pointed out to Henriette some of the minor inaccuracies of the models. This visit, too, had served as a reminder to Wilhelm that he was the prince of a great city, that whatever challenges arose, he would conquer them, that like the spirit of the German people, he could not be broken.

There was much to challenge his spirit these nights. As if the curse were not enough, Gustav was proving as obstinate and confrontational as ever. Wilhelm protectively stroked the flawless skin of Henriette's forearm. The scars that she carried from Gustav's tortures were not visible to the naked eye, but Wilhelm could see them when he looked at her face—the doubt and fear in her eyes. *How could I have risked her? Why did I send her as the messenger?* he asked himself. But risking her could have saved the city, if only Gustav had, for once, proven reasonable and sane, and Wilhelm knew that he would make the same decision again, as did Henriette. And thus the pain in her eyes.

Doubtless some of the passersby who saw the prince and his childe leaving the museum wondered how they had managed to be inside so late in the evening, but power, Wilhelm knew, carried its own rewards. Probably few of those same passersby, captivated by Henriette's beauty and Wilhelm's charming smile, would notice the presence of Peter Kleist several paces behind the couple he so capably guarded. Without drawing attention to himself, Kleist constantly scanned their surroundings. No one in the vicinity of the prince escaped Kleist's awareness. Occasionally he would move off to one side or the other or out in front, his mere presence subliminally warding off potentially rowdy or troublesome mortals. The Kindred of Berlin knew better than to try anything while he was on watch.

As Henriette and Wilhelm crossed the street from the museum, she squeezed her sire's arm warmly. "It's been so long since we've gone out for a pleasurable evening."

Wilhelm patted her hand gently. It had been a long time since he'd been able to do *anything* pleasurable, but being with his beautiful childe could almost take his mind off his omnipresent responsibilities. He had opened his mouth to respond when Kleist brushed past him. At the same time, Wilhelm noticed the attention of the mortals on the street shifting down the block. Around the cor-

ner came a man running. Not a jogger, or someone late for an appointment. This was a Turk,
Wilhelm saw, dressed casually, but not appropri-
ately for an all-out sprint. As Wilhelm and
Henriette watched, the man passed Kleist, who had
positioned himself between them and the fleeing
Turk.

"He's frightened to death," said Henriette.

"Of what, I wonder," Wilhelm pondered.

The nearby mortals also watched with curiosity
and some confusion as the man continued frantically on his way, panting, speaking to no one. They
shared the common thought that if the Turk were
running, someone was chasing him—the police? a
jealous husband? No one knew.

Wilhelm was more curious than concerned. He
was a predator in his city, not prey.

"Look!" Kleist was the first to catch a glimpse of
the mob swarming around the corner from the direction the Turk had come. They were young,
fair-skinned men for the most part, some with
shaved heads, many wearing jackboots, all yelling
and angry. They wielded clubs or beer bottles, and
they spread out to occupy the width of the street.
Traffic stopped. The members of the mob poured
around and over the cars in their way. If the driver
was the least bit darkly complected, the hoodlums
dragged him or her from the vehicle and began
beating and kicking.

Wilhelm's first response was anger. His instinct was to dive into the mob and put a stop to their racist violence. He cared less for the well-being of the individual victims than he did for the image of his city. Such riots only served to blacken the image of Berlin across the world.

But the crowd was too large. Many sported swastika armbands or tattoos. Wilhelm saw two neo-Nazis smash a windshield. Nearby, a shop window shattered. The throng was surging down the street, seemingly swallowing all that stood in its way—automobiles, pedestrians. The mortals near Wilhelm, captivated until now by shock, began edging nervously away. Then, one by one, they turned and fled headlong.

"This way!" Kleist grabbed Wilhelm's arm. They were too far from the museum already, so Kleist pulled them toward a nearby sidestreet. Once the three were moving, Wilhelm and Henriette needed no further encouragement to vacate the main thoroughfare. Twenty yards down the sidestreet, they stopped and turned back to watch.

"Damn them!" Wilhelm muttered. It was not his nature generally to openly criticize. Such was not politic. Even those of whom he disapproved had agendas that Wilhelm could discover and use to his benefit. Every enemy was a potential resource, but these riots, these acts of senseless violence and destruction only harmed his city. There were elements of German society that abhorred the immigrants Wilhelm had welcomed with open arms for the diversity of skills they brought to Berlin. *Let the dissenters address that issue, not lash out with this barbarism! How have we Germans achieved the peak of world civilizations with such cretins as countrymen?*

The head of the crowd pressed past the street where Wilhelm, Henriette, and Kleist had sought cover. The sound of more shattering glass filled the air. The racist chants of the mob took on a rhythmic, fevered pitch. Turks, Jews, Pakistanis—all were targets of the free-flowing hatred.

As he watched, Wilhelm only grew angrier. He strongly believed that the majority of Germans favored liberal immigration policies as did he, but that majority did not demonstrate, did not make its voice heard so loudly and consistently.

"Dear God!" cried Henriette.

As Wilhelm's anger was channeled into sociopolitical theory, a portion of the mob suddenly broke away from the main body and rushed down the sidestreet. Either they had lost track of what direction the Turk had run or, more likely, the riot had grown beyond the original purpose of apprehending a particular individual, and these people were intent only on spreading destruction wherever they might. With unusual speed, the first of the hoodlums covered the yards that had separated Wilhelm and the others from the bedlam.

"Here!" Kleist shouted again, as he quickly ushered Wilhelm and Henriette toward the edge of the street. They turned their backs to the buildings. With their vampiric powers to influence mortal minds, they should have had little trouble blending into the thronging mass of people, but though the first of the rioters did pass by, seemingly oblivious to their presence, a ring of thugs from the following ranks quickly formed around the prince, his childe, and the bodyguard.

"This shouldn't be happening," said Kleist.

"Not if this were a normal mob," Wilhelm agreed, but as he said so, he sensed among those surrounding them several ghouls and at least one vampire, probably an anarch judging by the weakness of his aura. But numbers could make up for power.

After a moment's hesitation, the gang pounced. Kleist whipped a Luger from beneath his jacket and began firing. Wilhelm, too, was taking no prisoners. He crushed the skull of the first skinhead who rushed him. The prince was distracted slightly by concern for his childe, but a quick glance revealed that, for the time being, she was holding her own, dodging the larger men who were trying to tackle and weigh her down. She lashed out with kicks and claws, hamstringing an opponent here, slashing eyes there. She was by no means defenseless.

All around, chaos swept through Kreuzberg. The rioters were destroying cars, setting buildings ablaze.

Kleist rapidly emptied his clip and was then swallowed by the tide of mortals and ghouls rushing toward him. Wilhelm warded off blows as best he could, but the press of the thronging attackers limited his movement and the effectiveness of his own blows. A club to the back of his head, a blow hard enough to kill a mortal, drew blood. Someone hit his knees. The prince faltered, stumbled. And then he was on the ground, and people were piling on top of him, the weight of their bodies full upon him. He heard and felt his own ribs snapping.

This was no random mob. Not even the Final Reich, that collection of fascist Brujah and Malkavians, could assemble this many foot soldiers. Wilhelm could feel the presence of other vampires in the crowd. They were moving in. The smell of death brought them strong and thick. This riot had the mark of Gustav all over it. He used hatred and fear to manipulate all those around him.

Wilhelm could struggle no longer. Even with this preternatural strength, his movement was so hampered by the horde atop him that he could mount no effective defense. He had no idea if Henriette or Kleist were faring any better.

As the prince's head was kicked to the side, he saw the ring of rioters part. A man in Nazi garb stepped through and threw something. Instantly, the entire world was a flash of fire and pain. A *Molotov cocktail*. The flames seared away Wilhelm's skin. Screams of agony filled the air, as did the smell of petrol and burning flesh.

♀

Kli Kodesh opened his eyes upon riot. His eyes were glossy black and expressionless. It was as if the artist who had carved the marble features had, as an afterthought, added two quick daubs of paint to the smooth sockets.

Kli Kodesh quickly took the measure of this city divided against itself. Its most telling feature was a fresh pink scar that seemed to cleave the city in two. It was as if the metropolis had built itself around some great scab and then worried it until the wound bled afresh.

Berlin.

He needed no atlas to put a name to this place or its people. Among the sharp young businessmen, he recognized many of the same faces he had seen waving torches in the Forum in the last days of the Republic.

He wondered that those who burned the treasuries of Rome now found themselves the champions of an economic community that spanned all of Europe. People, like cities, Kli Kodesh reflected, are continuous in time. They are often, however, discontinuous in purpose.

He banished such conjectures from his mind. Thoughts of the City of Seven Hills always put him in a foul humor. Images of Caesar, minted in silver, often intruded upon his rest.

To banish the lingering doubts, he threw himself into his work. The violence spread out below him like the face of a shattered mirror. There were clues here for those with eyes to see—hints of a pattern of great subtlety.

With exacting precision, Kli Kodesh traced the familiar lines of a pattern he had first discerned thousands of miles away, in the City of Angels. Like the augurs of the accursed city upon the Tiber, he had little difficulty reading the portents—distilling the flashing arc of a knife, the spurt of blood, the tumble of entrails.

One could not be immersed in violence and betrayal for as long as he had without acquiring an intimate knowledge of the rituals that adorned these crimes. Yes, the omens ran true. Surely some great reckoning was at hand.

Kli Kodesh blinked and looked again. The pattern had shifted slightly. Somewhere, in the heart of the riotous maelstrom, someone was manipulating the delicate strands of emerging truth.

He focused on the heart of the disturbance. The anomaly was spreading out in languid circles, originating from somewhere deep beneath the streets of the city. Kli Kodesh could get no bearing, however, on the power behind the disturbance. It was alien, not of his kind.

The art of weaving the ancient prophecies had been lost long before Kli Kodesh had first awakened to this nightmare. He could only watch in wonder as one dark thread of the pattern doubled and then redoubled itself—gathering power, tensing to spring.

Suddenly and silently, it streaked off into the night, like a shooting star run in reverse. Kli Kodesh doubted that he would have been able to pick it out at all if he had not been watching it directly.

His mind, however, was honed to this work by centuries of waiting. Before the new star had reached its zenith and burned out amidst the smudge of the Milky Way, he had already calculated its exact angle of descent.

Without a second thought, he turned his back upon the carnage still raging through the streets of Berlin. With a twist of will, he caught the tail of the vanishing comet and rode it westward—toward Iberia and the man that awaited at the far edge of the strand of dark prophecy.

Walking through the narrow, twisting streets of Toledo brought memories of bygone years flooding over Owain. Not so much in the early evening when the tourists were wandering about, but after the shops and restaurants that catered to the foreigners closed, he was hard-pressed to tell if this was a city of the twentieth century or of the fourteenth. The Moorish architecture still caught his eye. The sprinkling of Gothic, Renaissance, Baroque, and modern buildings were an anomaly to Owain, centuries of window dressings by people who had occupied Toledo, but never captured its heart. The austerity of the Moors, the plain, rounded arches, the relatively unadorned facades, these held for Owain the measure of the city—a sense of hidden brooding, of schemes behind faceless walls, of traps laid for the unwary. Ignoring the presence of automobiles and other obtrusive reminders of the modern age, Owain could imagine the year was 1380, or 1830, but even those were not fabled golden years. Plotting, politics, death. From the day of his birth, they had been everpresent. There was no time Owain could think of, spanning ten centuries and two continents, in which pain and suffering had not followed him like his shadow.

Most of the other Cainites that Owain had known here had perished over the years. All save El Greco and Miguel. Owain was not surprised that Miguel had survived. *A cockroach among men.*

The previous night, or early morning rather, Miguel had arrived and consulted with El Greco shortly after Owain had left him. Then Miguel had informed Owain that he would not have to go even as far as Madrid to locate Carlos. El Greco's enemy was much closer. "Why is he here in Toledo?" Owain had asked incredulously upon hearing that news, but Miguel had offered no further explanation.

"You will leave here tomorrow evening," Miguel informed Owain, "and not return. If you must contact us, there is a small pottery shop across from *la Iglesia de San Nicolas*. Ask for me. You will be given instructions."

"And if I would like to confer with El Greco...?"

"Contact me *only if you must*. You will not speak with El Greco again until this matter is resolved," Miguel said bluntly. "We have already taken too many chances in keeping you here." He handed Owain a small, sealed envelope. "This is the address and the key for a small house where you can stay."

At that point, dawn was rapidly approaching and the debate was cut short. *Besides*, Owain had thought, *eternity is too short to spend it arguing with Miguel*. Owain had won the concession that Kendall Jackson would remain, for the time being, with El Greco. "Until I make contact with Carlos, she will only be in the way. Afterward, I may need her." Miguel, pressed by the need to return to his haven, reluctantly acquiesced.

Owain gave brief instructions to Kendall. "Keep your eyes and ears open here. Each night at midnight, wait at the Puerta del Sol. Come and go by different routes. Make sure you are not followed. Stay for no more than fifteen minutes. If I need you, I will meet you there."

Tonight, with little more in the way of preparation for this deadly quest, Owain had left the colorless house that was El Greco's—and yet strangely was not. *I know El Greco,* Owain pondered. *Or at least I did. He could not be content in such a dwelling. It lacks all the trappings, all the aesthetic touches that were so important to him.* After all, it had been not even a century since Owain had seen El Greco last. Could a Cainite change so dramatically in such a short period?

Owain's wanderings took him east past the cathedral and then south to the edge of the Rio Tajo. The river surrounded Toledo on three sides, all but the north. The often steep and rocky banks lent natural defense to the city which, nonetheless, had changed hands numerous times over the ages— Romans, Visigoths, Moors, Christians. The struggles for control were by no means restricted to the mortal world. The clans of the undead had just as long and bloody a history here. Young Spanish Brujah had fought both their own elders and the restrictive Ventrue hierarchy. The fiendish Tzimisce, as well as the Lasombra and the dreaded Assamites, had joined the Brujah. The Anarch Revolt, as the conflict had come to be known, had failed, but from its ashes rose the Sabbat, carrying on to this day the battle against Cainite tyranny.

How ironic, Owain again thought, that it was the Sabbat with its doctrine of freedom that was tyrannizing him. Just as with that brief experiment that had been Soviet Russia, there was theory and there was practice. The utopian ideals of communist theory were no more immune to the abuses of corruption and megalomania than were other social structures. In much the same way, the Sabbat had come to resemble its nemesis, the Camarilla, in all the worst ways. Self-aggrandizing leaders pretended to act in the interest of the sect while actually doing everything they could to maintain their personal grip on power. Underlings struggled aggressively and treacherously to climb the ladder of status and prestige, only to fall victim to the frequent purges orchestrated by the elders. Chaos and violence had superseded freedom.

None of this was new to Owain. He had seen the cycle of decay through a perspective of years that few Cainites could match. He had been part of the charade. Centuries before the Anarch Revolt, before the Sabbat had added its bloodlust to the night, and the Camarilla its hollow Masquerade, he had perpetrated the basest cruelties, ostensibly in the name of freedom. But he had learned that the roads to freedom and to power follow similar routes, and not until they diverge does the traveler truly know where he is. And maybe not then.

Owain moved quickly as he followed the course of the river northwest. Did the Tajo protect the city of Toledo, he wondered, or did it constrain it, cutting off avenues of expansion and growth? It was not a question he could answer. Owain shortly found himself at the base of the Puerta del Cambron. The gate had been altered many times since that night when he had perched atop it and watched as the Jews had been expelled from the city. Two additional towers had been added and the facade extensively redesigned. The gate had once been known as Jews' Gate, but after the Jewish quarter of the city was emptied, the sobriquet was something of a misnomer.

With grace and ease, Owain scaled the tower wall and found a comfortable perch from which to gaze out over the city of his past. It was difficult for him to believe that among the United States, Spain, France, and his native Wales, he had spent the most time residing here, even discounting the two and a half centuries of torpor. Still, he felt a stranger. Despite the general familiarity and the nostalgia of remembrance, he had never felt at home in Spain. The people, the language, the terrain—none were above mastery, but neither were they his beloved Wales.

Owain refused to follow that vein of thought. He

was too easily swayed into romanticizing what had gone before. How many years in Atlanta had he dwelled in the past? That same siren song that had reawakened his ability to feel the past, rather than merely to long for it, had also enabled him, once again, truly to experience the present. Such was the gift of life to a vampire. To become stagnant in the past was to wither and die, as surely as if he had succumbed to the blood curse.

The reality of the present, however, was grim as well. El Greco held all the cards, or so it seemed. If Owain refused what El Greco had requested, what El Greco had *ordered*, then El Greco would expose Owain. He would be found out as both a traitor to the Camarilla and to the Sabbat, to be hunted down to the end of his nights. Never again would he have a moment's peace. His unlife would consist of fleeing from one temporary haven to the next, always wondering how long his luck would hold out. Though his appearance was that of a mortal slightly over twenty, Owain was too old for that type of existence. He would rather meet final death—not altogether out of the question considering his current mission.

If any trace of his and El Greco's friendship survived, Owain decided, El Greco would not have coerced him into such a course of action. Together, they could have come up with a more reasonable plan; but El Greco had made up his mind about what needed to happen before Owain had even arrived. *I could have admitted that I didn't write the letter,* Owain pondered. *But would he even have believed me?* It would have seemed too convenient, as if Owain were merely trying to avoid the service he had sworn to provide so many years ago. Also, for whatever good it did him, by not admitting that he hadn't written the letters, Owain had the advantage of knowledge denied to El Greco. Owain knew that someone had perfectly forged not only his handwriting, but his tone and word choice as well. Reading the letter, even Owain could have believed that he had written it. Who could know his mind so well?

So Owain played along, and here he was, charged with the task of infiltrating Carlos's faction, finding the secret laboratory in which the curse was allegedly devised, and then securing proof to fulfill a vendetta which, in the first place, was expressly forbidden by Archbishop Monçada. Owain sighed. He watched the water flowing serenely beneath the bridge to the south, the Puente de San Martin. Was there ever a Cainite, Owain wondered, who had found serenity? Perhaps that was the worst of the curse of vampirism. Though the lives of mortals, too, were consumed by fearful striving, they at least enjoyed the solace and the release of death. For Owain and his kind, there was no relief in death, only continued fear, continued striving.

Whether it was fear or hatred, or both, that motivated El Greco, he was certainly striving to rid himself of his enemy. Owain could sympathize with that desire, but the manner in which El Greco had enlisted Owain's aid left Owain cold. El Greco could at least have explored the possibility of Owain offering to help of his own volition. As far as Owain had read, the letter had not been an offer to solve the problem but rather a sharing of information. No, as with any interaction among the Cainites, beneath the obvious topic, the destruction of Carlos, there was a subtext of control, and Owain had already decided that he would not be controlled. If he were able to fulfill this mission, if he managed to contact Carlos and to live to speak of the encounter, it must be in a manner that would ensure that El Greco no longer exercised control over Owain. It was unlikely, Owain suspected, that El Greco, out of the goodness of his heart, would release him from his commitments. That left trickery or violence, or both, to eliminate El Greco's advantage.

Owain believed he could probably destroy Miguel, and the task would not be without its pleasure. Owain might also be able to destroy El Greco himself, though that would be a closer task. But even if treachery succeeded, how many servants or allies of El Greco would be aware of the deed? The driver of the Mercedes, the ghouls Maria and

Ferdinand—were there others? If so, would they rejoice at the downfall of their master, or would they seek vengeance, and spread word of what Owain had done? There was no way to know, and Owain was not one to leave a foul deed only partially done.

He would bide his time, Owain decided. He would pursue this goal of finding Carlos. The opportunity would present itself, Owain knew. He would remain watchful, and he would be rid of El Greco.

Finding Carlos, however, meant taking action, not perching atop a gate to history and reminiscing about the past. Owain made his way down and headed back toward the heart of the old city. He had not seen any Cainites earlier, but he had not been looking very diligently. He had been playing the tourist, strolling through the streets and soaking up the ambience but noticing little of detail.

It was late now, and few mortals roamed the dark streets. Again Owain climbed, taking to the rooftops of the low buildings. Walking down the street, he would more likely be the observed rather than the observer. Owain made his way back toward the cathedral, moving from building to building with powerful leaps and silent landings. No mortal, on the street below or in the buildings beneath Owain's feet, would be aware of his passing. The north wind carried away the sound of his steps, the very darkness cushioned his every footfall. Even among his own kind, Owain was skilled at moving unnoticed through the night; an odd gift for a Ventrue, but one that had served him well.

Thus, after perhaps two hours of searching, Owain felt an unmistakable sensation, the innate awareness that alerts a Cainite to the presence of another of his breed nearby. He was not surprised when he came to the edge of a shop above a narrow alleyway and peered down, careful not to present a clear silhouette against the sky above.

At first, he saw only shadow. The position of the moon did not allow any of its reflected light to penetrate the depths of the alley. The darkness, however, was no match for Owain's vampiric eyes. He saw in the mask of the shadows the individual he had sensed moments before. The Cainite was hunched over a still body—as he fed from it, no doubt—and gave no indication of having heard Owain. The intensity of the shadows in the alley suggested to Owain that this vampire did not want to be seen. Only Owain's acute awareness had cut through the other's powers to obscure.

"Greetings, friend," said Owain from the rooftop, confident of his ability to conceal his exact whereabouts.

The vampire below swung about quickly, flinging blood from his fangs. He glared all around, then upward, but his eyes, glowing red as he scanned the night, passed over Owain without pausing. The Spanish Cainite appeared to be in his twenties or thirties, the receding of his hairline eternally halted at midcourse. The boy he fed on was younger, perhaps fifteen, and had certainly paid the price for violating his curfew. "*Come here*," said the vampire.

Owain recognized the tone of voice, he felt the power in the words, but to one of his age, the command of a brash youngster was but a trifle. "I think not."

The Cainite in the alley continued to scan his surroundings. Clearly, he was not close to determining Owain's location. Not yet. "Where are you?" the vampire demanded, but received no response. "*Who* are you?"

"Save your questions and answer mine," Owain taunted, careful still to mask his presence, lest his voice give him away. "I am searching for Carlos. Do you know of him?"

The vampire below smiled. He stepped over the unconscious boy, more interested now in this strange disembodied voice in the night. "Do I know of him?" The vampire laughed. He was addressing his comments upward now. He had discerned that much of Owain's location. "This is his city. I serve him."

Carlos's city? Owain was taken aback by this. *What of El Greco?* Toledo had long been the province of the Greek. "You are not from here," Owain accused.

The vampire squinted, puzzled by that. He was staring very intently now at a spot not too far from Owain. "Carlos does not tolerate trespassers in his city. Who are you?"

"Tell Carlos," said Owain, "that Morgan has arrived, and I would offer him a bargain."

"What is your name again, friend?"

"You heard," Owain again taunted, "and you will tell him."

The balding Sabbat vampire launched himself into the air, razor-sharp claws swinging as he landed on the roof, but Owain was already three rooftops away. Silently, Owain lowered himself from the building and was off through the city streets.

Carlos. This is his city, the vampire had said. The words echoed in Owain's mind. How could it be? El Greco had said nothing of this. *This is his city*.

Nicholas almost didn't notice when the city first became visible. It blended somewhat with the low hills, dried by winter; many of the stone buildings shared similar shading with the rocky soil on both sides of the river that snaked around Toledo. Nicholas had not seen this city before. He was familiar with much of Germany, France, his native Russia, but he had roamed little across Spain. His unfamiliarity with the region was only one reason, however, that he happened upon the city sooner than he had expected.

Distraction was not a malady that normally affected the Gangrel. A clan of hunters conditioned to the wilds, they were known for their awareness of their surroundings, for noting every rustling bush, for taking account of every depression and rise beneath their feet. But Nicholas's mind was absorbed by thoughts of vengeance—no, by more than vengeance—by pure animal fury. A rage far more primal than anything Blackfeather could comprehend burned deep within Nicholas's breast. The Cherokee Gangrel had spoken of harnessing the inner rage, of learning the lessons it had to teach. But there was no taming that which was growing within Nicholas. To attempt such was to deny his own nature, to live as pretender within the confines of mortal society. Nicholas could pull it off when he had no other choice, but the task was becoming more and more difficult.

The trip by boat across the Atlantic had been less arduous than Nicholas had remembered. He had traversed the ocean several times in his existence, but his more recent crossings had been by air. Though always vaguely uncomfortable with the idea of flying in a man-made contraption, he had been seduced by the rapidity of the transport. This trip over the surface of the sea, however, had not seemed cumbersome. Nicholas had rested deep within the hold by day, while at night he had come out on the gently rocking deck to gaze at stars, the sight of which revived memories of other nights long ago watching the same points of light above the ocean. He could again hear the rhythmic swash of the oars and the steady drumbeat as the oarsmen silently propelled his Viking ship forward. Then he had been going west, not east, and the route had lain far to the north. He could note easily the altered position of the familiar constellations. *Ragnar.* Nicholas was Gangrel, wanderer of the world, teller of stories. He knew well the tales of his great-grandsire. But these were not mere stories that he remembered. He saw the stars that Ragnar saw, felt the same swell of ocean lifting the hull. Traveling, on the move, he was content. For a few brief nights, Nicholas found the serenity of his ancestor. The solitude of wide open plains was replaced by the expansive calm of the ocean, the purple-black sky that spread uninterrupted from horizon to horizon.

Nicholas was almost able to forget that which drove him, though it was Ragnar's blood, too, that screamed for vengeance. As the boat had chugged into Lisbon harbor, the modern world again thrust itself upon Nicholas. Piers and other boats closed in upon him; the sounds and smells of humanity stole away the quiet of the ocean at night. The city lights on the horizon too quickly enveloped him, rekindling his resentment, his hatred, his fury.

He slipped off the boat without a word to Blackfeather's captain friend, not because of ingratitude, but because the fury was once again upon him and he could not restrain it. Amidst the renewed stink of humanity, Nicholas hunted and fed, fiercely, roughly. He left the man lying in the gutter, perhaps still living, perhaps not. Nicholas could no longer bring himself to respect the Masquerade. It was a concession to the mortals who had ravaged the wildernesses. He continued quickly east and that same night was far away from Lisbon.

Blackfeather had said that Evans had touched down in Madrid, but Nicholas could now feel that his destination had shifted. Not from Madrid but from Toledo the blood called him. The contentment of the ocean voyage grew increasingly distant as Nicholas made his way across the arid interior of Iberia. This was a land of human poverty, of small villages cloistered among barren soil and tenacious brush. A determined ruggedness pervaded all that survived here, and the untamed wildness stirred the blood rage that had been growing within Nicholas. *Owain Evans. Defiler of Clan Gangrel. Reclaim the blood.* This became Nicholas's unspoken mantra. The sentiment, if not the words, measured his every stride. He could feel his claws rending flesh, taste the tang of vitae reclaimed. His thoughts were occupied thus when he crested a bluff and nearly missed the outline of Toledo in the distance.

Nicholas could still feel the energy of the ritual he and Blackfeather had performed. The power of the blood could not be silenced, and it called to the Gangrel across the miles. Somewhere in the city ahead was the violator of the clan, and Nicholas was very close.

CHAPTER EIGHT

Never before had Eleanor set foot in Hannah's private office, and the prince's wife could not help but suspect that the disorder within was a result of the crisis gripping the Kindred world. To many, the disarray might not have been apparent—notes and papers spread across the desk, open books stacked atop one another on every table around the room, several vials scattered about, empty except for the darkened residue of blood—but Eleanor was familiar with the completely fastidious state in which Hannah normally maintained her chantry. The only thing more amazing than the current state of the office was the fact that Eleanor was allowed to see it so. One of the neonates had led her here to wait for Hannah.

After a very few minutes, Hannah walked briskly into the room carrying an armload of aged, leather-bound books, which she almost dropped upon seeing Eleanor waiting for her. *"Eleanor!"* Hannah quickly regained her composure. "What a pleasant surprise." Eleanor suspected more *surprise* than *pleasant*. "Kathleen showed you in?"

"Yes. She was such a dear." How embarrassing, Eleanor knew, to be caught unaware in such a manner. It was not intentional that she had been allowed to view this inner sanctum. Undoubtedly, Kathleen was supposed to seat guests in one of the more comfortable and tidy rooms. Hannah, Eleanor was certain, would not permit such a lapse to go unpunished. "I received your message that you had completed the experiments."

Hannah set down the books she carried on one of the smaller piles of books she could find. "I see," she said. "I did not expect you to stop by so soon."

"This is an important matter," Eleanor explained sweetly.

"I see," said Hannah again. She opened a cabinet behind her desk and removed a pillow covered by a white silk cloth. She placed the pillow on her desk before Eleanor and removed the cloth. Nestled atop the red velvet of the pillow was the sparkling steel and gold of the dagger Pierre had found while following the Gangrel. Pierre having been scared off the job, and the Gangrel not available for questioning, Eleanor had brought the dagger here to the Tremere chantry. If anyone could help, Eleanor reasoned, it would be the Atlanta regent. Even should the task have proven too much for Hannah, then at least Eleanor would have had that to hold over her friend.

"Have you had any luck?" Eleanor innocently inquired.

Hannah's fatigue was readily apparent. She was harried and short-handed. Before the curse, several neonates would have been evident scurrying around the large chantry on Ponce de Leon Avenue. Today, Eleanor had seen only Kathleen briefly, and now all was quiet. Most of Hannah's time, no doubt, was taken investigating the dread curse. She was attempting to satisfy Benison, her prince, as well as her Tremere superiors around the world who were also occupied trying to unscramble the mystery of the curse. On top of all this, Eleanor had asked a personal favor of Hannah: *Examine the dagger. Tell me whatever you can about it.*

Eleanor had been no more specific than that. She realized that it might have been helpful to Hannah to have more information to go on, but the chance that the dagger would prove to be anything meaningful was minuscule. Just because Pierre had followed some strange Gangrel to the burned-down church and found a dagger did not mean that it would prove useful. It was only Eleanor's dream that the dagger was somehow connected to Owain Evans, and she had seen too many dreams left unfulfilled in her time. There was always the possibility that Pierre, trying to retain a scrap of dignity, had been less than forthright in relating how he had come to possess the dagger. With so many possible avenues to failure, Eleanor was not about to reveal her desire to discredit Owain or, more importantly, the reason underlying her quest for justice.

Hannah let the dagger rest on the pillow between them for several moments without comment. With her left hand she rubbed her eyes, then massaged the bridge of her nose. "What I did," she explained at last, "was to trace the auras with which the dagger has been associated. Normally, I should be able to divine information of a general sort about whoever had possessed the object." Hannah looked up to make sure Eleanor understood so far. "The stronger the attachment to the object or the more intense an emotional experience connected to the object, the clearer the picture I am able to envision of the individual involved."

Eleanor nodded. She was hopeful, but at the same time was preparing herself for disappointment.

"The passage of time," Hannah continued, "weakens the links to the object, obscures the associated auras. So except for the most recent or emotionally charged situations, this process often proves fruitless."

Eleanor was still nodding politely. Her patience was waning. She did not need a discourse on the arcane practices of the Tremere. "I understand."

Hannah paused. She stared at the dagger for a long while. Finally, she removed it from the pillow and cradled the blade and hilt gingerly with her fingertips. "In my investigation, I found several auras connected to the dagger." Eleanor edged forward on her seat. "The first, though most recent, was very faint," Hannah said. "I sensed fear, and little else. This individual was definitely Cainite; my guess would be a Toreador, but that is far from certain."

Eleanor nodded knowingly. *Pierre, no doubt.*

"Before that is a stronger aura," said Hannah. "Not necessarily strongly associated with the dagger, but quite bestial, predatory."

That description, Eleanor knew, could fit any of thousands of Kindred, but it certainly was not inconsistent with the story of the Gangrel that Pierre had related. So far, Hannah seemed to be on target with her magical sleuthing, but she had told Eleanor nothing that she didn't already know.

Again Hannah paused. She continued reluctantly. "Before I go on, Eleanor, I feel I must request it be remembered that, though I uncover information that may be displeasing to yourself or to the prince, I am not associated with the information except as messenger. I do not wish to be held responsible for any unfortunate knowledge my investigation might bring to light."

"Yes, yes." Eleanor waved away Hannah's concerns. "Completely understandable. The prince can be rather...abrupt in his judgments at times, but by doing this favor for me, you have earned my support, and I will allow no misdirected criticism to fall upon you." Somewhat reassured, Hannah still hesitated. "Of that," Eleanor added, "I give you my word." Eleanor knew that for Hannah to delay or negotiate further would be tantamount to questioning the word of the former archon of Clan Ventrue, and of the prince's wife.

Hannah, having little other choice, continued. "The third aura I observed was the most intense I have ever seen...."

Eleanor absorbed every word, each nuance and implication of Hannah's description. She allowed the Tremere chantry leader to finish her account uninterrupted, then asked her to repeat it again. Only then, after two tellings, did Eleanor begin to ask questions. She demanded elaboration of one point after another, both of the details Hannah had divined and of her certainty of their accuracy. The two women talked deep into the night, and for the first time since Eleanor last felt Benjamin's gentle touch, her heart warmed with anticipation. She and Benjamin would be together again. She would have her day.

And Owain Evans would have his.

Owain stood motionless in the shadows near the Iglesia de San Nicolas. He was perhaps too near the quarter of the city where El Greco resided, but Owain's prey had led him there, and considering the imposition that El Greco had become, Owain felt little need to go out of his way to protect his former friend. Had it not been for the mysterious mention of Angharad's name, he might never have undertaken this mission, treason or no. But, again, her name *had* surfaced. There was no possible way a mortal woman, over eight hundred years dead, could be connected to the havoc wrought upon the Cainite world. Owain kept telling himself that. Still, he felt there was more at work than coincidence.

From his place of concealment, Owain could see the pottery shop across the street that Miguel had mentioned as a contact point should Owain require assistance. Owain snorted. *Does Miguel really think that I will continue to play his little games?*

Owain's prey had not, in fact, led him to his place. More accurately, Owain was lying in wait. For so many years Owain had shied away from contact with other Cainites, especially his lessers, those of more recent Embrace whose vampiric vitae was diluted by time and distance from the Dark Father. Over the past few nights, Owain had been somewhat surprised at how effortlessly he evaded the young whelps. Three nights running, like the first evening preceding them, he had contacted vampires in the city. He had hidden himself from them each time, and each time he had found them proud and boastful. They were Sabbat. They were followers of Carlos. Not once had Owain come across a Cainite avowing loyalty to El Greco. These young fools did not speak with the caution of interlopers invading a rival's territories, but rather with the swagger of the victorious. *Carlos. This is his city.* Owain had heard variations on this theme with each neonate he taunted, and each time the assertion was made not merely as boast, but as simple statement of fact.

Not once had Owain stumbled across an El Greco loyalist. *Surely El Greco would have mentioned something as vital as having lost control of the city,* Owain imagined. How could someone left in the dark about such facts be expected to complete a mission? Yes, Owain realized, El Greco was arrogant, but he had always been a passable strategist and tactician. There must be some explanation, though Owain had not yet arrived at it. He had stalked different parts of the city, in case various quarters were loyal to opposing masters, but he had found only Carlos's influence, never El Greco's.

Approaching footsteps attracted Owain's attention, footsteps that in all likelihood a mortal would not have heard, but in many ways, Owain was as superior to these foot soldiers of the Sabbat as a vampire was to a mortal.

"*Buenos noches, Señor Brillante.*" *Mr. Shiny.* It was what Owain had taken to calling this balding vampire he had first encountered four nights ago.

Brillante stopped in his tracks, let out the slightest of hisses as he casually scanned his surroundings. He wore all black this night—shirt, tie, leather jacket, pants. Unable to locate Owain, he stretched his neck, rolled his shoulders back. "So you are still here, Señor Morgan." The vitriol of his words betrayed the intent of his disarming smile. "I have heard. You must know that even the streets have ears in Toledo."

"But does Carlos have ears?"

Brillante stiffened slightly. He cocked his head trying once again, Owain knew, to trace the voice from the darkness. "He has ears, *señor*. And he has claws, and he has fangs."

Owain did not respond. He had no desire to reveal prematurely his whereabouts. With each word he spoke, the Sabbat lackey was more likely to pinpoint Owain's position. For all that concealed him were the shadows of the night that he wrapped around himself, and the slight disorientation that he projected into the mind of the younger vampire.

"Come out here!" Brillante snarled, but then his tone immediately softened. "So we can speak. Face to face." Their was no hidden power in the challenge. He remembered how his preternatural command, which would be law to a mortal, was ineffectual before. "Or maybe you are Nosferatu, and you do me a favor by hiding your face."

Strangely enough, Owain found the pure defiance of the Cainite on the street more compelling than any vampiric power. Brillante's complete assurance that he could take any comer, his unwavering self-confidence provoked Owain. For the past few nights, Owain had accosted those who were his lessers from the shadows, and though he was a creature accustomed to years of tedium and plans that unfolded over decades, he found himself short of patience, a fleeting virtue when dealing with his lessers. Impulsively, Owain stepped forward, first one stride then another. Even the movement did not completely undo Owain's power. Not until they were only a few paces separated did Brillante start at Owain's sudden appearance.

"So we can speak," said Owain. "Face to face."

Brillante's surprise quickly receded. Again he smiled. "That is much better. Now we can speak properly." Without warning, he swung claws instantly called into being.

Owain caught the blow inches from his face. He did not release Brillante's wrist but held the clawed hand suspended aloft. "This is how you would speak?" Brillante tried to pull his hand away, but Owain did not let go. Owain could feel strength in this one, but not an unmanageable degree. Staring down his would-be assailant, Owain still made sure to listen for others approaching. The Sabbat typically roamed in packs, and four or five of these whelps would undoubtedly prove a more serious test. "You gave Carlos my message?" Owain asked.

Brillante stopped trying to pull his hand back. "You are nothing to Carlos."

Owain tightened his grip until he knew pain must be shooting up Brillante's arm, but Brillante did not so much as flinch. "You told him," Owain said smugly. "And the others told him as well." He knew baiting these violent Cainites was dangerous, but he also knew they were easily goaded into action. "Tell him again that I would offer him a bargain, and tell him that I would speak of Angharad."

Brillante did not react to the name. It meant nothing to him. Or perhaps he was too intently concentrating on the pain in his wrist, or on his seething hatred for Owain that grew more fierce with each passing second of humiliation. Owain's thumb and razor-sharp nail were digging into Brillante's flesh. Blood began to trickle and then to run down both of their raised arms.

"I will tell him," said Brillante, still defiantly. "I

will tell him, Señor Morgan. Or do you prefer Owain Evans?"

Owain tightened his grip even more, but otherwise hid his surprise.

"You are not the only stranger in town. Someone is asking about you," Brillante said with self-satisfied bite.

"Who?"

Brillante shrugged. "Some Gangrel. Some of *mi hermanos* had been telling me of how they had talked to this invisible Morgan, just like I had, and then this stranger Gangrel with dirt in his hair shows up and wants to know where is Owain Evans."

Owain was trying to remember the Gangrels he knew—there weren't many—and which could have discovered that he was in Toledo.

"You don't have to tell me you are Owain Evans if it makes you feel better to pretend, *Señor Morgan*. I thought it strange that we should have so many visitors in our quiet city. But we get two for the price of one, eh?"

Owain released Brillante's hand and took a step back. "Tell Carlos."

"I will tell him," said Brillante, flexing his injured hand as Owain stepped around the corner of San Nicolas. "And I will tell your Gangrel friend that I talk to you. I do not think he is happy with you."

Once out of sight, Owain made a few quick turns

in case Brillante was following, then climbed to a low rooftop to wait and see. *Someone is looking for me*, Owain thought. *A Gangrel*. He couldn't think offhand of a Gangrel that would want or need to find him. That would bear some looking into. *And so much for keeping secret who I am*. It was not the end of the world that his identity was revealed, but he would have preferred anonymity.

The minutes passed. Owain saw no signs of pursuit. Apparently Brillante did not have the stomach for a chase. Perhaps he was nursing his injured hand. Owain knew his claw had penetrated well into flesh and tendon, probably to the bone. It would have been exceedingly painful. At least he hoped so.

Nen caught himself before he had drawn blood. He stopped scrubbing his hands, gently patted them dry on a clean white towel, and then rubbed in hand cream, making sure to wipe the residue from his wedding band. *I really should get home*, he thought as he glanced at his watch. But he was finally ready to begin his report, and Leigh would understand.

Another body had arrived, this time from the medical examiner in Chicago. Again, fresh blood but tissue samples that indicated the subject had been dead for weeks. Nen had seen enough in the past weeks to feel confident that this was not localized cult activity. No one was dumping blood on these bodies. In every case, the internal organs and many of the muscles were atrophied, but the blood was only hours old. Add to that the repeated presence of multiple blood types within a single body.

For weeks, Nen had worked on little else. He had double-checked lab findings, researched case histories, visited sites where bodies had been found. He had ignored his supervisor Dr. Blake's advice to drop the case and had even gone as far as to enlist the aid of his pathologist friend Martin Raimes. Now Nen held the report that Raimes had sent after examining the blood samples Nen had provided from cases JKL14337 and JKL14338. For probably the twentieth time, Nen thumbed through the summary.

He wasn't sure why Dr. Blake was so opposed to this research. The situation appeared quite serious to Nen. Even at the start, before his investigation had heightened his alarm, he had felt that merely the *possibility* of the presence of some strange new contagion was reason enough for the Centers for Disease Control and Prevention to direct some attention toward the enigmatic cases that were popping up.

The disturbing deaths were still occurring, and at an increased rate, or perhaps Nen merely knew what he was looking for now. By actively searching recent autopsy reports, he had noted another disturbing trend as well: Even in cases where the strange blood mixture and tissue decay anomaly were absent, there were increases in deaths from unexplained massive hemorrhaging. *Very much as if there were a contagious hemorrhagic fever on the loose*, Nen surmised, and that was the missing piece of the puzzle that Martin Raimes's data had provided. *Maureen Blake or no*, Nen decided, *this needs to be pushed forward, and if she can't see that, then I'll have to go over her head.*

Nen pulled up the computer file he had been working on and began to type. He had no way of knowing that eyes were watching him, that a figure clung to the wall just outside his window and took in every word that he wrote.

Owain did not leave early from the house where he was staying. He did not want to fall into too predictable a pattern. Certainly Brillante and some of his ilk were growing tired of an unwanted stranger in their midst, and now that Owain had revealed himself, he would have to be even more careful on the streets lest he be recognized.

Not once had Owain, in his contacts, come across a follower of El Greco. That was befuddling. None of the Sabbat that Owain had antagonized had even mentioned El Greco. Not only had none of them accused Owain of being in league with their rival, they seemed oblivious to the very existence of any rival, as if El Greco were not even a factor in the equation. Owain could not make sense of it.

Perhaps it is the curse, Owain wondered. *Perhaps more of El Greco's followers have been claimed, or it could be that he has ordered them off the streets*. There were many possibilities, but none sounded plausible to Owain. He glanced at the clock on the bookshelf. In a few moments he would leave to meet Kendall. Perhaps she could provide him with information of value.

Owain paced restlessly around the tiny house that El Greco had provided for him. This restlessness, the sense of directionless agitation, had been growing in him lately. For decades in Atlanta, he had been numb to the passage of time, whiling away years as if they were mere minutes to be squandered, but now a delay of only a quarter hour drove him nearly to distraction. So much had changed since the siren had entered and then been torn from his life. Or was it the visions that had changed him? Or the curse? There was no way to tell.

The furnishings and decor of the house did little to soothe Owain. They were similar to what he had found at El Greco's—vaguely impersonal, chosen for no one in particular, and for no other reason than to be inconspicuous. As inconspicuous, perhaps, as El Greco had become in this city where he used to rule. As he paced through the kitchen, Owain knocked over a chair, deliberately left it on the floor. At least it was a sign that someone, anyone, an actual person, inhabited this space.

The time was at hand. Owain left the house and made his way north-northeast, keeping to the shadows that welcomed him. The streets were so quiet. Aside from the nearby tourists at the plaza and the occasional pedestrian or motorist, no one was about, a circumstance that would have made Owain easy to spot had he not taken precautions. He kept away from the broad thoroughfares—broad only in comparison to the other streets—favoring instead the dimly lit, narrow passages between the austere building faces. Owain remembered from earlier years the feeling that there was more going on than one could hope to see; that, behind the nondescript facades, plots were being formed, taking shape. If anything, he was more sensitive to that mood now. Back then, he had been brash, confident, too sure that he was destiny's hand, that he was the author deciding the plot.

Now, he wasn't so sure. In recent years, he had wanted mostly to be left alone. He had strayed from his relative seclusion to savor a few inspired memories of a better time, a time that, if not placid or tranquil or even happy, had at least known him to feel, to have the capacity for emotion, to *live*. But the song that had brought those memories was stolen from him. He had wanted only to listen, but the curse had pushed Benison over that edge to which, Malkavian that he was, he had always walked so closely. And now Owain had been brought back to Spain by a friend turned tyrant, set upon some death-wish mission, lured along by the name of his long-dead beloved. Looking up at the triple-crowned spire of the cathedral of Toledo, Owain knew afresh that a spiteful God looked down upon him and laughed. *It wasn't enough to take her from me in the first place*, he turned his face to the darkened heavens, *to drive me from the land I loved as well. They were all I cared for, and you left me neither. And now you taunt me with her.* Owain had often wished that, when final death did some day take him, that he might at least glimpse paradise—even from a distance, for surely the streets of gold would be denied him—only so he could spit in the direction of the Almighty. Perhaps he would be lucky, and his saliva would go as far as to moisten the hem of St. Peter's garment, but Owain would not hold out for such phenomenal success.

As he approached the   he saw Kendall standing alert in a recess of the gate, her dark hair and clothing rendering her virtually invisible to lesser eyes. Owain checked carefully to make sure he was not being followed, then crossed the final yards to her.

"What have you learned?" he asked without preamble. Owain knew his ghoul better than to think she had been idle these past days, but also he sought unfiltered information, so he did not prejudice her view of what was important by directing her report. There would be time enough for specific questions shortly.

"I have not seen El Greco since the night he first appeared," Kendall began. "He could have been coming and going without my knowing," she grimaced briefly, probably remembering how the elder vampire had caught her unaware that night, "but I have not seen him again."

Owain did not stop her, so she continued. "Our friend Miguel, on the other hand, has still been stopping by regularly, once in the early evening, once in the morning, sometimes with his ghoul driver, sometimes without."

"Whom does he speak with? What does he do?" asked Owain.

"He ignores me, or tries to."

That sounded likely to Owain. Miguel had been less than pleased at Owain's insistence that Kendall remain at the house, but there had been more urgent arrangements to attend to, and Owain had persevered on that point.

"Mostly he bosses Maria and Ferdinand around,"

Kendall elaborated. "They would both be glad to be rid of him, not that they would ever say as much. Otherwise, there's only been one visitor, a Cainite, Javier. From the sounds of it, he might be Miguel's childe. I tried to listen in, but Miguel is careful. All I heard was something about a Gangrel."

I will tell your Gangrel friend that I talk to you. I do not think he is happy with you. Owain remembered Brillante's words from the previous night. Whoever this Gangrel was, he was interfering with Owain's plans. He had already given away Owain's identity. Who knew how he might further jeopardize the situation? "Anything else?" Owain asked.

Kendall shook her head. "No. That was all I heard, and nothing else has happened."

"Does anything strike you as particularly strange about this city?" Owain pressed.

"Too damned quiet." Kendall thought for a moment. "I mean, for Sabbat territory, I'd have thought there'd be more activity. New York, Miami—there's chaos; the Sabbat packs run wild. As far as the mortals can tell, the social fabric is unraveling. Here..." Kendall gestured to their surroundings, "nothing."

Owain smiled. "Your New World is a brash, young thing, Ms. Jackson, as are the Sabbat there. In this part of the world, our kind are more staid. There is the lingering memory here of the Inquisition, of mortals rising up in fear and anger." Owain tried not to think of his own first ghoul and companion, Gwilym, who had survived so long only to fall to the Inquisition in this very city. "But do not mistake caution for inactivity. Toledo has changed hands many times over the centuries. Today's lord is tomorrow's pariah. It is safer to keep one's allegiances to oneself. Do not allow yourself to be lulled to sleep by guarded ways."

Kendall absorbed Owain's words. She was a quick study, Owain had noticed. *Perhaps worthy of the Embrace.* She would be even more useful entrusted with more power. But could Owain subject another to that curse? In all his years, he had propagated numerous ghouls, but never had he created progeny.

"Have you seen or heard of any other followers of El Greco?" Owain asked.

Kendall thought for a moment. "Just Miguel and the driver, Maria and Ferdinand, and now Javier. No others."

"I see." Kendall stood quietly waiting for any other questions while Owain pondered what she had said and what he had seen. "I have encountered no one else loyal to El Greco. I do not know if they have been destroyed, or are in hiding, or simply do not exist, but every Cainite I have spoken with has been in Carlos's camp." El Greco had volunteered no help in sending Owain on this task; perhaps the old Toreador had none to offer. "Keep listening. There must be other Cainites than Carlos's. We may need to call on them, if we can find them."

They may want to be rid of El Greco as much as I, Owain thought, *if they exist.* More and more, he was beginning to flirt with the idea of eliminating El Greco, of having done with his secret connection to the Sabbat and returning to his unlife in Atlanta. Why, Owain wondered, was he holding to those old, tired oaths? If there were no others over whom El Greco held sway, it might be conceivable for Owain to challenge him.

But that would not answer Owain's questions about Angharad, about how her name came to be involved with the blood curse. So there was still reason to proceed with his plan. And there were other immediate considerations.

"How long since you have fed?" Owain asked.

"Quite some time." Kendall did not seem desperate. Owain suspected she would die stoically should her master decide to end her service. She was not the type to make demands, to mistake her ghoul status as a right rather than a privilege.

Privilege or curse? Owain was not certain. In many ways, the existence of a ghoul was more subtle, more insidious than that of a vampire, and more tenuous. For now, though, he needed her service, and with a flick of his wrist, the stiletto from his forearm sheath was in his hand. Owain drew the blade quickly across his palm. He offered his hand to Kendall as the blood welled up, and she drank.

She did not take much, but Owain could feel his power flowing into her, could sense her muscles and flesh invigorated, strengthened. For some, this sharing could carry emotional entanglements. It had not been so for Owain for many centuries, and never had he been able to decide whether this loss was a relief or a burden. As Kendall drank, he watched her lips against his skin, felt her tongue caressing his wound. With time, could she come to mean more to him than any of the string of servants who had come and gone over the years, now that the siren had reawakened certain impulses, certain capacities for feeling within him? As Kendall drew away from his hand, Owain pushed away such thoughts. As ever, time would be the final arbiter.

The shadow of Time is not so long that you might shelter beneath it.

The words from his vision came unbidden to Owain. Those, too, he pushed away. He would not afford them reality by devoting thought to them. Not now.

Without another word, Owain left his servant.

He couldn't allow himself the luxury of introspection. He had lost too many years already in brooding and grieving, and now the pendulum had swung back. The time to act was at hand. He had yet to contact Carlos, and the added complication had arisen of a Gangrel searching for Owain. That, he decided, would be the first order of business. There were some Gangrel who were at home in cities, but they were few and far between. Most members of that clan preferred to roam the wilds, and ventured into urban areas only out of necessity, perhaps to evade hostile lupines.

Owain began his search along the northern edge of the city. He made his way to the Puente de Alcantara then circled back west, keeping to the shadows. It was not so late that the streets were deserted, but this portion of the city was quiet. The earthen brick structures held their secrets as silently as ever. There were not a multitude of kine about, nor of Cainites. By the time Owain wound his way to the familiar Puerta del Cambron, he had seen two vampires searching the streets, for food or perhaps for Owain himself. The first was Sabbat; Owain had met her a few nights before and had given her his message to relay to Carlos. The second was a stranger but not Gangrel. Owain avoided both. The Sabbat, if not Carlos himself, would be easy enough to find, Owain hoped, after he had found and dealt with this Gangrel.

Owain followed the old city walls around to the Puente de San Martin. Looking across the bridge to the countryside beyond, he was struck by the peacefulness of the land, at the same time both comforting and desolate, lacking the trappings of civilization, the secrets, the intrigue. Forcing himself to keep moving, he turned eastward again. Even with a systematic sweep, this blind search of the city, Owain knew, could take several nights, and even if he covered every inch of Toledo, he could not expect necessarily to be in the right place at the right time to come across the Gangrel interloper. Owain was considering the risky option of continuing with his attempts to contact Carlos and ignoring the Gangrel, or of letting the Gangrel find him, when he was overcome by an unusual urge.

Without intending to, he had veered to the south, and with each step he was drawn more inexorably forward. He quickened his pace; he was moving rapidly now but still concealing himself from any casual observers. There was something important ahead. He didn't know what it was, and he didn't know what drove him, but there was *something* ahead. He was sure of it.

Owain rounded a corner and froze. Movement caught his eye as he entered a long, open plaza. At the far end of the square was a person, a mortal, an *agente de policía*, by his uniform. The police officer strolled along past the storefronts, checking to make sure the doors were locked, shining his flashlight down the alleys between buildings. Watching the officer, Owain began to question the impulse that had led him here. But then movement from a different direction attracted his attention.

Several dozen yards behind the police officer, another figure crept forward. Crouched low, stealthily moving only a step or two at a time, the hunter possessed the shape of a human, but its movements were more instinctive, sprung from the low cunning of a predatory animal. Now that Owain had spotted it, he could make out the long, untamed hair, the ragged clothes, and the more he observed, the more the wolfish mannerisms called out to him, *Gangrel*.

The Gangrel was closing the distance to the oblivious policeman with deceptive speed. Owain realized that, in the wilds, he probably never would have seen the hunter until it had pounced upon its prey, but here in the city the Gangrel made the same mistake that many Cainites did, growing so intent on its hunt that it did not maintain complete awareness of its own surroundings and the approach of other predators.

Owain could have waited for the Gangrel to strike, but he decided instantly to do otherwise. "You!" he called out across the plaza. His voice echoed against the cold stone, took on a larger, more ominous sound.

The policeman jumped, his hand moving to his holstered sidearm. Owain was gratified to see the Gangrel start as well, but still the officer was not aware of the nearby danger. Owain began across the plaza, each deliberate step punctuated by the staccato click of his heel against the cobbles. For the moment he ignored the Gangrel, other than to remain aware of its location. Halfway across the plaza to the policeman, Owain stopped. He glared until he could feel that his ever-black eyes had captured the policeman's gaze. Owain pointed eastward, away from the plaza. "Go."

The officer's hand dropped away from his holster. He straightened and walked quickly out of the plaza.

Owain turned to the Gangrel. "I hope you weren't too hungry. We need to talk."

The Gangrel, not having moved appreciably since Owain had first spoken, now came forward, slowly. A low growl rumbled in the back of its throat. Owain held his ground and tried to place the vaguely familiar Gangrel, now within leaping distance. *I have seen him before*, Owain realized. *But where? And when?*

The Gangrel came even closer, the growling more noticeable.

Owain was quite aware that he was placing himself in harm's way, but he knew he had met the Gangrel before. *Not since I left Atlanta…* And then it came to Owain.

"The courier." The Gangrel had brought the most recent chess move. He was the strange fellow who had broken into something of a fit of hysteria in the study. "I don't remember your name," Owain offered almost apologetically. He was not taking for granted that this would be a violent confrontation.

"You never asked my name," the Gangrel snarled. He was only feet from Owain now, poised to strike. "Just like you never asked my great-great-grandsire's name."

This sounded very like an accusation of some sort to Owain, but of exactly what, he was uncertain. There were countless sins of which he could be rightly accused. "I am asking."

The Gangrel was both perfectly still and balanced to spring. It flexed its claws. "My name is Nicholas." An animal glint shone in his eyes. "My great-great-grandsire was Blaidd."

Blaidd. Wolf. The sound of his native Welsh instantly took Owain back hundreds of years, back to the days before he had ghouled his nephew Morgan. Owain had just returned from England, forty years after his Embrace, his heart filled with black hate, his head full of grandiose plans, some of which had taken shape.

Blaidd. Wolf.

Nicholas lunged. Owain snapped back to the present just quickly enough to dodge out of the way. Nicholas's claws sliced through the air where a moment before Owain's throat had been.

Owain landed hard but rolled and was on his feet

within seconds. Only the reflexes of a Cainite of his seasoned age saved him. Nicholas, too, recovered quickly. He feinted, then sprang again.

Even Owain's speed couldn't spare him the full force of Nicholas's fury. Owain sidestepped and blocked the Gangrel, but Nicholas's claws dug through Owain's coat and into his forearm. and scraped bone. Owain stumbled backward, the pain jolting through his entire body. He could not keep himself from crying out.

Nicholas paused in his attack, lifted his hand to his face. He sniffed his claws then licked a bit of the fragrant vitae. A mixed sigh and snarl escaped his lips, and as Owain watched, the Gangrel's eyes glazed over. He still looked at Owain, but distantly, as if through a haze. When he spoke, the words were deep and throaty, noticeably different from how Nicholas had spoken before. *"Trespasser. Defiler. Murderer."*

As Owain clutched his left arm, he saw the eyes of the staked Gangrel that he had stood above so many years before. He saw the hatred, the penned rage. Owain shook his head violently. He didn't have time for these memories that were forcing themselves upon him. *The pain. Cling to the pain*, he told himself. It would keep him in the here and now. He flicked his right wrist and held in his hand the stiletto that earlier had drawn his own blood. No more would he be a target for this raging

Gangrel; he would carve him and leave the pieces to feed the night's rats.

Nicholas charged again. Eschewing subtler tactics, he dove low and was met by Owain's blade. It dug deeply into the Gangrel's shoulder. Nicholas tried to knock the legs from beneath his prey, to bring him to the ground, but Owain was too quick. He jumped clear, jerking his stiletto upward and to the side, slicing muscle and tendon and opening a deep, jagged gash.

The blood of Gangrel and Ventrue mingled as it splattered on the ground, slickening the uneven cobbles. Nicholas flexed his arm and hand, determining how much damage had been done. He felt the wound, Owain was sure, but was nowhere near debilitated. Owain wished for his sword.

Before Nicholas could attack again, gunfire rang out in the plaza. Owain's head whipped to the side, and the next he knew he was sprawled on the ground. All he could feel was the throbbing in his head. He had fallen and hit his head. Slipped on the blood. No. More than that. He was shot. Owain reached up and felt the bloody mess of scalp and bits of skull at his temple. More blood. He smelled it, tasted it.

He felt faint, weak, and for the first time in ages, hungry. Owain rolled to his side and began licking his own blood from the cobbles. His vision danced; his hair fell across his face, grew thick with blood from the open wound and from the ground.

The Gangrel. Owain had forgotten about him. Where had he gotten a gun? No, it wasn't the Gangrel that had fired. Owain's thoughts were jumbled. He had been shot in the head. He was losing a great deal of blood…so quickly.

More gunshots. They sounded so far away. Still, Owain knew he should take cover. He wanted to move, but his body would not obey him. He was lying now in a deepening pool of blood. His own blood.

Suddenly he was moving but not of his own volition. Hands were lifting him, none too gently. And then a muffled but familiar voice: "This is him. This is Señor Morgan, or Owain Evans, or whoever he is."

Owain wasn't sure if his eyes were closed or covered with blood. He thought he could make out shapes, but perhaps they were just the stones of the plaza beneath him. He raised his head, or maybe someone was lifting it by the hair. For a moment he saw a figure standing above him, a hard face full of metal studs. Glaring down, leaning closer. But Owain's vision was failing him. A sickening grayness was falling around him, taking him in. *Carlos*, he thought. *I have found him. Carlos. This is his city.* And then the gray turned to black.

CHAPTER NINE

The first gunshot struck Owain Evans in the head and slammed him to the ground. Blaidd, bleeding from his wounded shoulder, stood over his downed prey, but the gunshot itself was a befuddling incongruity. The plaza was spinning, the cobbles shifting and flowing together, forming the inner wall of a cave, then the face of a sea-swept cliff. But this was neither the land nor the age of Blaidd, and the stones would not conform to his memories. Back into the mists of time he was reined; he retreated, leaving only Nicholas, disoriented, standing over his downed prey.

Confused or not, bullets Nicholas understood, and several were flying toward him. He dropped sideways to a crouch, no time for the pain and distraction of his shoulder. His arm was still functional. That was the immediate concern. He launched himself toward the edge of the plaza, toward the cover of buildings, instinctively changing directions every two or three steps. Bullets ricocheted off stone around him.

Closer to the buildings bordering the plaza, Nicholas leapt. He latched onto the side of a wall. The sun-dried bricks crumbled beneath the force of his claws, but he dug in more deeply and scrambled up to the roof.

Two armed Cainites awaited him. They fired their pistols, but Nicholas had already sprung high into the air. He landed on the vampire to the right, knocking him to the rooftop and slashing into his neck and face. The upended vampire's gun clattered over the edge of the building.

The second Cainite recovered his wits quickly and fired several shots at Nicholas who, having lost only half a step in his attack, was bounding off the building. One slug caught him in the back of the same shoulder that Owain had slashed. The force of the shot knocked Nicholas off balance. He crashed to the ground below.

Other Sabbat were closing in from the direction of the plaza, but they miscalculated how quickly Nicholas would be back on his feet after such a fall. Before any of them had fired a shot, Nicholas was sprinting down the street. He ducked down a narrow avenue to the right and kept making turn after turn, racing along the winding streets, the names of which meant nothing to him.

At first, there were shouts and a few more shots behind him, but these sounds quickly died away as Nicholas's speed carried him beyond their reach. When he no longer heard pursuit, he stopped only briefly. With a towel snatched from a clothesline, he tried to stanch the flow of blood that might give away his route. For who could track a trail of blood if not a vampire?

After a very few minutes, he was on the move again. He moved more cautiously now, confident that he had lost the Sabbat and not wanting inadvertently to rush headlong into them again. As he ran, Nicholas cursed the Sabbat who had cost him his kill. For several nights, he had searched for Evans, had asked those Cainites he had seen. The Sabbat did not automatically assume that a Gangrel was an enemy, Nicholas knew, because members of the wandering clan would come and go frequently and seldom become connected to larger political matters. So most of those Sabbat he had encountered had spoken with him, and they had turned out to be of little help.

But apparently Nicholas had been of help to them. They had followed him, *tracked him*, a great embarrassment for a Gangrel, though not inconceivable in the city. Nicholas had been preoccupied by his task, and by his visions—by the ancestors who, more and more, wanted exposure to the modern world. Ragnar and Blaidd were close to the surface now, and oftentimes Nicholas could not keep them down. Sometimes he did not try.

The bullet in his shoulder and the gash from the knife began to throb more forcefully. Though painful, they were not fatal wounds, Nicholas knew. The prospect of infection meant little to a vampire. With blood they would heal.

He had come very close. But he had not crossed the Atlantic to come close. Perhaps if the old debt of blood were repaid, the ancestors would again sleep. This was Nicholas's hope; it was what he chose to believe, no matter what Blackfeather said about the rising beast.

Nicholas was still very close. And next time he would strike true.

☥

"So it is as I suspected. Gustav." Wilhelm rubbed his face gingerly in the darkness. His eyes were still particularly tender. Nearly two weeks later, not all the scars from the mob attack had healed completely. The Molotov cocktail had badly burned Wilhelm. He had found himself blinded, his eyelids melted shut, flames searing the flesh all over his body. Were it not for Henriette's determination and an inordinate amount of luck, he would have met his final death there on the street.

The initial blast of the homemade explosive had also killed or dislodged many of Wilhelm's attackers. Henriette had pulled him, still burning, from the carnage, and somehow to safety. That she had been able to get him away unseen was nothing if not miraculous. Also fortunate was the fact that pursuit had never developed, for the blind prince and his injured childe would have been easy marks. The chaos of the rioting mob that was to have been his destruction had made possible his escape.

Closing his eyes, Wilhelm could still feel the blows as Henriette beat out the flames that burned him like the fire of the sun itself. He could hear her whispering gentle warnings in his ear: *Hush now. Quiet, my dear.*

"Gustav." Wilhelm spoke the name again, savoring the hatred it evoked.

Ellison stood silently, listening, watching—ever the charge of a Nosferatu. In the shadows of the park where Ellison had asked to meet, Wilhelm could almost ignore the blue-tinted, warted skin of his informant, the mangled ears, the deformed arm, the pained way in which Ellison held himself. Almost. But what did Ellison's freakish countenance matter? For years he had provided Wilhelm with accurate intelligence that had helped him stay a step or two ahead of his rival.

There was very little that happened in Berlin that remained unknown to Ellison for long. Besides, since the attack, Wilhelm's own visage was marred and disfigured.

"So Dieter Kotlar and the Final Reich were the foot soldiers," Wilhelm pieced together the information that Ellison had related, "but Gustav was the general giving the orders." Wilhelm was not surprised. "Do you have proof of this?" he asked.

Ellison took an almost imperceptible step back from Wilhelm. "I deal in information," said the Nosferatu in a near-whisper. "Not in proof."

Wilhelm knew this to be the case. He did not need proof to believe this news. It fit too perfectly, and Ellison had never before delivered questionable information. Wilhelm believed all too well that Gustav had orchestrated the mob rampage, but aside from personal vengeance, Wilhelm was attempting to construct a case against Gustav should the Camarilla powers-that-be decide that arbitration was required to preserve the Masquerade. They would want proof. Although if Karl Schrekt, the Tremere justicar with whom Gustav had had such acrimonious dealings in the past, sat in judgment, he would be certain to rule against the eastern prince. Ruling against Gustav, however, would not necessarily mean ruling for Wilhelm. Much better for Wilhelm to take care of this problem on his own, once and for all.

"I provide information," Ellison added, his voice barely audible. "What credence you place in it is completely up to you."

"You have always proven yourself reliable," Wilhelm assured the Nosferatu. It was not the prince's intent to affront this, his most valuable of allies. "I am in your debt."

It may merely have been a trick of the shadows, but Wilhelm thought he saw the faintest of smiles flutter across Ellison's grotesque features. *Of course I'm in his debt*, thought the prince. *He remembers every favor, every service, each and every scrap of knowledge he's ever conveyed to me*. Nothing, Wilhelm knew, was free, and Ellison was not shy about asking for favors in return when he needed. *And he always makes sure the balance of debts is in his favor. Always.*

"I am always pleased to serve the prince," Ellison whispered, and then he was gone.

The lethargy clung to Owain as his eyes fluttered open. Lethargy brought on by weakness of body, not the even more debilitating weakness of spirit that had once led him into torpor for over two centuries. Only slowly as the fog receded did he become aware of his surroundings. He was beneath blankets on a large four-poster bed, veils draped all around, and next to him lay an unconscious man, naked above the waist, young, perhaps twenty—very close, Owain realized, to the age that he himself appeared to be. The young man's skin was dark and smooth. The sound of blood pulsating through his veins was torturous to Owain. It was rare for Owain to thirst, to desire blood. He'd assumed it was another passion that had dulled over the centuries, a pleasure that had lost out to encroaching ennui. But Owain remembered his blood thick upon the plaza, and he felt the weakness of his undead body. To heal, he needed blood, so from an ingrained sense of self-preservation more than any thrill, he turned to the body next to him.

Owain reached over and touched the man's carotid artery. The flowing vitae just beneath the surface caressed his fingertips. Tilting the man's head, Owain drank. He was prepared for the wracking headaches and nausea that assaulted him on the rare occasion he fed from those of less than noble birth. Every member of his clan held to similar proclivities of one type or another. It was a sign, Owain believed, of the inherent Ventrue sense of order and form, and was only one indication of why his clan was most suited to guide the destiny of the Cainite race. To Owain's surprise, the vitae of this dark Spaniard flowed smooth and true. Owain drank deeply and could feel as his undead body began to repair itself. The gash on his forearm would require time to mend. There was a certain destructive quality to the claws of a Cainite that produced a wound of a more lingering nature, even for another vampire. The gunshot to Owain's head, however, though more potentially dangerous, began to heal. Skull, veins, skin, all began to knit together.

Owain continued to feed, and the blood that was his curse also gave him life. As his rejuvenation progressed, he felt just how close to final death he had come. A gunshot to the head, from closer range or in a slightly different location, could quite definitely terminate the existence of a vampire. Owain wished for a return to the nights when a blade was the weapon of choice for noble or for low-born. A confrontation between men or Cainites was more complete when they stood face to face. No strength of character was required to shoot from a distance, but to face an opponent over crossed steel—that was how men should settle differences.

Strangely enough, even as Owain fed, his thoughts remained fairly rational. He followed the recovery of his body with interest, tracking to what degree the gaping head wound had closed, noting the fatigue which would recede only with much more blood than this one mortal could provide. Owain could remember the frenzied passion of his feeding as a more youthful Cainite. In those days, the kiss was overwhelming, providing a glorious rapture that more than compensated for the vampiric lack of interest in other mortal niceties such as sex or gluttony. But now he fed dispassionately, drinking only because he knew he must. Where were the pleasures, even the shallow titillations, of this extended unlife to be found? Why, he wondered, did he bother to refurbish his damaged body?

Angharad. Only his feelings for her had truly survived the test of time, though even they had resurfaced only haltingly over the past millennium. Her name had somehow been dragged into this affair, and Owain had long ago ceased to believe in coincidence. With a spiteful God hell-bent on torturing him throughout eternity, nothing fell to chance.

"Not too much," said a voice from beyond the veil.

Owain withdrew his fangs from his provided meal. Already he felt much improved, but it would be some time and several feedings before his strength returned in earnest, as much blood as he had lost. His immediate needs satisfied, Owain peered through the bedcurtain but could make out only the general shape of the person who had addressed him. Pulling back the drapery, Owain rose to sit naked on the edge of the bed.

Before him stood Carlos, his dark hair severely short, his square jaw jutted forward, his ears, nose, and eyebrows adorned with at least a dozen rings and studs. He indicated the sleeping man. "He's the son of one of the first families of Toledo. Drugs, prostitutes," Carlos shook his head disapprovingly. "It's a sad story. They don't care for him and wouldn't be that upset if he turned up dead, but he's worth more to me alive."

Owain glanced back at the vessel he had very nearly drained of blood.

"I assumed you to be Ventrue," said Carlos. "All my people reported that you were arrogant beyond belief, so what else could I think?" He shrugged. "You were mumbling about nobility when I asked about feeding, so I took a chance."

On a chair by the bed were fresh clothes—a crisp white shirt, black pants, Owain's own shoes, cleaned and shined. Gone were his coat and other bloodstained clothes. Also noticeably absent were his stiletto and sheath. While Owain dressed, he was struck by the familiarity of the room. The roughly hewn stone of the walls and the high ceilings were unmistakably distinctive. These were the chambers beneath the Alcazar that El Greco had occupied when last Owain had been in Toledo. El Greco had demanded that the stonemason ghouls he employed raise the ceilings to fifteen feet, an exorbitant height considering the labor involved. The small team of five masons worked diligently for just over three and a half years to create each room to the exacting specifications of El Greco, a

290   **Gherbod Fleming**

taskmaster as demanding as he was unforgiving. He'd displayed artwork of his choosing, large paintings of his own and of various mortals who had fallen under his influence over the years. The texture of the walls and ceilings, the refraction of light from the surfaces, had to meet El Greco's wishes exactly. No matter what political instability or deadly conflict had raged in the Cainite world, El Greco had overseen the transformation of these rooms into a shrine to the finer pursuits.

No artwork marked the walls now. The cold, empty stone stared back at Owain. El Greco's signature was as completely absent from this, his former palace, as from the small, anonymous building in which he now resided. The cavernous room was too large for the bed and two chairs which were its only furnishings. Carlos sat in the second chair and watched silently as Owain finished dressing and then brought his chair near the Sabbat bishop and sat.

Carlos's appearance was that of a street punk. When he spoke, he revealed a metal stud through his tongue. He looked to be of the same mold as Brillante and the other Sabbat that Owain had contacted. Carlos's mannerisms and speech, however, were more refined, almost aristocratic. From his accent, Owain guessed that Spanish was his native tongue, but his English was flawless as well. He appeared to be in his late thirties or early forties, but this, as Owain could attest, meant very little.

"I hear that you have come to Toledo to offer me a bargain?" said Carlos.

Owain did not respond at once. "You are difficult to find."

"I am pleased to hear that." Carlos waited patiently. He had asked a question and expected an answer.

"Your friends are not particularly hospitable," said Owain after a moment.

"Santiago?" Carlos made a pistol shape with his fingers and bent his thumb for the hammer coming down. "He is what you would call quick on the draw."

"Santiago." Owain rubbed his forehead to indicate the ill-tempered, balding Cainite. "Brillante."

Carlos smiled. "*Brillante*. You called him that? That would explain why he shot you. Or maybe it was a lesser reason." Carlos waved dismissively. "At any rate, he is not my friend. He is an associate. And you are here. You wanted to see me." He laid his hands open before him as if to say, *You see me*.

"I do have an offer to make you," Owain began. He'd planned this conversation in his mind dozens of times, but still he went slowly. He was venturing far into unknown territory, making assumptions from the portion of the letter he had read at El Greco's. Assumptions that, if incorrect, could well lead to his destruction. *Angharad*. It all came back to her, and this was the only way Owain would find out how. If he stepped carefully. If he survived. "I know about Angharad," he lied.

Carlos did not respond to the mention of the name. He was not about to give anything away. Could it be coincidence, Owain wondered, that after four fruitless nights of accosting Sabbat vampires on the street, the night after he had mentioned Angharad he was face to face with Carlos himself?

"I know about the blood curse," said Owain. "I know how it began. I know how it spread."

Carlos nodded thoughtfully. "Very interesting. Tell me what you mean."

Just as Carlos was being careful not to give away the truth, Owain had to be certain not to give away what was fabrication. He had to conceal the fact that everything he said was pure conjecture, for if the mysterious letter was inaccurate, revealing details would only advertise his duplicity. But at the same time, if he did not reveal enough to convince Carlos, Owain would end up just as dead. He would have to gamble on certain facts. "Does the name Grimsdale mean anything to you?"

Carlos said nothing, did not so much as move a single muscle.

"He came to the United States, to Atlanta." Owain knew he was pushing his luck but felt that he had little choice. "He brought the tainted blood to sell to the highest bidder, but he never had a chance to sell, did he?"

Carlos leaned forward in his chair. "I find your story fascinating. Please tell me more, Señor Owain Evans of Atlanta," he said, reminding Owain that he was no longer shielded by anonymity, that he had nowhere safe to run where the Sabbat would not be able to find him.

Owain could sense the trap that Carlos was attempting to lay. He wanted nothing more than for Owain to give himself away, and when that happened, despite his refined manners, Carlos would take great pleasure in rewarding Owain for his impertinence. "Why should I waste our time telling you what you already know?" Owain postured. "You never recovered the blood, and Grimsdale managed to set the curse loose. To devastating effect, I must add. You must be proud." Owain stopped. He needed some sort of reaction from Carlos, some indication of whether the truth lay in this direction.

"And what does this Grimsdale have to do with me?" Carlos prompted.

"He took the blood from laboratories under your control, probably without your permission. But that matters little, no? I wouldn't want to be the vampire responsible for destroying practically all of my Sabbat brethren. Wouldn't engender enormous goodwill."

Carlos sat back, crossed his legs. His face betrayed nothing. "This story of yours—if there were any truth to it—it does not cast me in a very favorable light. Who did you hear these things from?"

Owain smiled incredulously. "You don't expect me to *tell* you that."

"These are serious allegations you make," Carlos explained. "Should I not know those who attempt to sully my good name?"

"I imagine you would merely ask them to stop spreading such rumors?" Owain shook his head. "I can no more tell you their names than I can tell you the names of the people *I* have told this 'story,' as you call it. For then I would not be safe, and it would do me no good to tell you that I have instructed at least a half-dozen of my *associates* to make 'this story' known, should I fail to return from Spain."

Carlos sat back in his chair. He stared unblinking at Owain. The nearby bed and the unconscious mortal in it might well not have existed for all the notice the bishop gave them. The creak of the chair as he shifted his weight was the only sound to be heard. Something in his expression had changed; he looked at Owain in a different way, with a mixture of respect and ire, Owain guessed. "You have yet to make me an offer," Carlos pointed out. "But let me warn you that I would rather have my reputation marred by baseless allegations than submit to blackmail."

"Baseless?" It would be dangerous, Owain knew, to antagonize Carlos further. He should reach some accommodation with the Sabbat bishop, an agreement that would allow Owain the opportunity to spy around this underground cluster of corridors and chambers that, once, Owain had known very well. That would be his best chance to learn the whereabouts of the laboratory. It might be here beneath the Alcazar. More likely, it was hidden somewhere in Madrid. Then, if he found the laboratory where the blood had been magically altered, he could obtain the proof that El Greco desired.

That was what Owain knew he should do.

But Carlos's thinly veiled threat did not sit well with Owain. He considered it a challenge; he resented the fact that this probably younger Cainite would dare lord his position as one of the most preeminent officials of the European Sabbat over Owain. First Benison, then El Greco, and now Carlos was attempting to exercise control over Owain. He had taken as much of that as he could stand, so Owain raised the stakes of his bluff.

"Baseless allegations?" he repeated. "Do you think me such a fool as to come here with nothing more than unfounded rumors?" Owain stood. He stepped around behind his chair and spoke down to Carlos. "Grimsdale may have loosed the curse before his demise, but he did not dispose of *all* of the tainted blood. I have acquired a portion of the blood and, no, I will not reveal how I came by it. But this does bring me to the heart of my offer." Carlos sat, his expression again blank. He listened but did not appear agitated by the condescending manner in which Owain addressed him. But appearances, Owain well knew, often did not hold true when put to the test.

"Every Tremere across the world," said Owain, "is trying his damnedest to unravel the curse, to find a way to counteract it and become the savior of the Cainite race. With the number of dead claimed by the curse mounting every night, this discovery may well shift the balance of the conflict between Camarilla and Sabbat. Whoever solves the riddle of the curse will win this war. Not only will that sect survive, it will be victorious. It will watch its enemy defeated and utterly destroyed!"

Carlos did not disagree, nor did he interrupt.

"I believe that your sorcerers, Tremere or whomever they might be, as the originators of the curse, will be the first to discover a protection against it." Owain pounded the back of his chair with his fist. "If I've predicted the wrong outcome in this, I am already Camarilla. I will survive. If I am correct, I want protection from you. Protection from the curse, whatever your people have learned, and protection from the hordes of Sabbat who will sweep over the territory formerly held by the Camarilla."

"Your loyalties run deep, Owain Evans," Carlos said dryly.

"My first loyalty is to survival."

A long moment of silence passed between the two. Owain still gripped the back of his chair. Carlos regarded him thoughtfully. "You have told me what you want, but every bargain has two parts. What am I to receive?"

Owain slowly stepped back around his chair and sat again. "I will agree not to present the tainted blood to Archbishop Monçada and reveal to all the Sabbat that you were responsible for the plague that has nearly destroyed them."

"You claim a great deal of knowledge about the Sabbat," said Carlos.

"I have many sources," said Owain and almost left it at that, but his personal curiosity got the best of him. "Though I believe I was misled on one point. I was led to believe that you had a rival for power here in Toledo. Is that not the case?" Owain knew this to be a dangerous admission of ignorance, but he could not believe that the situation was, as it had all appearances of being, so completely other than El Greco had represented it.

Carlos laughed quietly. "You have been misinformed, unless your information is fifty years old. I have no rival here." To Owain, the words thundered across the cavernous room. *I have no rival here.* Not boastful. A mere statement of fact. "But as to your offer," Carlos added, "how could I ever be assured that you would maintain your part?"

"You would have my word," Owain responded.

"I see." Carlos rubbed his stubbly chin. "Perhaps if you presented me with this allegedly tainted blood…"

"Then I would have no guarantee of my safety."

"You would have my word," Carlos echoed Owain.

Again the two Cainites regarded one another silently. Carlos sat at ease, deep in thought. Owain remained calm—what else could he do?—wondering if he had pushed the game beyond an unspoken boundary, if he had too blatantly affronted the Sabbat bishop.

Carlos uncrossed his legs and straightened in his chair. "I do not believe that you have any of this blood that you speak of, Owain Evans." Owain glanced at the two thick, wooden doors on either side of the room, expecting Carlos's lackeys to rush in any moment, guns ablaze. Carlos saw Owain's reaction but waved away his concern. "If I wanted you dead, you would already be dead," said Carlos. "Just because I do not believe you does not mean that the cost of what you ask is not worth the assurance of your silence. Dead you would be silent, true. But there is the chance you may not be lying."

"Why would I bother coming here if I were lying?" Owain asked.

"Why, indeed?"

From the four-poster bed, Owain's recent meal moaned. Carlos looked that way. Owain considered rushing for a door, trying to escape the Alcazar before a proper alarm could be raised, but that would doom him to failure, and he would never find out more about Angharad.

A moment's hesitation and the opportunity was gone. Carlos turned back to Owain. "I will think about your offer for one evening. Return here tomorrow at midnight and I will give you my answer." As if on cue, the door to Owain's right opened and Santiago and the female Sabbat that Owain had contacted a few nights ago stepped inside. "As a show of good faith, I grant you safe passage from here tonight, and tomorrow night. On that, Owain, *you have my word.*" A mischievous glint shone in Carlos's eye; it was the playful look of a victor, of one who could afford to be magnanimous.

Santiago and the woman escorted Owain through the hewn tunnels that had once belonged to El Greco. As they progressed, Owain was surprised by how many of the turns and barely discernible landmarks he remembered. With each step he grew more confident of his ability to navigate the maze-like corridors, so much so that he had to make a conscious effort not to outpace his escort and give away his secret.

The tunnel through which they exited surfaced

just beyond the Iglesia de San Miguel, as Owain knew it would. There were probably a dozen entrances to the catacombs beneath the Alcazar that he could think of, and it was just possible, Owain realized, that not all of those tunnels were known to the most recent residents. He would not try to sneak back in tonight, for there might still be headway to make with Carlos tomorrow night, but if that failed, Owain would not give up. He would find the laboratory, whether it was here or in Madrid or somewhere else. He would find the birthplace of Project Angharad.

CHAPTER TEN

"For God's sake, Bill. It's Saturday. Weekend. You remember that quaint little idea—those couple of days that separate one work week from another?" Leigh had been somewhat perturbed. She had made reservations at Dante's Down the Hatch—steaming fondue on the old ship in the middle of the restaurant—a surprise for her husband.

But Nen was mere hours away from completing the task that recently had taken hold of his every waking hour, and many of his nonwaking hours as well.

Leigh had stood with her hands on her hips as he put on his coat that afternoon. "We need to leave here at 7:15." That was all she had said. William had nodded.

At each red light on his way to the office, he looked at the occupants of the cars around him. Though the people were light-skinned or dark-skinned or any of various shades between, Nen saw superimposed over each the image of one of hundreds of Sudanese that he had seen over twenty years before—skin flushed, eyes sunken yet bulging, moments before the final hemorrhaging began. Death was not long in coming. That was the only merciful part.

He would work only until 6:30, Nen decided. That would give him plenty of time to get home and change. There was only the summary of his report to conclude, and there was always Sunday afternoon and evening, as he wanted to hand the report to both Maureen and her superior, Dr. Andrew McArthur, the Research Director, first thing Monday morning. Nen had raised more questions than he had answered, true, but certainly the CDC administration would not be able to deny that the matters he had been investigating deserved more attention, perhaps even priority status. Public education was one of the most powerful tools in heading off an epidemic, and in a society so saturated with print and broadcast media, there was no excuse for the general populace to remain ignorant of a potential hazard. Granted, the information needed to be presented in a way so as not to cause panic, but dissemination of facts was vital, and even a good scare could sometimes prove beneficial.

Much to Nen's chagrin, he struggled with the conclusion to the report. What should have been two hours' work stretched out to three, at which point he decided he was taking the wrong approach and started over. Already it was five o'clock. Why, he wondered, hadn't he come in earlier, in the morning? Why had he wasted those hours trying to fulfill Leigh's expectations that he spend more time around the house? He would be done by now.

Finally, the words began to flow. One idea led naturally to the next. The proper details revealed themselves to illustrate his points. Still, there were facts to check. In his notes, Nen had at one point transposed two case numbers, an error that had crept into the report and managed to corrupt several calculations. Accuracy was everything in this type of case. An unreceptive superior would all too willingly turn away at the first sign of inaccurate data, never mind that the original hypothesis remained unshaken.

When Nen glanced again at his watch, he was shocked to see that he had overshot his 6:30 quitting time by half an hour. But he was so close. Surely he and Leigh could be a little late for their reservation with no harm. That way he could finish and spend all of Sunday with her. He decided against calling. The explanation would take longer and make him that much more late. Besides, having established a productive rhythm, he was loath to abandon the moment. Better to finish up quickly.

But *quickly*, Nen found, was a perception not completely correlating to reality. As he triumphantly printed the final copy of his report, he was horrified to realize it was 8:15. As the laser printer hummed in the background, he dialed home. "Can I meet you there?"

"I canceled the reservation," Leigh said.

Nen tried to read her mood, a trick at which he had never been overly skilled. "Tomorrow. I'll make it up to you tomorrow."

"Fine." And she hung up.

Fine. William knew that word had been used in a way diametrically opposed to its actual meaning. Once, long ago, when they were first married, he had believed that Leigh, being a psychologist, would be more straightforward and open in telling him what she was thinking. He had since come to realize that her background merely made her perfectly aware of the wild goose chases she led him on through the labyrinth of female thought.

The printer had resumed its stoic silence. Nen removed the report, made thick by the attached data files. Just thumbing through, he spotted formatting changes he would need to make. Maybe he would read through his work tonight and mark changes for tomorrow morning. Leigh wouldn't begrudge him the morning, or so he hoped. He tucked the report into a manila folder and that into his briefcase.

Outside, the air was crisp. The marginal warmth of the afternoon was hours past. Nen buttoned the top button on his overcoat. Atlanta had its winter days, but chances were that next week it would be in the sixties again. The parking lot at CDC was relatively bare, but still Nen did not notice, at first, the man approaching him.

"Dr. Nen?"

Nen looked quizzically at the smartly dressed young African-American. His tweed jacket couldn't be enough protection from the cold, but the man did not appear uncomfortable. Nen wondered if this were someone he should remember having met before—it would not be the first time—but he could not place the face.

"Dr. William Nen?"

"Yes?" Nen was sure he had never met this person.

"It's a great honor to meet you, Dr. Nen. My name is Thelonious. I've read about your work in Zaire." He held out his hand.

Nen felt relieved, his suspicion confirmed that he had not, in fact, met this man before. And never before, that he could remember, had he been stopped on the street to be praised for his work. It was a situation to which Nen had no experience responding. "Why...thank you," he stuttered, the mist of his breath hanging between them as they shook hands.

Thelonious smiled warmly. *"I would greatly appreciate the chance to look over the report you've been working on."*

Nen cocked his head for a moment, then reached into his briefcase. "Of course. That would be no problem at all. It's not quite finished, mind you. A few formatting problems I need to neaten up, but the content is complete."

Thelonious took the offered report, slid it under his jacket. "I'm sure your sterling analysis makes up for any cosmetic lack, Dr. Nen."

Nen beamed at the unexpected compliments. *Such a knowledgeable and well-mannered young man,* thought Nen.

"And one other thing, Dr. Nen," added Thelonious, *"you decided to take the rest of the night off, and tomorrow. Your wife would like to spend some time with you."*

"Of course," Nen agreed. "I expect I should be going."

"Yes." Thelonious nodded. "And thank you again, Dr. Nen. You've been a great help."

"Think nothing of it." Nen continued on to his car, looking forward to spending the rest of the weekend with his wife.

Owain threw open the front door of the small house of El Greco's, determined to have his answers. Startled by his violent entrance, Maria fled the front room. Just as quickly, Miguel rushed in, a snub-nosed pistol aimed and ready. A second armed Cainite, short and squat, followed Miguel. Seeing that the intruder was Owain, Miguel put up his hand. "Hold your fire, Javier." But Miguel's anger was kindled. "Owain! What in God's name…?"

Owain let loose with a backhand blow that caught Miguel squarely across the side of the face and sent him stumbling into the wall. Three powerful strides carried Owain past Miguel and the surprised Javier and up the stairs. A moment later he was before the door to El Greco's study. Without pausing, Owain kicked open the door. The top hinge ripped from the wall. Splintered wood flew across the room.

Owain stepped into the unoccupied chamber. The desk that held the letter he had not really written stood before him. He bellowed, "Where are you, El Greco? Damn you!"

Only a few steps behind Owain, Miguel stepped through the remains of the door, his weapon again leveled at Owain.

"Where are you?" Owain yelled again. He scoffed at Miguel and his gun. "I've been shot by little girls with bigger pistols. Don't hurt yourself. Where's El Greco?"

Miguel did not lower the gun. "What is the meaning of this? Are you insane?"

"I'm sorry," Owain mocked him. "Was I supposed to go by the bread shop to ask for you?"

"*Pottery* shop," Miguel tersely corrected him.

"Damn you and your worthless store, Miguel. Where's El Greco?"

"You idiot!" Miguel spat in Owain's direction. "How many of our enemies have you led to our doorstep?"

"Do you think they don't know where you are? Do you think they care?" Owain asked. "There's no one in Toledo *except* your enemies. They would have killed you already if you were worth the trouble." Owain kicked the chair. It slammed into the rolltop desk. "Come talk to me, El Greco, you lying, insane bastard!" he shouted.

"You must go," Miguel hissed. "Now! And stop your yelling," he added. "Otherwise, half the city..."

Miguel stopped short as both he and Owain saw the seam appear in the ceiling. As they watched, a trapdoor that had been completely concealed before lowered, revealing steps to a hidden attic, and coming slowly down those steps was El Greco. First his booted feet and then his legs came into view. His dark cloak clung tightly about him. He stepped from the stairs, and the trap door closed silently behind him. "Hello, Owain. I wasn't expecting to see you so soon."

Miguel began stammering at once: "He completely disregarded my instructions to…" but stopped as El Greco raised a finger for silence.

"Leave us," said the old Toreador, altogether calm in the face of his servant's consternation and Owain's fury.

Miguel self-consciously lowered the gun that he had still pointed at Owain, and slinked out of the room. Ever so slowly, El Greco righted the chair that Owain had kicked over, then sat. He indicated for Owain to do the same, but Owain refused.

"What has happened to you?" Owain asked, his voice full of disgust.

"Nothing that has not happened to you, Owain." El Greco scratched his pointy chin.

This was not what Owain wanted to hear. He was nothing like the pathetic creature sitting before him. "You rave," he accused. "You are a doddering, insane fool. You sent me on this chase after Carlos as if he were your rival, as if you were equals. But you are nothing! You gave me none of the information that might have helped me. You were willing to risk my destruction because you couldn't bear to face the truth."

"What truth would that be?" El Greco asked quietly.

Owain began pacing the room. "That truth would be that Toledo is no longer your city, hasn't been for years, as far as I can tell. That truth would be not that Carlos is invading your territory, but that he is the master here." As Owain spoke, he could see El Greco's color rising quickly, as well as the tension in his gnarled fists. "Why did Monçada really summon you to Madrid? Not to demand peace between you and Carlos, because the war has already been fought, and you lost. Did he ask Carlos to suffer your presence? Was that his way of repaying old debts to you, his faithful lackey from centuries ago?"

With a terrible scream, El Greco shot to his feet and took his chair in his hands. He smashed it down upon his desk. The chair disintegrated into countless pieces, and the blow crushed inward a portion of the rolltop. "This is my city!"

The two old friends stood facing one another. A wildness, a desperation had crept into El Greco's eyes. As withered as his body had grown, there was still strength there. He still held the back of the destroyed chair in his grasp. Owain noticed the sharp ends of the wood.

How far El Greco had fallen, Owain realized. The Toreador had indeed been the most influential Cainite in the city once. While the mortal reins of power had changed hands time and again, El Greco had survived by accepting each new occupying force, by drinking in whatever it was of beauty they had to offer. It was perhaps his greatest legacy—that he had befriended the human artist most widely associated with Toledo, Domenicos Theotocoulos. The painter, who coincidentally enough hailed from near the Toreador's own homeland, had affectionately taken on his mentor's *nom de guerre*, El Greco.

That legacy would live on, but it meant very little to the famed artist's vampiric namesake at present. Owain could see the despair in El Greco's eyes as he was confronted with the truth of the situation, and all of Owain's questions were answered by that one sight.

"Yes," said Owain quietly. "This is your city." El Greco had not kept anything from Owain out of sheer perversity, as Owain had suspected. El Greco could not face the truth, couldn't grasp it. There was no way he could convey it to another. He was a relic of bygone days, just as Owain could easily have become had not the siren jolted him back to the present by reacquainting him with his feelings from the past. What had happened to El Greco? *Nothing that hasn't happened to you, Owain.*

"The dreams, Owain," said El Greco, his eyes sad and worried. Owain wanted to believe that he could see a hint of lucidity breaking through. "The dreams are the worst. I see how it was." He dropped the remnant of the chair to the floor, then stared in horror at his own hands, turning them over and over to inspect every bone, every vein. "It's the curse. It brings the dreams. It takes me back." Now he looked at Owain with a pleading gaze but unspoken words.

Owain looked at his own hands. *The curse brings dreams.* Owain had been suffering his own dreams. He'd wondered if the curse had anything to do with them, but he had put the thought out of his mind whenever it had arisen. *The curse brings dreams.* It could very well be so. Was the insanity anything more than a waking dream? Owain could not discount the insight of the pathetic creature standing before him. El Greco had too often proven the strength of his intuition.

The dreams.

The curse.

Project Angharad.

Whether they were connected or not, Owain would undoubtedly discover. Or he would perish.

"I will find a way to stop the curse," Owain said, and a small degree of comfort shone in El Greco's expression. "But know this," Owain added defiantly. "I do it out of no sense of obligation or duty to you. I do it for my own reasons." *For Angharad,* he almost said. *And for the old friendship of a pitiable wreck.* He resisted the urge to reach out and touch El Greco, to place a hand on his arm. It was a gesture Owain could not bring himself to make, a gesture somehow too…human. Owain gladly let his sentimentality wash away. He knew he could destroy this creature if need be. There was no need to worry overly much about anything El Greco tried to hold over him.

"You do have obligations to me," El Greco protested weakly. He motioned toward the chess board on the table by the desk, the game pieces still arranged as Owain had seen them several nights before. "Yes, you have bested me on *that* field of battle, Owain."

Owain did not completely understand. The Toreador seemed to think that was the game they had been playing, that Owain had proven victorious. *More raving*, Owain thought. *The dementia runs deep*.

Painfully, El Greco reached over and took the nearly defenseless white king in his gnarled fingers. He clenched the piece tightly in his fist, and as he squeezed, the cheap plastic melted and dripped between his fingers—into his lap, onto the floor. "That is but a game," said El Greco. "You, however, have sworn oaths to me, to the Sabbat."

"My oaths are centuries old," Owain replied. "Words only. No promise is meant to live so long, on into eternity."

El Greco frowned. "*Every* oath should live through eternity. Otherwise, it *is* only words."

Owain turned and left his old friend. Downstairs,

Miguel was in the sitting room with Javier. Owain stepped into the room. Miguel and Javier both looked up. "Miguel," said Owain, "cross me again, and I will kill you." He left the house.

Kli Kodesh loosed his grip upon the writhing strand of prophecy. It tore free of him, the friction burning a weal of raw pink across his marble-white palm. A single drop of rich red pooled in the cup of his hand, like holy water in a font.

The tail end of the prophecy flicked once, disdainfully. Then, cracking like a whip, it snaked from view.

Kli Kodesh stared after it impassively. He let his hand fall to his side and clenched his fist. When he opened it again, the hand was bloodless and unblemished. It might have been a work of sculpture rather than a thing of flesh and blood.

If Kli Kodesh noted this miraculous change, he gave no outward sign. His attention was fixed on the slowly resolving cityscape. With growing anticipation, he watched the city draw into focus. Something within him stirred at the first hint of the Moorish architecture. As the tangled sprawl of the Old Town unraveled before him, he found himself racing ahead, tracing half-remembered routes through the unfolding labyrinth of docks, alleyways, marketplaces.

The city struck him like a blow. Certainly much had changed since his last sojourn here, but that was perhaps inevitable. He must have been away for…well, far too long.

The entire city spread out below him now. He drank deeply of it. It bore the reminders of its bloody history openly, in plain view.

Toledo, the City of the Sword.

The city itself was a peninsula, besieged by water on three sides. The unique property of Toledo, however, Kli Kodesh reflected, was not that it formed a peninsula in space, but rather that it comprised a peninsula in time. Throughout its turbulent history, Toledo had been surrounded by three cultures in conflict, changing hands repeatedly throughout the Middle Ages as Moors, Crusaders and Jews vied for dominance. Kli Kodesh had found himself returning to the familiar confines of this place time and time again.

The trained eye could still pick out the pattern of the city-that-was lurking just beneath the veneer of the modern city. To Kli Kodesh, it felt almost like a homecoming.

He had not expected the prophecy to carry him so far so fast. It had seemed mere nights ago that he had walked dripping from the sea into the neon blare of the City of Angels. It was there that he had apprehended the first subtle hint of what was surely the Final Pattern.

From that time forward, he could not escape the growing sense that his actions were somehow prescribed by some greater force, almost predetermined. He had tracked the evolving pattern further, of course, back to the tangled black web of omen that was the City of the Scar.

At the heart of that web, deep beneath the streets of that city, he could feel a dark presence brooding. An alien power lurked there—a black widow tickling the delicate strands of prophecy. Kli Kodesh could feel the thrumming message she sent out. She was calling home her own.

It was not difficult to follow the course of that vibrating strand. It had released him here—in the City of the Sword. Somewhere within this ancient labyrinth, between the press of the three besieging beliefs, he knew he would find the one for whom this message, this omen, was intended.

He knew little of the one he sought. His only advantage was an ancient name, a title that had survived the passing of centuries sealed in the words of ancient prophecies, like a moldering scroll sealed in a bone tube.

Undeterred, Kli Kodesh descended upon the city to find the one the ancient songs called the Kinslayer.

CHAPTER ELEVEN

J. Benison Hodge, prince of Atlanta, sat motionless at the conference table in Rhodes Hall. His officer's saber stood embedded deeply into the table, neatly slicing the thick Sunday newspaper in half. Each tick of the clock's pendulum behind him roared like thunder in his ears. Benison's every ounce of energy was fueling his restraint. It was a supreme effort of will that kept him from completely destroying the room, from rampaging through the house and smashing everything in sight—a supreme effort of will, and the thought of Eleanor's extreme displeasure should he further mar the furniture.

A prince must be moderate of temper, he told himself over and over again. *I must prove myself worthy to lead the shining city of Primus, and this is one of my tests.* His hand quivered as he struggled to keep from tearing the sword free from the table so that he could hack the bookshelves to bits. He wanted to pull down the very foundations of the building.

A prince must be moderate of temper.

A prince must be moderate of temper.

Unable to resist, like picking at a scab that should be left to heal, he looked again at the headline that had greeted him when he rose this evening: *CDC FEARS WORLDWIDE EPIDEMIC.* His hand quivered more forcefully. The prince closed his eyes, drew in a deep, calming breath.

For weeks since the outbreak of the blood curse, Benison had been working nonstop to preserve the Masquerade, to ensure that the death and chaos of the Kindred world remained hidden from the eyes of mortals. The story was the same across the nation, across the world. Cainites were being struck down by an angry God, and as existing vampiric power structures were destabilized, the survivors contested viciously for preeminence. The mortals had felt the tremors, but they were used to the rule of fear and uncertainty. They would look the other way as long as they could.

Benison opened his eyes and glared at the headline again. *This* would not allow them to look the other way. From the sound of the reported facts, the blood taint had even spread among the kine somewhat, claiming victims among the old and the infirm. What the papers mentioned only in passing, the enigma of fresh blood found in apparently weeks-dead corpses, was the greatest danger to the Kindred. If investigators should pursue this matter...

The news in the papers—and they were all largely the same—was a catastrophe, but equally disturbing was the fact that the reports had begun with the *Atlanta Journal-Constitution* and spread to the other news services. Not only might Cainites the world over be found out and hunted to extinction, but it would appear to be Benison's fault! The final blow to the Masquerade had come from within the city that was his charge. And Benison had no doubt as to how it had happened.

Thelonious.

A knock at the door interrupted the prince's dark thoughts.

"Enter."

Vermeil opened the door and ushered in Xavier Kline, the giant Brujah. As Benison's ghoul closed the door, Kline stepped forward somewhat sheepishly, a rather amusing display if Benison had been in a mood to be amused.

"Well?" asked Benison, already knowing the answer.

"'Scuse me?" Kline turned his head to the side.

His hearing had never come back completely after his attack on the cursed Daughter of Cacophony.

"What happened?" Benison asked more loudly.

"No sign of Thelonious at his law office or his known haven," Kline reported. "Looks like he packed in a hurry."

Benison nodded. He was not surprised. As soon as he had seen the paper this evening, he had sent Vermeil for Kline with instructions to find his Brujah elder and bring him to the prince regardless of Thelonious's wishes in the matter. Benison had not expected that Kline would find the Brujah primogen. He had undoubtedly acquired the CDC reports, set the story in motion, and then fled the city or gone into hiding. Kline was nowhere near smart enough to find Thelonious if Thelonious didn't want to be found.

"This mean I'm Brujah primogen?" Kline asked.

Benison looked up at the Brujah of towering stature and ambition. "This means," said the prince, "that the Brujah no longer have any seat among the primogen. Thelonious has proven your clan unworthy. You have shown yourself loyal to your prince, but any other of your clan who does not personally swear fealty will be exiled or destroyed. Let it be known."

Kline took a step back as if struck a blow by this pronouncement against his clan.

"But I will tell you this, Xavier," added the

prince. "Find Thelonious. Bring him to me, and his former seat in the council of primogen is yours."

Kline's eyes brightened at this, as Benison had expected. *I might as well be training a two-hundred-pound pigeon*, thought the prince. Kline excused himself and backed out of the room. Benison, still only half-decided on the next steps he would take, returned to contemplating his sword buried in the table.

Eleanor poked her head out of the living room when she heard Xavier Kline tromping down the hall and out the front door. Perhaps this was the time to present her findings to Benison. Earlier in the evening, Vermeil had hinted that the prince might not be in the most receptive of moods, but that was hours ago, and she had heard no yelling while Benison conferred with Kline. *If J. Benison can speak with that hired killer, then he can certainly speak with his wife*, she decided.

Eleanor turned back to Hannah and Aunt Bedelia, who had consumed all but the last of the blood crumpets. No one would ever take the last of anything. "It is time, ladies." Eleanor and Hannah had spent their bridge time last night explaining their plan to Bedelia. It had been a lengthy and rather disconnected conversation, consisting of much redundancy to ensure that the old dear could anchor basic facts in her sieve-like mind. It was always a matter of speculation exactly what Bedelia would say, but Eleanor was as sure as she could be that the prince's sire agreed with her. And Benison would never go against Bedelia's wishes.

Hannah rose and wheeled Bedelia into the hall. Eleanor took up a parcel from its resting place on the couch. She held, wrapped in a cloth of crushed velvet, a gilded dagger. With her husband's help, she would have her Benjamin back, and Owain Evans would have his due.

It should have worked, damn it! Dieter is an idiot, a buffoon. Even after two full weeks, Gustav was still incensed that the riot he had helped to bring about had not claimed its intended victim. Wilhelm still walked the streets of Berlin. *I take Dieter's pathetic little Final Reich and give them direction and force, and still they are incompetent!* The mob was indirect enough a phenomenon that Wilhelm could not have foreseen it nor prepared against it. By all accounts, the western prince, his childe, and his bodyguard Kleist had all been overwhelmed and immobilized by a veritable legion of skinheads. Yet the three Kindred had escaped.

Foul play! had been Gustav's first thought. How else could such an exquisite plan have gone awry? He had spent much of the past two weeks questioning many of the participants, trying to discover who was to blame, trying to uncover the turncoat. All for naught. He had found no signs of treachery, merely incompetence. But still, the suspicion lingered. It gnawed at him constantly. His mind had a way of latching on to such disturbing possibilities, of turning them over and over, all through the night. Gustav had lived too long to think that paranoia did not have its proper place. He did not casually dismiss the prospect that he might have been betrayed, and as he made his way down through the lowest sub-basement of the Berlin Palace, he knew that this night he would learn the truth.

The basement was a maze of ladders and tunnels, of pipes venting steam or leaking from their decades-old seals. The sound of dripping water and the vague odor of sewage were inescapable. At least one of the pipes running through the palace proper above was empty, Gustav knew, because whenever he needed to meet with a certain individual, he would place a message in the pipe. Then it was only a matter of time.

I will know who betrayed me, and they will pay! Gustav promised himself as he stepped off another ladder. Whatever ancient lightbulb was installed nearby flickered erratically, its scant light shrouded by the thick steam.

"Gustav."

The eastern prince heard the near-whisper and turned to see an obscured form in the shadows. "You have news for me?"

"As you have requested." Ellison stepped forward, but rather than coming into the light, the shadows seemed to move forward with him. Gustav could just make out the crippled shape of the Nosferatu. "You seek those who turned on you, those who sabotaged your plan to rid Berlin of Wilhelm."

"Yes," Gustav answered tersely. He hated this overblown sense of secrecy and drama that Ellison always employed—*Just tell me what I want to know, you walking birth defect!*—but the accuracy of the Nosferatu's information was beyond question.

"You were betrayed," said Ellison.

"I *knew* it." Gustav smashed his fist into his palm, imagining as he did so the way he would crush whomever had crossed him.

"You were betrayed by the ineptitude of those you chose to do your bidding," Ellison explained. The words were spoken softly, almost inaudibly, yet they rang in Gustav's ears like a hammer striking the steam pipes. "There was not a traitor, no one who willfully blocked your plans."

Gustav could not believe what he was hearing, did not want to believe. He wanted very much the name of someone he could pound into submission, someone he could personally draw and quarter and leave staked out for the sun. But Ellison was telling him that he was to be denied this rightful satisfaction. "Are you sure of this?" Ellison responded only with affronted silence, until Gustav realized what he had asked. "What am I saying? Of course you're sure. You 'provide information...'" Gustav mocked the Nosferatu's stock answer for whenever he was questioned, then laughed. "You tell me what you know rather than what I want to hear. You are not like the others."

But Gustav realized suddenly that he was speaking to the empty darkness and the steam. Ellison had slipped away. *One day you will push me too far, you palsied simpleton, and I will crush you and drive your entire tainted bloodline out of my city. One day.*

Before Gustav even realized that he was gone, Ellison was slipping out of the bottom-most level of the Berlin Palace and into the storm sewers that crisscrossed beneath the whole of Berlin, the passageways that blurred the distinctions of east and west for the Nosferatu more so than for any other clan.

It was perhaps unwise, Ellison realized, to anger Gustav by slipping away so, but the eastern prince in particular needed constant reminding that the Nosferatu would not stand by to have abuse or doubts heaped upon them. Ellison provided a service. He was not duty-bound to provide information to any prince, and as long as the hostilities continued between Gustav and Wilhelm, they both needed the Nosferatu more than he needed them. As long as the hostilities continued. If one prince should prove victorious, or should one find out that Ellison was less than exclusive in offering his services, the Nosferatu position would suddenly become considerably more precarious.

Ellison moved through the sewers more sure-footedly and more rapidly than other Kindred would have imagined. His physical deformities served to disarm the concerns of others far more than they inconvenienced Ellison in any meaningful way. He might lack the particular grace to which surface dwellers were accustomed, but his shriveled arm and misaligned legs did not actually hinder his movement.

As he made his way more and more deeply into the tunnels that were his refuge, he clutched to his chest the locket that hung on a string around his neck. The locket was crafted of beautiful gold. Ellison polished it each night without fail, and was never without it, pressed against his chest beneath his filthy clothes. If need be, he would trade the favor of both princes to safeguard this, his greatest treasure.

Finally, he crawled into a small compartment, little bigger than a casket, that was one of several scattered throughout the sewers he'd made his havens. Nestled in among the rags and crumpled paper, he opened the locket, oh so carefully, so as not to dislodge the picture within, though it had never come loose during the many years he had possessed it. The picture was a simple line drawing in black ink, but it somehow managed to capture the very essence of its subject—Ellison's lost love, Melitta. *Lost only for now,* he reminded himself. During the final days of World War II as the Allied forces had moved to occupy the city, a bomb had detonated and one of the sewer tunnels had collapsed upon her. Melitta had crawled out of the rubble, but then had slipped into the torpor from which she still had not awakened.

Ellison held the locket to his breast, to his heart, and as he did so, he could feel her presence. He knew that the blood of unlife, the smallest trace, still flowed in her slumbering veins. Warmth flooded his body, as if he had just fed upon three mortals. She would return to him. All he had to do was remain patient. Her body was entombed far beneath the city, far beneath where he now lay. He had seen to her safety and would allow himself only one visit to her body each year. Though incredibly remote, there was the slightest chance that someone could follow him to her, and that was not a chance he was willing to take merely to satisfy his own personal longings.

So he would wait. He would hold the locket to his body; he would pray to the picture like some icon from the east, and he would thank the gods that Isabella had given it to him. The price she had asked had been so small. He would gladly have given so much more. He had thought at first that the locket was a mere trinket, that the drawing was just some sentimental rendering of her image. But he had quickly learned how much more they really were.

Closing his eyes, Ellison could imagine that his beloved Melitta was lying there next to him, that she was reaching out to stroke his cheek...but it was his own hand that touched his face. Still, he could touch her mind, could *almost* make out her thoughts. The locket brought him so close to her. It was almost unbearable.

A few more minutes. He would allow himself just a little more time with his beloved, and then back to other matters. *Come back to me, love.* It was these brief respites that gave meaning to Ellison's nights. Otherwise, he was completely alone in the world. Other Nosferatu were like distant cousins perhaps, but it was for Melitta that he tried to carve out a secure home. *Come back.*

Owain stepped out of El Greco's house and the world closed in upon him. What had begun as a clear evening was now dark. Churning clouds had rolled in from the west and hung so low in the sky that they threatened to swoop down and swallow the entire city. The faceless buildings of Toledo loomed, crowding together, leaning forward, ready to crash to the ground and crush Owain should the blustering wind but change direction. Crevices opened in the street to sabotage his footing, or certain cobbles rose to cause him to stumble.

Again, certainty had fled Owain. Mere hours ago, he had been secure in his hatred of El Greco, a hatred that he had been cultivating since setting foot in Spain. How dare his onetime friend summon him from across the Atlantic and try to assert control over Owain? There could be no worse crime. Owain had spent nearly a thousand years ensuring that no one controlled him, striving to become the master of his own destiny. El Greco had breached the wall of isolation that contained the fury within Owain's soul and Owain, seeing tyrannical designs behind El Greco's demands, had been ready to destroy the old Toreador. What had slowed the progress of Owain's advancing hatred had been surprise—surprise that none of the vampires he'd accosted had acknowledged El Greco's existence.

Even when Owain had stepped into El Greco's abode this very evening, the Ventrue had been ready to decide upon a death sentence for his old friend. Nothing so rash as a personal assault, but Owain had been ready to make the decision that El Greco would have to be removed from the picture once and for all. Owain would have killed Miguel first and enjoyed the act, then found out what other supporters remained, if more than those he had seen, and taken care of them. El Greco, Owain would have saved for last. There would have been no more loose ends. Still, Owain would have pursued his charade with Carlos, for Owain had to find out what improbable coincidence was behind the reemergence of Angharad's name. But at least he would have been acting unquestionably of his own volition.

But there are always complications, he thought, as freakish winter thunder rumbled in the distance. The clouds appeared even closer now, if that was possible, close enough, almost, to touch the upper towers of the nearby Alcazar. There were unusual numbers of people on the street. Perhaps the kine, too, sensed the barely restrained force of the stormy heavens. Owain would have preferred empty streets. He was distracted by his recent encounter, and with so many mortals about, concealment would be plentiful for any spy or lurking Sabbat. It was quite possible that word had not trickled completely down through the ranks that Owain and Carlos were in the midst of negotiations, and some Sabbat flunky might want to vent a grudge against the uninvited guest to the city. There was the Gangrel Nicholas, as well, who might be stalking the streets. Owain had forgotten to ask Carlos what had happened to the beast back at the plaza, but then again, what reason would Carlos have had to tell him? Better that Owain had not brought up the subject, rather than admitting something else that he did not know.

Complications indeed. It would have been much simpler to have written off El Greco, to have made plans and then destroyed him at some point. But just as the very heavens and the city itself now conspired against Owain, his emotions had conspired against him. He had seen his old friend left by the years withered and irrelevant, and Owain had been surprised by his own pity. It was very nearly a first for Owain, as kine or Kindred. He felt sure that he could influence El Greco easily enough. After seeing just how far the Toreador had fallen, and just how fleeting was his grasp of reality, Owain did not feel threatened, and where normally he would have felt revulsion for this Cainite, a weak specter of El Greco's former self, Owain felt pity.

Lightning played among the black clouds. A far-off tower clock chimed midnight, but even at this late hour, mortals thronged the streets. Some curiously admired the sky. As Owain looked more closely at the people, however, he noticed that many were carrying loads of clothes and household goods—old pots, a mirror, a chicken. These same people wore not modern attire, but the frocks and knee-pants that Owain had seen five hundred years before…when he had previously resided in Toledo, when the Jews had been expelled from Spain.

He continued on his way, already late for his appointment with Carlos, and saw more and more of the dark-haired denizens of the past. They were somber, carrying what they could of their lives on their backs, and they were oblivious to the dynamic rumbling of the storm above. Owain stopped and looked around him. For a moment he could not tell who was out of place—the fifteenth-century Jews fleeing their homes, or the twentieth-century young people with their good looks and bottles of wine. As the rain began to fall and the storm hit in earnest, the streets were left to the somber ones who cringed as the raindrops struck. The more modern inhabitants scattered, seeking the shelter that, then and now, was denied their counterparts.

Owain walked as if in a dream. He could feel the onset of the vision, was fully aware that, already, he was stepping into it, but he resisted. *There is no time*, he told himself. Just as there was no time to pity his old friend, there was no time to investigate these unfortunate sojourners, be they apparitions of his mind or of the city itself.

He approached the Iglesia de San Miguel and the concealed tunnel from which he had been led the night before. There, Owain was greeted by one most definitely not an apparition. Santiago stepped forward out of the shadows, and behind him the female Cainite, also of dark Spanish complexion. Owain, his mind awhirl with what he had seen and felt the past hour, offered no witty banter, and Santiago did not seem to grieve overly much. He turned and led Owain into the depths of the earth, the woman following behind.

The tunnel, lit by occasional torches on the wall but dark for long stretches, was even more familiar to Owain this time. For many of his years in Toledo, he had more or less stayed with El Greco here. Owain knew, before he and his escort turned the corner, that there would be a passage leading down on the left, and another on the right several feet further along. Only twice did he misremember a turn or incorrectly predict the lay of the next passage. The apparitions did not follow him beneath the surface of the earth. No beings from the past greeted him. Unexpected from the darkness, however, appeared Carlos. The silver rings through his eyebrows and nose shone in the torchlight.

"You're late, Owain Evans," said Carlos. "I was afraid you had rescinded your offer." He spoke almost playfully, belying the fact that he would have had Owain hunted down had the Ventrue not returned tonight. "Come. Walk with me." Carlos wrapped his arm around Owain's shoulder and led him deeper along the tunnel. Santiago and the woman remained behind.

"You are an intriguing individual," said Carlos. "You make your residence in Atlanta in the United States, have for just over seventy-five years. Never have caused a stir there, a very well-behaved Camarilla elder. And now suddenly you are in Toledo attempting to blackmail a bishop of the Sabbat." Carlos cheerfully squeezed Owain's shoulder.

"'Blackmail' is such an ugly word," Owain commented. "I prefer to think we are reaching a mutually beneficial agreement."

"Call it what you like. Whatever eases your conscience."

They walked in silence that way, Carlos embracing Owain, through the tunnels for some time. Carlos neither spoke nor indicated that he expected Owain to offer any information. Owain tried to record their path in his mind, but they were very deep now, in corridors that had been mostly the province of El Greco when Owain had been here, and still descending.

"It was very foolish of you contacting me like you did," Carlos said at last. "Every tender young recruit in the city knows that you were demanding an audience. They see it as an affront to my authority. Besides," he squeezed Owain's shoulder again, "a Camarilla elder meeting with a Sabbat bishop. What will people say?"

Owain could not argue. He had not been particularly discreet. Perhaps it was a reaction to the extreme precautions Miguel had taken in smuggling him into Toledo. Owain had gone about his assignment with all the subtlety of a bull racing through the streets of Pamplona. Or perhaps, as with the clumsy threat he had cast toward his fellow Ventrue Benjamin several months ago, Owain was just getting careless, sloppy. It could happen quite easily after nine hundred or a thousand years—an elder Cainite grown weary of the elaborate precautions and wiles that had enabled him to reach such a ripe old age, or just not caring about the consequences of missteps, either out of a sense of invulnerability or ennui.

"Ah, but you do not care," said Carlos, slapping Owain on the shoulder and letting go of him at last. "You do what you want regardless, and if you die in the process…that is the end. You fear the curse that much?" Carlos's words followed Owain's thoughts, but diverged to arrive at a different conclusion. "You decide, if the curse will snatch me away like a giant eagle swooping down from the sky, then why fear death otherwise. Why fuck around, eh?"

As Carlos led Owain around one final corner, a sudden shock of recognition flashed through Owain's mind. He knew exactly where he was in the labyrinthine tunnels beneath El Alcazar, and trepidation followed closely upon the heels of the realization. They descended a long straight corridor, the floor leading down as the ceiling leveled off, forming a hallway that was easily twice as tall as the other portions of the cramped tunnels through which they had traveled. The passage ended at a massive stone door, its surface carved with wards older than El Alcazar, older than the Sabbat itself. Owain had felt the energy of those wards once, though he was not privy to the arcane rites by which the symbols were empowered.

Carlos touched the door lightly and it swung open surprisingly smoothly on some unseen pivot. "These passages are very old," said Carlos, his tone of reverence unusual for a member of the Sabbat, most of whom thrived on violence and destruction. "Older than the nation of Spain. Perhaps as old as the world."

A fine sand of ancient days covered the floor of the small room beyond the door. The walls were covered with more runes, as was the stone sarcophagus that occupied most of the space in the room. Owain's knees buckled as he again was assaulted by the disjointed sense of time that he had felt upon the street. The visions were reaching for him, but he could not submit. Not here, not now, in the presence of Carlos. Owain saw the carved wards shimmering with light and power, as they had been when activated by a Tremere—Tanzani, that was the name—who had served El Greco. The lid of the ornate sarcophagus was slid down, open, but Owain could not force himself to look inside. He was suddenly fearful that he was in that distant time, that he would look into the ornate coffin and see himself, for he had crawled into it late one night and not emerged for over two hundred years.

"Don't you think so?" Carlos was asking something. Owain couldn't catch all the words, but he and Carlos were in the here and now, the present. He latched onto Carlos's presence, forced himself to nod. Cautiously he gazed over the edge of the sarcophagus and saw that it was empty. The visions again receded. The wards were a dull gray, lifeless, devoid of power.

Owain looked up at Carlos. The Sabbat bishop's expression gave away very little. He appeared slightly amused, almost as he had from the first moment Owain had seen him. Why had Carlos brought Owain here? Had the bishop learned of Owain's relation to the former master of these halls? Did Carlos know that Owain had spent centuries of torpor in this very room?

Carlos smiled. "I like this place." He edged around the sarcophagus, caressing the cold stone, running the tips of his fingers through the indentations of the runes. "I like it because it is as silent as death." He paused, raised his head to listen to the emptiness. "Many of my followers, they know nothing of quiet, Owain. This tomblike silence…"

he paused again. "It is the sound of victory after your foes are vanquished, as they lie staked at your feet, their blood on your lips, before the sun burns away their flesh. Can you hear it?" He raised his head again. "Skin, muscle, fat—sizzling as surely as if they were on a gridiron."

Carlos lapsed into silence, and Owain could feel the weight of the quiet, heavier than all the tons of earth that separated them from the storm above. Owain had wished for death here once, but he had been too much the coward but to hide away from the world. Perhaps his desire would be fulfilled belatedly. Perhaps Carlos planned for Owain never to leave this tomb. In the age of swords, steel upon steel, Owain would have had little concern for his escape. It was quite possible for one superior swordsman, especially a Cainite, to hold his own against impossible odds. But firearms evened the score in the favor of the unskilled masses. One shot from afar, one burst of a machine gun, could shatter the skull of the most adept swordsman.

"You have spoken," said Carlos, breaking the silence, leaning forward, both arms braced atop the sarcophagus, "of things that no one should know. You have spoken of secrets and threatened to bring them to the light of day. You also speak of mutually beneficial agreements. I offer you an agreement."

Owain listened carefully. Apparently Carlos did

not know the relevance of this room to Owain. Instead, they were meeting here for purely symbolic reasons. In a strange way, Owain found himself liking this predator who leaned over Owain's former resting place. Like a snake sunning itself, Carlos appeared disarming, yet he could be coiled and deadly in an instant, Owain was sure.

"As you mentioned before," said Carlos, "'blackmail' is an ugly word. I like to think of this as an opportunity for us to trade favors, and possibly to build the foundation for a mutually beneficial relationship. Do you object to this approach to our…our situation?"

Owain shook his head. He was trying to measure Carlos's words, to read beneath them. Could this proposal be serious, or was it merely a ploy to find out what Owain knew and then destroy him?

"Good." Carlos clapped his hands together. "This is my offer: First, I will not kill you; second, I will extend my protection over you, as you asked, when the Sabbat rules supreme. In return, I ask two favors of you: First, you turn over to me the vial of blood you claim to have. You still have a series of individuals whom you have told what you know. It is easier for me to buy your silence and theirs than to torture you and find out who they are and then kill you all. You must see that this is true. Your safety ensures their silence, for with your death, they would spread their secret. Second, you will remain amenable to providing certain information to me on occasion when I request."

The agreement sounded surprisingly even-handed, though two facts jumped out at Owain. Regardless of what he said, Carlos would undoubtedly try to discover the identity of those in whom Owain had allegedly entrusted the secret of the curse's origin. It would be a slow, arduous process, but Carlos would certainly make every attempt to find out, with an eye toward killing the entire lot once he knew, including Owain, his erstwhile ally. More importantly, even were Owain inclined to make the deal, he did not have the vial of blood that Carlos wanted. Owain's mind raced. He needed access to the magical laboratories, he needed to find out about Project Angharad, but he couldn't turn over the blood.

"That sounds very charitable," said Owain, "and I could agree to your terms, except I should keep the vial."

Carlos laughed aloud. "Ah, you do not feel safe." The amicable tone which he had maintained rapidly faded. "You come here," he gestured around them, "into my lair because you think possession of the vial protects you." Carlos stepped back around the sarcophagus to Owain, who had not ventured far from the single door to the room. "Do not overestimate the power of your shield. Yes, it would be...inconvenient for me to be linked directly with the curse, and even some proof of my culpability would be problematic. I would choose to avoid that situation. It would be troublesome...but not insurmountable.

"The vial does not render you impervious. I could have killed you last night...as easily as I could kill you tonight. I will bend only so far for expediency. That I allowed you to leave last night should show that I am willing to be more than reasonable. The anonymity of your confidants will protect you as well as any vial. For me," his jovial manner returned, "it is a loose end I will not leave untended. It is not a point of negotiation."

Owain nodded thoughtfully. His translation: *Turn over the vial or die.* This left him in a rather precarious position. Owain smiled in turn. "You are quite persuasive." Carlos seemed pleased with himself. "I agree to your terms," said Owain, "with one added stipulation."

Carlos's smile turned skeptical. "That being...?"

"I will turn over the vial, but first I must see the laboratory from whence it came. I must speak with the sorcerers who unleashed this curse upon us." It was a weak gambit, Owain knew, but he needed to find the laboratory if he was to discover anything. He would worry later about how to circumvent the tiny detail that he didn't have the vial.

"That would serve no purpose whatsoever," Carlos dismissed the idea out of hand.

"I am bargaining that your followers will unravel the mysteries of the curse," Owain pointed out. "I deserve to have first-hand knowledge of them, to speak with them."

"You *deserve?*" Carlos repeated incredulously. He took a deep breath; his hands balled into fists. "Please choose your words with care, for you *deserve* nothing! And you could quickly find yourself with no bargain at all."

Carlos's patience had run out with little warning. Owain could feel the negotiations slipping away from him, but without this one concession, the dangers he had survived would be for naught. He quickly tried a different tack, shrugging disarmingly. "What harm could it do? It would ease my mind…and you would have your vial."

"You think yourself knowledgeable enough to judge them and their work?" Carlos asked mockingly.

"You would be surprised what I know," Owain answered.

Carlos took a step back at this comment. The smile crept back across his features. "I have been, at that." He reached over and brushed the dust from Owain's shoulder. "I like your audacity, Owain Evans. It speaks of forthrightness—either that, or you are the greatest fool I have ever met." Carlos took Owain's lapels in his fingers and leaned close until their faces were mere inches apart. "I will grant this final request."

Final request. Owain didn't care for that particular turn of phrase.

"But do not mistake my graciousness for weakness," added Carlos. "There will be no more favors. Deny me what I ask, suggest a new limitation on our bargain—any of that, and you will die. Vial or no vial. I will deal with the consequences." He stepped back and straightened Owain's jacket. "Our deal, then, is struck."

Owain nodded, but any comment he might have made was superseded by the sound of many footsteps in the hallway beyond the door. Carlos, an eyebrow raised, glanced in that direction. "We have guests."

Santiago stepped halfway into the room. "Many pardons," he said to Carlos, "but there is important news."

"I see." Carlos turned to Owain. "You will excuse me for a moment." Without waiting for any response from Owain, Carlos followed Santiago, who paused only to direct a brief glare at Owain.

After a moment, Owain could hear whispered comments down the corridor. He had no way of knowing that the conversation was about him, only the inborn paranoia that had helped him to this ripe old age. Owain glanced at the door. He was relieved to note that it had not been modified over the years. He could not be locked in this room. The solid wooden beam and iron latches were designed to keep others *out*, as he well remembered. If the wards were activated, then the chamber was impenetrable, but that availed Owain nothing, for he lacked the knowledge to empower them.

Easily suspecting sinister intent from Santiago, Owain stepped closer to the door. It was half open still, and he could see Carlos, Santiago, and a third Cainite some yards down the way. They were speaking in low tones, and the acoustics of the stone tunnels further served to render their speech incomprehensible. As the stranger spoke, Santiago looked on malevolently while Carlos listened with interest.

It was the third Cainite who captured Owain's interest. His face was familiar. Owain had seen him before…not one of the Sabbat that he had contacted trying to reach Carlos…

And then Owain knew.

Just as he remembered where he had seen the third Cainite, Javier looked up. His eyes met Owain's, and he smiled. Javier pointed to Owain at the half-open door and said loudly enough for Owain to hear: "Yes, that is him."

Suddenly the door slammed open into Owain. The woman who had been with Santiago earlier shoved the barrel of a large revolver into Owain's face. Over her shoulder, Owain could see the others rushing down the corridor.

With preternatural speed, he grabbed the

woman's wrist and twisted the gun away from his face. Her only other choice having her forearm snapped in two, she spun, turning her back to Owain who now held her wrist and revolver pointed at the charging Sabbat trio.

The woman struggled, but the blood was not strong in her, not as old and rich as in Owain. He shifted his finger over hers on the trigger, still holding her before him as a shield against the weapon that Santiago had drawn. Owain fired two deafening, thunderous shots down the corridor. Carlos, Santiago, and Javier dove for cover.

The Spanish woman tried to twist away from Owain, but his left arm was tight around her throat. He pulled her back into the room and gave the door a shove. But already, Santiago was back on his feet and lunging forward. He smashed into the door before it could shut completely, before Owain could slam the wooden beam down and into place.

It was all Owain could do to hold on to the woman and lean with his back against the door that Santiago was pushing furiously against. In a moment, Carlos and Javier would lend their strength and the door would swing open. The stone door weighed several tons but was balanced well on its pivot. Once it began to swing with any force, there would be no stopping it. Time was running out.

CHAPTER TWELVE

It was all Owain could do to keep pressure against the stone door at his back and not lose hold of his prisoner. The female Sabbat would not release the revolver. She reached with her left hand back over her shoulder, her claws searching for Owain's eyes, biting into the flesh of his face. Owain stretched his neck away from her. She turned her head to the side, hissed in his face.

Owain heard as much as felt the impact of a body against the door behind him. Either Carlos or Javier had joined Santiago pushing, and no doubt the other was right behind.

Again Owain twisted the woman's wrist. She growled in pain and anger but could do little beyond slowing the movements that Owain forced upon her. But the heavy momentum of the door was already starting to shift against Owain. Extra seconds might be more than he could afford.

Slowly, ever so slowly, he forced her hand around. Now the revolver pointed at her shoulder. Owain forced it farther. She screamed, full of rage as the last of her strength fled her. His face contorted with strain, Owain forced the muzzle of the gun into her mouth. He pressed his head to the side and squeezed her own finger on the trigger.

Owain tried to ignore the roar that left his ears ringing. He tried to ignore the fragments of skull, bloody scalp, and brain that pelted his face. He needed all his energies focused on closing the door, which was beginning to swing against him. The woman's body dropped to his feet.

Freed from distraction, every muscle straining, making use of the ancient vampiric vitae in his veins, Owain began to make headway. The movement of the door stopped, and then reversed. It had never been open enough that Santiago or one of the others could stick an arm in to block it, and considering the mass of the door, that might only have been a recipe for amputation at any rate.

Owain reached up with his right hand, tried to pull down the beam across the door, but the edge of the door was still in the way by an inch or two. Owain was already pressing against the door with as much force as he could muster. He had nothing else to add.

Then he felt his feet give way beneath him. He slipped on the blood pooling on the floor. As he fell, his full weight on the wooden beam was enough to jerk it down past the lip of the door. The bar slammed home as Owain landed in the blood on the floor.

He could only faintly hear voices and pounding on the far side of the door. It was so solid that breaking through or forcing the beam would be quite an undertaking. But not impossible. And Owain didn't know what unguessed resources Carlos and his Sabbat brethren had to draw upon. The black arts of one Tremere might suffice where the brawn of twenty other Cainites would fail. Owain did not know how much time he had.

He quickly surveyed the room in which he had spent so much time in bygone years. Were it not for the body on the floor, he could have imagined himself again emerging from torpor. There were also those pounding on the other side of the door to remind him of his current predicament, and among them Javier, one of the few partisans of El Greco and Miguel, apparently a spy for Carlos. But Owain didn't have time for those matters. He pushed them farther back in his mind.

He quickly scanned the small room, his tomb. Aside from the sarcophagus, the barred door, and the runes carved into the walls, there was nothing. The room was only a few feet larger on each side than the sarcophagus. Owain stepped around the ornate coffin and searched for a particular rune that he remembered. After just a few moments, he found it, and when he pressed his fingers into the deepest indentation and twisted, the sound of grating stone filled the room. A portion of the wall slid open, revealing a passage leading up and away from the tomb.

There were no torches along the exposed corridor. Owain hoped that this meant that Carlos and his followers had never discovered this passage—quite possible since they had usurped the catacombs from El Greco at some point, and there would have been no one to give them a guided tour.

Before he began his ascent, Owain listened again for the sounds of industry and outrage at the main door, but this time he heard nothing. Probably the close blasts from the revolver had left his ears ringing sporadically, he decided, and the door was thick enough to screen the rest of the sounds.

The revolver.

He grabbed it from the floor by the Spanish Cainite's body. He was no expert with modern firearms, but it could prove useful. He glanced once more around the room. It felt odd to be here again, and this time fleeing what before had been a safe haven.

As he closed the concealed door behind him, the light of the room was blocked and Owain found himself in darkness more complete than had he called upon it to hide him. Even his preternatural eyes strained, trying to make out any shape in the enveloping blackness. Only the feel of the rough stone wall against his fingertips betrayed the existence of a world around him. Otherwise, he might have been floating in the nothingness of torpor that had claimed him once before.

As he made his way up the unilluminated passage, he listened for sounds of pursuit. Not only did none materialize, but when he came to a halt, eliminating even the sound of his own echoing footsteps, the encompassing silence was eerie. *If I were ready to give up*, he thought, *I could lie down here and never be disturbed*. He contemplated that route. After all, he had failed. Carlos had been prepared to show Owain the laboratories. What Owain would have done from that point, he had no idea; neither did he know how he could have faked the vial of tainted blood he had claimed to possess. But he was sure he would have thought of something. Now the path was blocked. How could he hope to learn anything further about how Angharad's name had come to be connected with the curse?

Carlos had been ready to deal, even to take Owain into his fold, it seemed. But Javier had put an end to that. The one Cainite in Toledo who had worked for El Greco and Miguel—the one other than Owain, that was—was actually a spy for Carlos. *How ironic*. There was a certain completeness to the manner in which Carlos had superseded El Greco as master of Toledo. Only in El Greco's mind was it not so.

Damn Javier. But had not Owain himself dealt with Carlos under false pretenses? Owain did not curse the fact that Javier had lied, but that he had apparently lied so well. Perhaps Owain would have been more careful had El Greco and Miguel been more straightforward with him regarding the nature of the situation in the city. But they, too, were only playing their part. El Greco was, it seemed, incapable of viewing the situation as it was. Miguel either shared his master's delusion or was following orders from which he dared not stray. It mattered little which was the case any longer.

Keep moving, Owain told himself. Again, his footsteps clicked through the darkness, asserted his presence amidst the nothingness. Owain could only imagine that Carlos and his followers were not aware of this particular tunnel. Surely they had broken into the tomb by now. It would make more sense that Carlos had chosen that room to meet in if he did not know of the secret escape route. Owain had not needed to escape when he had emerged from his two-hundred-fifty-year rest, but the earlier precautions, the secret tunnel in particular, had proven serendipitously useful.

The secret path was less artfully hewn than the other tunnels beneath El Alcazar. The floor was not smooth or even clear in places; the walls and ceiling dipped and curved as if the long-dead miners had been attempting to maintain a certain bearing without boring directly through every expanse of solid rock that they encountered. Owain began to doubt his recollection of the route when he started happening upon side passageways. He did not remember tunnels leading off to either side. At first he passed them by, but when his count of the new tunnels reached half a dozen, he wondered if it were possible that the original route curved to follow one of these paths, while what continued straight ahead was actually a newer addition.

In the midst of this quandary, he began to hear the voices. Had they been the noise of angry shouting and the braying of bloodhounds, he would merely have hurried the opposite direction, but what he heard was...he couldn't decide at first, so out of place was the sound. But after a moment more, he was sure. He heard laughter, and mixed with it faint music.

Owain stumbled on through the darkness, fleeing the sounds that did not belong there, but the voices stayed with him, the chatty conversation and mirthful laughter of a social gathering, the smoothly plucked notes of a stringed instrument, perhaps a mandolin, an instrument which El Greco had favored when these halls were his.

An inexplicable terror began to rise within Owain. He feared this music more than he would the gunfire of pursuing Sabbat. The laughter and music could not be here. They were of a different time. Like the specters of Jews fleeing their homes, these sounds were real to Owain, but they could not be. The world of his memory was blending with the world of his senses, and in these sightless, soundless tunnels, memory was taking over.

Owain hurried through the darkness, trying to fashion a route that took him away from the sounds that could not be, but still they were with him. He tripped over the uneven floors, slammed into walls when the passage suddenly changed directions. If anything, the laughter grew louder. He began to run blindly, smashing his body against stone, crashing into one invisible wall after another. The past was reaching out to capture him, to drag him back to torpor, and for the first time in many years, that thought panicked Owain. He could see dim connections between his past and the present, connections that he still needed to discover, connections that were hiding just beyond his reach. He could not abide the thought of remaining imprisoned within these dark tunnels, not so soon after escaping his self-fashioned prison of ennui. The laughter grew louder, mocking his fear.

The unevenly carved floor took advantage of Owain's distraction as an unseen obstacle took hold of his foot. Owain stumbled and fell. He crashed to the ground and was still. All around him, too, there was only dark stillness. Only after several moments of silence did he realize that the voices were gone; the laughter had stopped.

Owain climbed back to his feet. Before him stood a figure of pure shadow holding before it a wooden chess board, pieces arranged in the later stages of a game. Owain absently wondered for a moment how it was that now he could see? But the shadow was moving its arm, reaching for a piece on the board. The dark hand and billowing sleeve were difficult to follow, but Owain saw the shadow grasp a knight, moving it one square to the side, then forward one square, and another. With the third tap of the piece to the board, the shadowy figure was gone, and in its stead stood an actual knight, an armored man in medieval garb, sword hanging at his side. Though he stood only a few feet from Owain, the knight's face was hidden in shadow.

Owain had heard no sound of this knight approaching nor of the previous shadow coming or going. The knight was equipped as a figure from Owain's early years of unlife would have been.

Suddenly Owain noticed a book that he did not believe had been there a moment before in the hands of the knight. As the knight opened the tome and turned the stiff parchment leaves, Owain recognized his own commonplace book that was so dear to his heart—except the cover was not the smooth, unadorned leather that Owain had added years ago. This book was bound in the original embroidered cover, complete with the crest of House Rhufoniog, Welsh grouse trussed, same as the day that Angharad had given it to him.

The realization was a shock to Owain, but now the knight was speaking in a rough gravelly voice that emanated from unseen lips: *"Hoard the nights that have fallen unto you. I tell you, it avails you nothing."*

Owain staggered as the knight spoke. These were the words of his visions, the words that haunted him, and by now he knew them well.

"This is the Endtime. This is the fading of the Blood. This is the Winnowing."

The words struck like a physical blow. Owain dropped to his knees. He wanted to snatch the book from the knight's hands, to stop the words that the voice spoke, but Owain was powerless in the face of the prophecy. He could coerce neither speech nor movement from his body.

"The shadow of Time is not so long that you might shelter beneath it."

As suddenly as the knight had held the book, he now held his sword before him, and as Owain watched in frozen terror, the knight drew back the blade to swing a mighty blow. *"Let it be thus. Thy will be done."*

The knight's stroke fell. Owain flattened himself to the floor in a desperate attempt to dodge the blow, but he knew he was too close. He lay with his face and body pressed against the cool stone, but the sword did not strike him. Owain glanced up from that spot where he should have been cleft in twain. He was greeted by the all-encompassing darkness. No sign of knight or sword or book or shadowy chess master. Silence surrounded Owain. Whatever illumination had allowed him to see his visitors was now gone.

This is the Endtime.

This is the fading of the Blood.

This is the Winnowing.

Owain rose to his feet. The words of his visions rang in his ears. He shook his head. There would be time enough later to understand what had just happened to him. His legs less than stable beneath him, Owain continued forward, not knowing if he chose the right direction.

No more sounds of voices or laughter came to Owain. No pursuit ever developed that he could tell. Twice more, he stumbled upon passages leading off to the right, but he continued straight ahead, and before long, the tunnel took on a noticeably steeper grade. Owain leaned forward as he ascended, climbing with his hands as well as his feet. Soon the tunnel turned nearly vertical. In the darkness, Owain felt carved handholds, a crude ladder. He began to see light ahead. Though only the faint illumination that the night provided, after the complete and possibly unnatural darkness through which he had just come, the scant light seemed as bright as the noonday sun.

Owain stepped from the ladder and slowly opened a door before him. He exited from the very wall of the Puerta del Sol, the Gate of the Sun. The threatening clouds of earlier had descended with full force. Owain could not remember seeing a storm so low before. The lightning streaking the sky seemed to be mere feet above the low buildings. As the door to the tunnel swung shut behind him, Owain could see the outlines of the portal only because he knew exactly what he was looking for. How many years, he wondered, had that passageway and door escaped the notice of Carlos and his faction?

Now that Owain had escaped immediate danger, he turned his thoughts toward what lay ahead. He had failed in his attempt to trace the origin of the curse through Carlos, to find out how Angharad's name had anything to do with the curse. Thanks to Javier, Carlos now knew something of the relationship between Owain and El Greco. There seemed little else to be gained in Toledo. Owain's ties to the Sabbat, for all practical purposes, seemed to be destroyed. El Greco was no longer an active player. Owain need not respond to summons in the future.

The only danger, Owain realized, would be if El Greco possessed any proof of Owain's association with the Sabbat. The chance was slight. The few times that Owain had utilized his Sabbat connections, such as when he had arranged for the war party to attack Prince Benison and himself outside the Cyclorama, that Owain might appear loyal in protecting his prince, he had communicated anonymously. There could be letters from the early days, perhaps, that in his initial enthusiasm Owain had written to El Greco. Not likely, but possible.

Owain pondered the matter for a few moments. Midnight was several hours past. If he was to leave the city tonight, make his way to Madrid, perhaps contact the Giovanni clan, he needed to leave soon. To completely erase the past, however, he needed to make sure that El Greco had nothing that could be used against Owain later. There was also Kendall Jackson. She obviously had left the prearranged rendezvous here at the gate hours ago.

Owain made his decision and began to make his way south through the deserted streets as the storm winds pulled at his hair, at his clothes. He would fetch Ms. Jackson quickly and then leave Toledo, traveling as far as Madrid before sunrise. Attempting to ascertain what evidence actually existed, if any, and then finding and destroying it would be quite involved, especially considering the unlikelihood that El Greco would prove cooperative in the matter. No, Owain would simply leave his old unstable friend to dodder off into obscurity, assuming that El Greco would not undertake coordinated action to gain revenge. And if Miguel again showed up on the doorstep in Atlanta, Owain would kill him.

Owain continued south, keeping to the narrowest byways, hugging the shadows in case Carlos had sent his men throughout the city in search of his escaped guest. The lightning constantly flashing above made more difficult this attempt to remain out of sight. The nature of Owain's escape had been incredibly lucky, he knew. If his luck held, he would gather up Ms. Jackson without needing to confront Miguel or El Greco. Then Owain and his ghoul would appropriate a vehicle of some sort and leave this city, which Owain hoped never to see again.

Luck, however, had never been a constant companion of Owain's. Instead, he had grown to rely upon suspicion. He was quite close to El Greco's now, which set him on edge. He was just emerging from the shelter of a darkened alley when a flash of lightning revealed a lone figure standing only feet away.

Before the light had flickered away, Owain was back within the shadow of the alleyway and on his guard. His eyes were locked on the spot where, a moment before, he had seen the other. The figure had not moved.

Owain waited patiently, scanning the street ahead for signs of activity, but there were none. He did not have long to wait. The lightning soon returned, striking quite near.

The figure did not stir. Owain was sure of it.

In that brief moment of illumination, Owain could make out little of the statuesque figure. Its head was unbent beneath the downpour. Its features were pale and looked chiseled—although this may have been a trick of the light, throwing the lines of its face into sharp relief. The figure seemed to stare fixedly back at Owain.

Minutes crawled past, but Owain could not discern the slightest hint of movement. The figure could have been a statue in a plaza, but it stood in the center of the dark street, and between Owain and El Greco's abode.

"I would not go there," said the stranger. "The others have already arrived."

His entire form seemed caught in the middle of flowing away to the pavement below. Water streamed freely over his unblinking eyes. Long white hair trailed off into runnels of dripping water. His robe clung heavily about him and dragged through the puddles underfoot.

Owain's initial surprise quickly gave way to anger. Again his plans were being altered by complications from an unexpected quarter. Each time he attempted to take control of a situation, it seemed his grasp was inevitably shaken by some such intrusion, and the pieces flowed away from him like rain through his fingers.

"I keep my own counsel. I go where please," said Owain.

This brought a smile to the stranger's lips. His thoughts, however, he kept more closely guarded. "There are those who think otherwise, *Kinslayer*."

Owain's head jerked up at the word—the familiar reproach. He had heard this challenge spoken only nights before, on the plane trip from Atlanta. On that occasion, he had wavered on the brink of dream and the accuser had spoken with the voice of his brother. The stranger who came to him that night had also used that epithet. *Kinslayer*.

Owain again felt control of the situation slipping from his grasp. "Who are you?" he asked aloud, echoing his unspoken question of that night on the plane. He could recall sitting across a chessboard from the same shadowy figure Owain had seen earlier tonight, trying to trick him into revealing the identity of his king.

Before he had gotten his answer, however, a third party had intruded upon their game. The critical center squares of the chessboard were suddenly besieged by warring factions on three sides—forming a peninsula jutting precariously out into the unknown.

"I only wanted to see for myself," said the alabaster stranger. "To set eyes upon you before the appointed end. You cannot imagine how many years I have waited."

"Speak plainly," Owain snapped. "Have you come only to mutter veiled threats? You may tell your master that I am not impressed."

The stranger smiled, indeed, at that. "You misunderstand me. It is not I who pose a threat. But you, your very existence, threatens all of our kind. *This is the Endtime. This is the Fading of the Blood.*"

As the words were spoken, a violent gust of wind struck Owain across the face. The words of his visions, the words the knight had spoken not an hour before—they were being repeated back to him by this stranger Owain had never seen before, neither in waking nor in dreaming sight. But the words were the same. "Who are you?" Owain pressed.

The stranger raised his black eyes to the heavens churning above. "It is I who shall remain when the world falls down around our ears, Kinslayer. It is I who shall testify that the doom you bring down upon our people was the one foretold from the time before time. Who but I keeps alive the sacred words? Who but I traces the course of the ancient prophecies? *This is the Winnowing, Kinslayer. The shadow of Time is not so long that you might shelter beneath it.*"

"You speak nonsense," said Owain, but the quiver in his voice betrayed his uncertainty.

"You must live to fight another day," said the stranger. "You must walk this uncertain road to its end, as damning as that end might reveal itself to be. The path ahead will take you to the center of the widow's web. It will take you to the very foot of the holy thorn. It will take you into the hidden presence of the sacred vessel. It is there you must speak the words of undoing for the children of Caine. This is the task that has fallen to you. *Let it be thus. Thy will be done.*"

"I will not—" Owain began to protest, but his words echoed across the empty street. The stranger and his infuriating smile were gone, vanished as completely as if they had never been. Had the lightning flashed? Had Owain blinked?

Only the words remained. They flooded Owain's mind.

This is the Winnowing.

Owain stood completely alone, oblivious to the torrential downpour. How many times had he himself appeared so mysteriously to a mortal and then vanished without a trace? But he was a vampire, and one with many centuries of experience to his credit. He was not one to be taken in by such tricks. Yet the stranger was gone.

The rain began to fall in earnest now. In but a few moments, Owain's hair was heavy and wet. Water dripped from his nose, was caught by the gusting wind and whipped away into the night. *I*

would not go there. The others have already arrived.
What others did he speak of? Could the stranger
somehow know where Owain was going? he wondered. *Impossible*, Owain thought. *As impossible as
him speaking to me the words of my own visions.*
Owain set his stride and continued south. *Damn
him! Damn him and his words!* Owain would not be
dissuaded from his goal by some white-haired interloper who might just as likely be apparition as
flesh and blood.

As Owain approached El Greco's house, the cathedral off to the west, El Alcazar rising to the east,
he was determined to ignore what the stranger had
said. Even so, he did decide to climb the row of
cramped houses across the street to get a better
view before barging in. Atop the buildings, Owain
was amidst the full fury of the storm. Static electricity crackled in the air all about him. Rain
pummeled him mercilessly. The wind greedily took
hold of him, tried to drag him to the edge of the
roof, over the edge. Owain resisted the storm. He
crawled forward, and mixed with the sounds of the
raging heavens, he heard gunfire.

Across the street, three black cars hastily parked
at odd angles were in front of El Greco's house.
Gunfire again, and screams, met Owain. From the
front door, he saw Santiago step out, pistol in hand.
The Sabbat lieutenant glanced around the street
but saw no one responding to the sounds of death

and mayhem within the house. Those nearby either did not hear over the storm, or they were clinging to their ignorance like frightened children.

Santiago's gaze lingered as he glanced in Owain's direction. Owain pressed his body against the roof. Apparently Santiago did not see him, for a moment later Carlos's follower went back into the house. More gunshots followed. Owain could imagine El Greco and Miguel overwhelmed by the sheer number of Sabbat that Carlos would have brought. They would be tortured and destroyed. The discovery of Owain's ruse had erased whatever truce had existed. El Greco, interfering in Carlos's affairs, was no longer protected; whether that protection had been accorded by Carlos's good will or by fiat of Archbishop Monçada mattered little. The household ghouls would suffer a similar, or worse, fate. And Kendall...Owain had left her to this.

As he looked on, flickering light shone through the windows of El Greco's house. Then tongues of flame began to lick up through the windows shattered by bullets. Owain found himself moved again by an unfamiliar emotion. He pitied his old friend, the end he was meeting. But such was the lot of a Cainite—warred upon and destroyed by his own kind. Owain hoped that El Greco would come to a quick end, less from any desire for mercy, but to keep Carlos from finding out any more of Owain's past. Despite his stirrings of pity, Owain still nursed his grudge against the Toreador. He had pushed Owain into involvement with Carlos, and even though El Greco was destroyed, it would not be hard for Carlos to track down Owain, not since that blasted Gangrel had given away Owain's identity.

El Greco deserved whatever he got, Owain decided. There was no kind and forgiving Providence. The powers of heaven had completely abandoned the Cainite race. Blood and death were their only birthrights and would find them all sooner or later.

Even over the storm, Owain heard someone approaching from behind. In an instant, he whipped the captured revolver from his belt and was pointing it directly at the face of the prone Kendall Jackson. She froze at the sight of the barrel, until Owain, recognizing her, rain-drenched and disheveled as she was, lowered the weapon.

She nodded toward the house across the street. "You've seen?"

Owain nodded.

Kendall crawled up beside Owain. She had to shout to make herself heard above the wind and heavy, punishing rain. "I barely got out when they stormed the house."

"El Greco?"

Kendall nodded. "Inside. So was Miguel."

The fire was burning strong in the upstairs across the street. Various Sabbat lackeys were wandering out of the front door, standing in the street to watch the house burn. They seemed unconcerned about the mortal authorities. Perhaps this fire would be passed off as an accident or an attack by Basque separatists. Owain's only hope was that El Greco and Miguel would die quickly, that they would not have the chance to give away any of his secrets.

Beyond hoping, there was little left to be done. Owain was not about to wade in, revolver blazing, among the numerous and well-armed Sabbat. Probably while they were still concentrating on El Greco would the best time for him to make good his escape.

"I have a car," said Kendall, as if reading his mind.

Owain didn't care where she had gotten it, from whom she had stolen it. It was enough that they should leave Toledo. Around them, the storm still raged, but despite the thick, black clouds, morning would arrive deceptively soon. Owain looked once again at the burning dwelling across the street. The flames were spreading despite the rain. The attic portion of the house, where El Greco's hidden resting place would be, was completely engulfed. Owain thought for a moment that he could hear his old friend's moans of pain as flames consumed his body. But Owain had seen and heard so much over the course of the night. He was no longer certain what was real and what was bleeding through from his visions and dreams to haunt his waking hours.

☥

For hours, Nicholas had huddled against the storm. It felt wrong to him. Not uncomfortable, but unnatural. The low-lying clouds had rolled in from the west, bringing with them the biting winds, the driving rains, the dangerous lightning that had already struck several times within the old walls of the city. The storm, a force of chaos and destruction, swept over the city.

Last night, Nicholas had fed upon a young couple enjoying a romantic night beneath the stars. He left them alive but unconscious on their blanket, probably no worse for wear. The rest of the night he had rested, feeling the power of the blood as it sped the healing of his injuries. By the time he had sunk back down into the earth at daybreak, he was recovered from the knife and bullet wounds of the night before. Tonight, he had awakened to the approaching storm and taken shelter in an abandoned building.

Owain Evans was out there somewhere. But where? For so long, Nicholas had been guided by what he could describe only as the call of the blood. His ancestor's vitae called out to him from the veins of a murderer, or rather, it had. His ancestors, too, had been quiet the past two nights, not battling for outlet, not forcing their memories upon Nicholas. He supposed that he should feel grateful, but he had grown used to the guidance of Ragnar, of

Blaidd. He felt lost without them. Their anger fueled his own rage, drove him forward.

As the wind battered his temporary shelter, Nicholas took comfort in the belief that his ancestors would not abandon him. Ties to the past were strong among the Gangrel clan, and he could feel stirring within him forces older and more bestial even than Blaidd. It was on such a night that Blackfeather had found him, had tried to instruct him in the ways of the Veil and the land beyond. But Nicholas felt more than he understood. He was driven by instinct, and though he had lost Owain Evans for the time being, Nicholas would have his revenge. Perhaps it was the curse that wakened his ancestors within him; perhaps the curse ate away at his very soul and would claim him soon. That only served to increase the urgency of his hunt. Nicholas knew that he was not the hunter of things spiritual that Blackfeather was, but in this chase for a creature of flesh and stolen blood, Nicholas would not be denied.

CHAPTER THIRTEEN

Kli Kodesh looked down upon the seven hills of the Accursed City.

Rome, the Throne of the Caesars. The city was both the crown of Western Civilization and the miter of Christ's Universal Church.

Another visitor might have been struck by the tawdry incongruity of the unbroken urban sprawl, the unceasing press of bodies and buses, the Babel of concrete and glass clamoring skyward.

To Kli Kodesh, however, these corruptions were only the most recent manifestations of the Unchanging City. He remembered vividly the angry mobs in the Forum trading insults, buffets, bribes, stealthy knife thrusts. He remembered the tramp of the legions spreading the benefits of civilization and enforcing them at swordpoint, all in the name of the Republic.

In Palestine, Kli Kodesh had learned to loathe the very sight of the golden eagle. He had been easily drawn into the intricate webs of conspiracy that roiled beneath the surface of the Roman occupation. It was, perhaps, this rebellious nature that first had drawn him to the Master and his dangerous teachings.

With the passing of so many centuries, there was certainly no man now walking who had better cause to hate the Romans and what passed for Roman justice.

Kli Kodesh wished he could look down into the heart of the Accursed City and see it for the festering wound that it was. He tried in vain to summon up the image of a decaying corpse abandoned at the crossroads of time. He wanted to force the city to wear its taint openly, to be revealed as an abomination in the sight of God and man.

But he knew, had always known, that when he at last returned to the City of Inequities, he would be greeted by quite a different scene. *Truly is it said that there is no justice within the walls of Rome*.

Kli Kodesh, however, would keep his promise. He had an important appointment here, in the crypts deep beneath the silent corridors of the Vatican. Something ancient awaited him in those crypts—

a certain crate, indistinguishable from its fellows and undisturbed since it was interred here at the height of the Church's power. That something must be loosed so that the appointed end might come swiftly now.

Reluctantly, Kli Kodesh braced himself and faced the city, the object of his enduring hatred.

On each of the seven hills stood an angel, stern and terrible of countenance. The seven burned with the brightness of a furnace and each carried both a golden trumpet and a flaming sword.

And as Kli Kodesh watched, the first angel raised his trumpet and blew upon it a mighty blast that shook the heavens and the earth. And there was the sound of a great company of men and angels crying, *"Glory to God in the Highest. Let it be thus. Thy will be done."*

Kli Kodesh hid his face and wept. *After so many years, has it truly come?*

It was a long while before he could force himself to stumble forward out of the piercing light and burning and into the welcoming shadows of the City of Inequities.

The VAMPIRE Epic
THAT SPANS THE CENTURIES